Praise for t

'If you want one of
Be

B

'I read this book 24/7. I can't wait to read book two!'
Annabelle, Year 6

'I really enjoyed the vivid descriptions of the beasts and creatures
that Jack encountered.'
Joseph, Year 6

'A thrilling style of science fiction, a sidestepping fantasy into
another world you've never seen before.'
Erin aged 11

'A spine-chilling, sure-fire hit!'
Courtenay aged 11

'This was a fantastic, gripping fantasy which I couldn't put down.
The story was so compelling at the end of every chapter I was left
thinking what happens next?'
Anna, Year 6

'I liked how real things were mixed up with fantasy. It made me feel
like I wanted to be in the book.'
Noah, Year 6

'My daughter read this book in 24 hours and has been nagging me
to buy the next in the series.'
Parent at Book Fair

'Chris Connaughton's fast paced adventure story is a very enjoy-
able and compelling read. The plot races from one dangerous scrape
to another. There are some echoes of Harry Potter and Lord of the
Rings, but the world Connaughton creates is distinct and his own.
You can see the author's reputation as an actor and storyteller in his
handling of speech and conversation.'
Amazon reviewer.

The Beltheron Darkness

CHRIS CONNAUGHTON

First published in Great Britain in 2011
by
Intext Publishing

A CIP Catalogue of this book is available from
the British Library

ISBN 978-0-9558707-3-6

Typeset in Palatino 10½pt and cover design
by Chandler Book Design,
www.chandlerbookdesign.co.uk

Printed and bound in Great Britain by
MPG Books Group, Bodmin and King's Lynn

With very best wishes!

DEDICATION

This book marks the end of the Beltheron story.
It is for the person who was the beginning of the
biggest story of my life.

Caroline, this one is for you. You've waited long
enough for it, I hope you like it.

About the Author

Chris Connaughton trained as an actor and has worked in all sorts of theatres and arts centres up and down the country. He has performed as Hamlet, Romeo and Macbeth, as well as Widow Twanky, the Mad Hatter and Mr Spoon on Button Moon! His television credits include *Byker Grove*, *The Tide of Life*, *The Man Who Cried*, *Tales from the Piano*, *Call Red*, *Throwaways* and *Harry*.

In 1997 he set up Intext Performance to write and produce stories and plays for children. He visits over 120 schools throughout the UK every year. Chris has also performed in France, Germany, Austria, Spain, Italy, Russia, Japan, China and South Korea. He has written (and co-written with Paul Harman) more than 15 stories and 6 plays. His two previous novels *The Beltheron Pathway* and *The Beltheron Select* have had great reviews from children and adults all over the country.

To buy copies of 'The Beltheron Pathway' and 'The Beltheron Select' or to find out more about the series, go to www.thebeltheronpathway.com

Acknowledgements

I started writing the first Beltheron story over ten years ago. The time since then has been quite an adventure, and the success of the books in classrooms up and down the country is due to the help and advice of many friends and colleagues. This final chapter of the story goes out with a huge thank you to all of the readers who have loved entering the worlds of Beltheron and Atros and who have given me such positive feedback.

SPECIAL THANKS TO:

Di Hewitson for her continued support of my theatre work in and around Gateshead schools.

Anna at Theatre Hullabaloo for her brilliant collective noun for dragons.

Portsmouth Grammar School for always making me feel so welcome, and for inspiration at their Summer Fete.

Prologue

The hills spread across the far side of the valley in the dawn light. Apart from the sound of a few birds singing there was silence; silence and stillness. Then, quietly at first, a low humming sound began. It grew in volume until the ground all around seemed to throb and shake. The birds stopped their singing, and flew into the skies, shrieking a warning to their fellows.

The source of this rumbling sound was the ancient generator in the outbuildings at the far end of the Thomas Family Stables and Riding School. Mr Thomas himself appeared around the corner of the outbuildings, wiping his hands on a rag which was already blackened with grease. The old generator often played up, but twice in the last two days it had packed in completely, refusing to start up at all. Mr Thomas grumbled to himself. He was sure it had something to do with the electrical storm he had seen the day before. There had been bright white flashes in the sky, the like of which he had never experienced before. He had called out to his two daughters to come and look. Mel had appeared straight away, she always did when he called, she was a good girl, good to her old dad. But Megan could not be found.

He was angry at first, thinking that perhaps she was deliberately ignoring him. Then Mel told him Megan had gone out riding with that Helen Day girl, who used to live down the valley in the big house by the pond on the village green. They'd ridden up Roseberry Topping, Mel told him. He was worried

1

then. He didn't want the girls out on the horses at all if there was going to be a storm, let alone up on the highest and most exposed hill for miles. Even as they looked up there was another bright flash, coming from Roseberry itself. Strange thing was, it looked to Mr Thomas as if the flash came from the ground, not from the clouds, like proper lightning should.

Anyway, whatever it was, no rain came of it. Soon Megan turned up, safe and sound. She looked shaken and upset though and wouldn't tell him anything the rest of that day. That Helen girl was nowhere to be seen. Not surprising, he thought. The whole family were in the habit of disappearing from the village without a moment's notice. He couldn't even remember the last time he had seen the girl's parents, Matt and Jenn, to talk to. Weird, he called it.

Now here he was again, first thing in the morning, and having to fix the generator for the second time. He lifted his gaze to the nearby hills to look for signs of another storm brewing. As he scanned the horizon he saw a figure silhouetted against the sky. The figure of a large man in a long coat. The man began to descend towards the stables.

'Tourist, out for a ramble,' Mr Thomas thought. 'Early though.' He continued to walk around the yard to check on the horses.

Five minutes later he reached the last stable. He looked in on Jigsaw, one of the smaller ponies that he took the younger riders out on. She was whinnying fearfully and he saw her eyes had grown wide as he entered her stable.

'What is it girl, eh? He asked her. 'What's troublin' you?'

The pony skittered backwards into the corner, her hooves scrabbling on the cobbles.

'Come on girl, there's nothing to be...'

A shadow appeared in the doorway behind him. Thomas spun around. There was a large bearded man standing there. He wore a long coat which hung down to the ground like a cloak. It was the same man he had seen walking on the hill, he realised.

'And what can I do for you?' Mr Thomas started to ask.

The bearded man raised his hand and extended it towards Thomas, opening his fingers wide as he did so. The man spoke a single word; 'Forget.'

A bright light shot towards Mr Thomas' eyes. He didn't even have time to blink.

When he could see again he was surprised at how bright that last flash of lightning had been. It meant a heavy storm for sure. 'Better get the straw in before it starts raining,' he thought to himself.

Mr Thomas started whistling cheerfully as he moved towards the stable door and out into the empty yard...

Megan saw the flash from the kitchen. Apart from her dad she was the first one up. She hadn't been able to sleep, not after all that she had seen yesterday. Her friend Helen appearing out of nowhere after such a long time away; that bearded man in the long coat attacking them on the hillside; those bright flashes of light from his fingers knocking Helen off Jigsaw; and Megan herself riding her own horse, Zarak, straight into the man, toppling him over the edge of the hill...

She shook her head to clear it of the images that haunted her. As she edged her way to the kitchen door it flew open.

Standing in front of her was the figure from yesterday. The one she had knocked down the hillside. He took a step into the kitchen towards her and she noticed he was limping slightly.

Megan was about to scream a warning to the rest of the house when the man's hand shot up towards her. There was a bright flash of light and she heard a single word.

'Forget.'

Later that day both Megan and her dad were convinced that the lightning must have struck the middle of their stable yard. They couldn't think of any other explanation for the dark, round scorch mark burnt deep into the earth...

The Plea of Vishan

Vishan awoke with a sharp stabbing pain in his lungs. It felt as though his chest was being squeezed by a giant hand. He coughed, and felt water surge up out of his throat and into his mouth. He spat it out frantically, and then gasped, trying to get his breath. He coughed again, spitting to get rid of the vile tasting water. He tried to swallow and a harsh rasping pain at the back of his throat made him wince with shock.

He opened his eyes but there was darkness all around. Vishan shook his head to clear it and tried to recall what had happened to him. He remembered struggling underwater. Someone had been holding onto his hair, forcing his head back under the surface. He remembered being spun around, this way and that, by the strong force of the current. He had opened his mouth in panic, but water flooded in, choking him. No matter how hard he had struggled, he could not get his head out of the water. Just as he thought he must pass out there was a flash of brilliant white light. Then nothing. Just blackness.

Like the blackness that surrounded him now.

As his senses began to come back to him, Vishan realised he was sitting in a hard chair. His spine was forced upright against the wooden back of the chair by a heavy rope. His arms were bent around behind him. They were twisted at a painful angle and he felt tight cords around his wrists and ankles. They were biting into his skin and he felt the wet slickness of blood running between his fingers. Tentatively he moved his hands. The pain increased with a sudden jolt. Similarly, when he tried to adjust the position of his feet he found that they were bound so tightly against the legs of the chair that he couldn't move at all. Instinctively he struggled more violently, trying to twist his body out of the cords. The chair did not even scrape a centimetre across the floor. 'It must be bolted down,' he thought to himself.

He tried to get himself to relax and focus his mind. This was not as desperate as it might be. Even though his strength was not sufficient to help him, all was not yet lost. His skills were not just limited to the physical training he had received as a pulver soldier and spy. He had discovered as a young boy that by focusing very hard on an object he could move it without even touching it. This was usually enough to undo even the tightest bonds. Vishan was proud of this talent. He knew it was rare. In fact, he had only ever heard of one other person who possessed it. That person was young Serrion Melgardes, a boy whose powers were like nothing Vishan had ever seen before.

Centering all his attention on the cords around his wrists he moved his fingers so that they were twisted back towards the knots.

He was aware of the usual green light that appeared whenever he used this skill. It glowed brightly in the darkness and he waited for the ropes around his wrists to fall away and free his hands.

Nothing happened.

By now the ropes should have untied themselves and fallen into a heap on the ground. That was what usually happened when he summoned his skills. But this time he remained tied as tightly as ever.

He rested for a moment and tried again.

Once more the green light shone from his fingers, and once more the ropes remained exactly as they were.

Vishan sat quietly for a few moments, thinking about his predicament. He was completely powerless. He was not used to feeling like this. Fear started to rise again in his breast. His heart began to hammer faster as panic started to take over. He bucked in the chair desperately, this way and that, trying to rock it over. But he knew in his heart that it was useless. The chair remained firmly bolted to the floor. All he managed to do by his violent exertions was bruise his arms and shoulders on the sides of the chair and cut more deeply into his wrists with the rope.

'Stop it!' he told himself under his breath. 'Calm down! Acting like this won't help you.'

He allowed his pulver training to relax him once more. There was no good to come of panic. That way lay certain defeat. He steadied his breathing and felt his racing heartbeat slow down.

Again he cast his mind back and tried to remember all that had happened to him before he had blacked out.

Water, swirling around him, the hands clutching his throat, holding him under.

But what had happened before that? How had he ended up in the water to begin with? And who had he been fighting?

Then there was a sound. It was so loud in the dark room that it startled him. The sharp click of a key being turned in a lock. The next instant the room was flooded with light. Vishan closed his eyes tightly as he was blinded by the sudden brightness. Squinting, he peered towards the doorway. Images came to him slowly through a swirl of colour.

Two figures appeared out of the glare. They stood in front of him, just inside the doorway.

The first one that he focused on was a tall man dressed in a tight fitting black leather waistcoat and breeches. His hair was cropped close to his hard, angular head and his sharp features were cruel and unforgiving.

Vishan looked at the second figure. He saw to his surprise that it was a woman. In such a dank and dismal place he had expected another man, a guard or soldier. The woman was dressed in deep purples and blues and her dark eyes were alive with malicious glee as she stared at him. In spite of the cruelty in her expression she was beautiful.

As he looked at the couple his mind cleared and things started to fall into place. All of a sudden he recognised both of them. Piotre and Sophia Andresen, the new Lords of Atros. He groaned to himself and closed his eyes again with despair as all hope left him.

'You are awake at last,' Piotre Andresen said. 'Good. Now we can begin to make you talk.'

Vishan's mind was racing. He had spent so many years as a double agent on Atros, convincing these two people in front of him that he was their friend and ally. Surely he could work that to his advantage now. As the Andresens walked slowly towards him he tried to piece together the last things he could remember before he had blacked out and woken up strapped to this chair.

The swirl of water, the gasping for breath.

No, before that. What happened to me before that? Come on Vishan, think!

As he struggled to remember, something else came into the room behind them. It closed the door and stood beside it impassively. A large, scaly creature with four long arms and an oversized, egg-shaped head.

It was a rish guard. One of the servants of Piotre and Sophia Andresen.

The sight of it caused Vishan to recall more of what had happened to him.

He had been fighting a group of these rish creatures. He was in the silver city of Maraglar. The boy, Serrion Melgardes, was in front of him, standing in the middle of a narrow bridge over the river. Sophia was also on the bridge. She was talking to Serrion.

But *why* had he been there?

The Andresens were getting closer to his chair. Only a few more paces to go.

'Force your mind back,' he told himself. 'You have to remember. Any detail might help.'

Why was he in the city of Maraglar to begin with? Think, Vishan!

And then it came to him. Of course!

He had been sent there to rescue Serrion Melgardes. The group of rish had arrived and attacked them both. He had fought and defeated the rish but then Sophia had appeared. He had raced up onto the bridge, towards them. He had knocked Serrion to one side and plunged into the waters with Sophia before she had a chance to harm the boy.

But in the back of his mind, Vishan knew there was more to it than that. Think! Another jolt of memory struck him.

He hadn't just been trying to protect Serrion from a physical attack by Sophia; he had been trying to stop her from saying something to him. Sophia had been about to speak when he had hit her with the full force of his weight and carried her over the edge of the bridge.

What was it? What was she about to say? Why had it been so important to stop her talking to Serrion?

There was no further time for him to consider this. His most pressing need now was to come up with a good reason to explain to the Dark Queen of Atros why he had knocked her into a roaring river.

However, Vishan was used to this kind of trickery and deceit. His training as a spy made it almost second nature to him. Like an experienced, accomplished actor he could improvise around any part that he was playing. He could rapidly invent a story even while he was telling it and think several lines ahead to create a convincing performance. This was the element of spy work he found the most thrilling. With every moment that passed he felt more of his senses coming back to him. The story to try to deceive the Andresens was already forming in his head. He could *still* turn this situation to his advantage.

Piotre and Sophia had crossed the room by now and were standing right next to his chair.

'My Lord, my Lady, thank goodness you are here,' Vishan spoke quickly and breathlessly. He knew he had to start his performance immediately. If he got his first words out before the Andresens even had chance to begin questioning him, it would put them at a disadvantage. 'And the Three Worlds be praised that you are safe my lady,' he continued

'No thanks to *you*,' she spat. 'If it hadn't been for you, the boy Melgardes would have been in my clutches by now.'

'I know, and I am sorry my Lady,' Vishan knew this would have to be the performance of his life. 'I made a mistake and I regret it deeply. I misjudged the moment. I thought you were in danger. I saw something flash in the boy's hand. I thought it was a dagger. I feared that he was going to kill you on the spot. I *rescued* you my lady!'

He beamed proudly at both of them, like a worthy servant who expects a reward.

For just a moment there was a flicker of doubt in Sophia's eyes. Could she and her husband still trust this man? He had given them such valuable information in the past... or had he?

She began to consider all that Vishan had told them over the years. Some of it had been very useful. After all it was Vishan who had first suggested that they should swap their own son Jacques for the Melgardes brat. It was Vishan who had told them that spies were stalking the backstreets of Atros and they must take care. But how much of that had really been useful? How much could have been just a ruse, an enemy plan to confuse her and her husband?

Piotre Andresen had seen the momentary doubt in his wife's eyes. He knew her too well and realised that if he didn't step in, there would be unnecessary delay while she considered the issue. There was no time for that. No time at all.

He moved his hand swiftly, signalling his displeasure to his wife. She stepped back into the shadows.

'We have wasted too much time on this man already, Sophia,' Piotre said. 'He is a spy, so we should not be at all surprised at his skills as a liar and manipulator. You know this, Sophia.'

She met his gaze evenly. She knew that her husband was right. She knew that the most important thing was to make those who had killed her son Jacques pay for what they had done.

Vishan recognised the change in her features. He quailed inside with the knowledge of what it meant for him.

'Sophia, you know what we must do,' her husband continued. 'There is no more time to be lost.'

She nodded. 'Yes, we must let Hethaloner Rasp question him.'

'No one can keep a secret from Rasp,' Piotre Andresen added with a gleeful twinkle in his eye.

'Rasp?' Vishan said. 'My Lord, who is Hethaloner Rasp?'

'You will find out soon enough,' replied Andresen. 'There is no one who can hide the real truth from him.'

'In that case my Lord, I welcome him so the truth can be known,' Vishan said. He was still desperately playing for time. He smiled up at his interrogators, but knew that a cold sweat of fear had broken out on his face.

The Andresens both moved towards the powerless Vishan. Sophia's hand reached inside her purple cloak and brought out a long, slim wand. Yellow fire flickered at its tip. Vishan bucked in the chair and twisted his head away from it. He could already feel the heat spreading across his cheek as she pointed it at him.

'Hethaloner Rasp will discover all of your secrets,' she whispered in his ear.

'But first,' her husband hissed. 'We can have a little fun...'

Farewells

People had been moving out of Beltheron City all morning. A steady stream of men, women and children made their way from their cottages, houses and apartments. They travelled through the streets and under the archway of the high gates that led to the Eastern Road.

Their destination was the cemetery. It lay beyond the stone walls of the city, high on a bare hill.

For two hours the crowds had gathered on the slopes and between the scattered trees that dotted the hillside. At first there were just small groups of families and friends clustered around, talking in hushed whispers. These groups had grown in number and joined together as more and more people arrived. Now there was hardly any space as far as the eye could see.

However, instead of the noise of conversation growing louder as more people arrived, it was as if some agreement had been made, and people stopped whispering until no one spoke at all. The silence in the middle of such huge numbers of people was eerie and unnatural.

The constant downpour of grey rain bled all the colour from the scene and made everything look like an old faded photograph. A monochrome memory of things long past; things best forgotten about.

The crowds gathered most thickly in a wide circle around a central raised platform. In the very middle of

13

this platform was a coffin. It took the form of a golden casket, beautifully decorated with formal wreaths of white hunnokken flowers along the top. Single stems of snowy roses and tumbling bouquets of pale lilies cascaded to the ground around it.

Three figures stood along one side of this casket. Their heads were all bowed down onto their chests. A fourth person, Harvus Goan, placed himself a couple of paces behind the top end of the coffin. Harvus Goan was the ceremonial master of such occasions. He held a small book of poetry in one hand, and a silver goblet of wine in the other. Raising the goblet above his head he waited until he felt the attention of the huge crowd had focused completely upon him. Then he took a deep breath and began to speak.

'Friends, companions, colleagues, we thank you for your support in this sad time.' His voice rang out clearly through the rain and could easily be heard at the back of the throng, high on the farthest slope of the hills.

'Today we celebrate the life of one of our greatest Lords,' he continued. 'And although this day is sad, we rejoice in the life that he led.'

There came an answering murmur of agreement from the other three people standing on the platform. The words spoken by Harvus and their responses to them were all part of a long tradition during Belthronic ceremonies such as these.

Harvus Goan's speech continued.

'Lord Ungolin's life was rich and full. He was a man with a great love of his people and this land, and we honour his memory.'

With this he lifted the goblet of wine to his lips and drank deeply. He passed the goblet to the man standing closest to him.

Matthias Dai, (or Matt Day as he was known on Earth) received it gravely and also drank. Next it was the turn of his wife. Jenia Dai (Jenn) took the wine from him with a slight bow of her head. She sipped gently before finally passing the goblet to their daughter, Helen.

Jenia's long, curling hair hung down in wet strands over her forehead as she watched her husband Matthias begin to speak about Lord Ungolin. His words came out slowly, with great respect and veneration. Occasionally he looked around at the huge numbers spreading across the field and up the side of the hills under the dark grey sky.

'We gather here today in memory of a great man,' he began. There was a murmur of assent among some members of the crowd, a low rumbling of 'Aye that he was' and 'the greatest of them all' rose up to greet the statement.

'Lord Ungolin, Protector of the Peace of Beltheron, High Councillor and Advisor to the Belthronic Mages, First Captain of the Pulver Guard and Keeper of the Seers is no more, and yet he will always be with us. In our memories, in our hearts and in our policies of fairness and forgiveness.' His voice rang out clearly across the hillside.

There was a ripple of applause from one section of the crowd. On such a solemn occasion, a state funeral like this, it was hardly appropriate. Matthias paused for a moment. There were a couple of 'Tut tut!' and 'Sshh!' sounds from those standing nearby. He waited for this small disturbance to die down again before he continued.

'Ungolin loved every one of you standing here today. He devoted his long life to the service of this great city of ours, and to the prosperity, peace and future wellbeing of all of our people. Even in his last days, weakened with age and worry, Ungolin did not forsake us. He died trying to protect the secrets of Beltheron that hold us all safe against the ravages and evil of the Atrossian Empire.'

There were many further nods of agreement at this, but now no one spoke. Every single person there knew the importance of what Matthias was talking about.

They all knew that Lord Ungolin had been mortally wounded by Piotre Andresen in a struggle to protect the golden staff of Beltheron, a powerful magical artefact. All knew that Piotre Andresen, and his wife, Sophia, were traitors to Beltheron, and now held positions of power and influence over the denizens of that dark and forbidding place, Atros City. Everyone in the cemetery that day understood that Beltheron would have fallen to the Andresens if Ungolin had not held out against them so bravely.

Matthias continued to speak. But the girl standing next to him could hardly bear to listen. His own daughter, Helen Day, struggled to connect what her father was saying with what she knew to be the whole truth about Lord Ungolin.

'Was Ungolin really a great man?' Helen wondered to herself. 'Would a great man have used an innocent child the way that Ungolin had used and manipulated Serrion Melgardes and his family?'

As she was thinking all of this through, her eyes came to rest on the distant figure of Serrion Melgardes himself. It was a figure she knew so well, a boy of fourteen years, just a few months older than herself. He was dressed solemnly in honour of the occasion, with a dark cloak covering his usual jeans and sweatshirt. As she watched him, the hood of his cloak was suddenly thrown back from his head in a gust of wind and rain. His face was revealed. Helen could see the white streaks in his long hair as it whipped across his features and tumbled around his shoulders.

Serrion stood apart from the rest of the huge gathering. His face showed little emotion. There was none of the sorrow in his eyes that was clear in those of everyone else. His thoughts were beyond what was happening there, on that hillside, at that moment. He was thinking about rain falling in a different place. He was concentrating on the memory of a swirling, raging river in Maraglar City, and two figures disappearing slowly under the foam and spray. Sophia Andresen and Vishan the spy.

As Serrion stood there, deep in thought, his memories were shattered by a bright flash of red light in front of his eyes. He staggered for a moment and reached out a hand to clasp the trunk of a hunnokken tree for support. He lifted his other hand to his head, the fingers digging into his eyes to clear the deep ache that had suddenly started there. He was used to this red light appearing and he knew that it always heralded a premonition of danger. He sometimes thought of it as being his own personal warning light that only he could see.

The image that came to him through the red haze was sharp and vivid.

There was a dagger flying towards him, the sharp silver blade getting closer and closer until...

Serrion gasped in shock. He realised that he had actually ducked to avoid the dagger in his mind's eye. Already the image he saw through the red light had changed.

...Now he could see the figure of a man whom he did not recognise. This man was old but powerful. Serrion caught a sudden close up view of his face and saw something strange about the man's eyes. One was pale, almost without colour, but the other flickered with a gleam of red and yellow behind wire framed spectacles...

The images cleared as unexpectedly as they had appeared. As he clung to the bole of the tree Serrion felt his knees give way and he almost fell to the ground.

A couple of people who had been standing nearby gave small cries of alarm and hurried over to help him. They all recognised the young man with the strange, streaked black and white hair, and they all knew how important he was.

In a few moments Serrion was back on his feet and he waved away the helping hands. He smiled his thanks to the worried faces of the people and looked around the hillside again. He spotted Helen standing close to her mother and father and began to walk towards her.

He realised that several minutes must have passed since his vision had torn his attention away from the funeral. The crowds had now thinned out and the casket bearers had finished lowering Ungolin to his final resting place beneath the earth under the wide spreading branches of a hunnokken tree. The broad silver leaves, and the tiny flowers (yellow and gold on alternate stems) would gently fall around his headstone every autumn and spring. The hunnokken was a traditional tree of mourning on Beltheron. Several could be seen around the cemeteries of every town in the land, and the flowers were often given in times of bereavement. Many people in Beltheron that day had been wearing one. As Serrion approached her, Helen reached up to one of the low branches of this particular tree and plucked a stem of blooms from it. She fastened it into one of her button holes then stepped away from her parents and walked over to meet Serrion.

She could tell that he was preoccupied with more than just the sadness of the occasion.

'Come on,' she said. 'Let's go, this place is creeping me out.'

He nodded his head briefly in agreement, but didn't say anything.

They began to walk down the hillside, away from the

cemetery. Both were silent, absorbed in their own thoughts. Soon they came to the dusty road that led back to the high, imposing gates of the city.

Helen's mind was turning one thought over in her mind again and again. She couldn't get away from it. The terrible secret was churning inside her all the time. She knew the truth about the man they had just buried. More than a dozen times during their silent walk she began to speak, then stopped herself again. Should she tell Serrion what she had discovered about Cleve Harrow and Lord Ungolin?

Even now it was difficult for Helen to believe the scale of their betrayal. The Cleve himself had confessed to her that he and Ungolin had worked together and how the two of them had masterminded a terrible plan which had threatened not only Serrion and his family, but Helen's as well.

Helen remembered how the Cleve had seemed proud of his actions when he spoke to her about T'yuq Tinyaz, the Seer of Beltheron.

The Seer was a witch like creature who lived in the caverns underneath the city. She could see into the future and had informed Harrow and Ungolin of her visions about how Piotre and Sophia would turn away from Beltheron and betray Ungolin and all his people. Using this information that the Seer had given him, Cleve Harrow and Ungolin had taken a terrible course of action.

This plan had led to deception, pain and sorrow for all those that Helen cared for. Her own family had been manipulated, tricked, and placed in the path of great dangers.

With a shudder Helen remembered how Harrow had even tried to kill her when she had discovered how he and Ungolin had used them all.

'And for what?' Helen asked herself over and over again. 'For a vision? For something that this woman, this *Seer*, T'yuq Tinyaz dreamt up?'

Helen looked across towards Serrion once more. It was only fair that he should find out who had really betrayed his family, she realised. He ought to know that he was being used as part of a huge conspiracy and that Cleve Harrow and Lord Ungolin had been to blame.

As they walked towards the gates of the City together Helen came to a decision. It wouldn't be easy, but Serrion had a right to be told these things.

And she had the responsibility of telling him.

Escape

Vishan was laughing hysterically. He knew that he was losing his mind. He had been moved to a different room for questioning. There was a cracked window high up in one corner of this room and he had been able to watch the passage of thin sunlight crossing the floor and finally sinking into gloom again as night fell. He had counted this four times before they moved him back to the original cell to be chained in the chair once more. Four passages of sunlight. Four days.

That now seemed like a long time ago. At least another couple of days must have gone by since then. He no longer had any real idea of how long he had been kept prisoner by the Andresens but he guessed it must be a week or more.

As far as he knew he had still not given them any of the information that they needed. No matter what shocks and pain they had subjected him to, he had stuck to his story of still being a loyal servant who worked and spied for them and them alone. But there had been terrifying dreams, as real as life, in which he had cried out for rescue and release. In those moments he could not be certain of what he had said...or who had been listening.

No one had come to him now for a whole day. Underneath the general haze of pain from his bruises, cuts and what he felt could be broken ribs, Vishan also felt the gnawing of hunger and thirst. They had given him a small cup of brackish water every day, and a couple of mouthfuls of a grey sludgy porridge. The water was oily on his tongue and the food tasted of something that could have crawled out from under a stone. Even so he always gulped at it eagerly and his stomach thanked him with grateful gurgles for minutes afterwards. Today though – if it *was* day, for there were no windows in this other room – he had not even been given that. Had they forgotten about him? Was this deliberate, had they decided to let him die of thirst and starvation? As his mind swam in its madness and confusion he didn't know whether he even cared or not anymore. It was hours since he had last bothered to struggle against the chains holding him in the chair. Now he slumped even further forwards against his bonds, exhausted by the effort of just staying upright.

He must have slept again for the next thing he was aware of was a large figure standing in front of him. Wincing as he raised his head, he could make out the shape of a hooded cloak silhouetted against the light coming through the doorway. The figure moved closer and bent down to him. Vishan thought that there was something familiar about it. It turned to check the doorway behind and he caught glimpse of a rough, dark beard in the face's profile. He had once known someone with a beard. He was sure of it. His hazed mind would not let him think though. He could not remember who it was or how he had known this person.

'Who...?'

'Hush!' It was nothing but a whispered breath, disguising the voice. 'Not a word!'

The figure was now behind the chair and for a quick moment there was a flash of white light. Vishan felt the chains around his wrists fall away and he almost cried out in relief as he moved his arms. He twisted round to look at his rescuer and as he did, there was another quick flash of light. This was just long enough for him to make out the glint of yellowy green eyes staring from the shadows of the hood.

The pulver felt himself being lifted from the chair into a standing position. His legs crumpled but he was held firm by the strength of the man's arms around him.

'Can you stand alone?' The question was still a whisper that disguised the voice. Vishan couldn't place it. He knew that the yellowy green eyes were very familiar, but hunger and the stinging pain of the blood returning to his limbs were fuddling his thoughts. He nodded dumbly in reply.

'Good.'

He felt himself being released and, even though he still staggered slightly, he managed to stay on his feet.

''Drink this.'

The stranger placed a small bottle against his parched lips. Vishan grasped at it and gulped greedily. A warming sweetness flooded his throat as he swallowed. Within a few moments he felt strength returning and his vision started to clear. Once again he could make out the dim light spilling through the half open door. The cloaked figure reached into a pocket and brought out a short dagger in a leather scabbard and another small vial of liquid.

'Take these.' He thrust them both into Vishan's hands. 'Save some of what is left in this other bottle for times when you need it most.'

He then turned to make towards the door. Vishan noticed a slight limp in the man's left leg as he moved.

'Wait here,' the man rasped.

'Where are you going?'

'Patience, I will return.'

'But..'

'Hush!'

Pausing to check either side of the corridor beyond, his rescuer disappeared to the left.

Vishan waited in the silence until his eyes had once again grown used to the dim light. He began to rotate his shoulders and flex his muscles. Whatever that liquid in the bottle had been, it was having an almost magical effect. Strength began to surge through his limbs. Even though his exhaustion remained, he now felt much steadier on his feet. He thought he might even be able to run a short distance if he needed to. He felt the weight of the dagger in the palm of his hand and took it out of its sheath. Holding it up to look more closely he saw the shape of the weapon was familiar. It was a Belthronic design, the metal of the blade and handle moulded together, continuing in one fluid shape that fitted his grip perfectly. It was a beautiful piece of crafting, he thought.

He did not have long to appreciate it however. Heavy footfalls made their way down the corridor towards his room. Vishan leapt to the wall behind the door without even thinking, his spy training once more kicking into immediate action. He listened intently as the footsteps drew nearer. Three pairs of feet, he could tell.

The footsteps stopped as the advancing figures noticed the open doors. Then gruff voices grunted.

'Here, what's this?'

'How did...?'

He heard them run towards the cell door. In another moment they were in the room. Two rish and another creature. It was shaped like them, with four strong arms, but much taller, and covered with a coarse black hair.

'A harch,' Vishan thought. 'I do not have the strength yet for him.'

He knew that these creatures were strong, but luckily

for Vishan, the rish and the harch were also stupid. All three beasts ran straight up to the empty chair. The two rish looked down at it in puzzlement. The harch, which had no eyes, sniffed with its long nose. Then, at exactly the same time, all three heads tilted to one side as they considered the problem. In less dangerous circumstances the image would have been funny.

Vishan had no time to find humour in the situation. Silently, swiftly, he crept around the doorframe. He moved his hand towards the door. A green light shot from his fingertips and the door swung closed. He just had time to see the rish and harch turn in surprise and begin to bellow a warning to each other before the door slammed to. The noise of the creatures inside was silenced instantly. He realised the room must have been soundproofed to blot out the screams from prisoners.

His fingers were tingling with a familiar glow. Was it the liquid that his strange rescuer had given him that had released his powers again?

With a quick flick of his hand in the direction of the door the green light intensified like a flash of lightning and the heavy iron bolts slid into place, locking the Atrossian monsters inside. Vishan grinned. He flexed his fingers. It felt good to have his old abilities returning. He thought about those yellowy green eyes again. As he did so his memory suddenly cleared and he knew who it was that had saved him. Vishan grinned. 'You old trickster, I *knew* you wouldn't let me down.'

Feeling much more confident again he turned and raced up the corridor. He followed the direction that his rescuer had taken minutes before. He sped on with his ears open to the tiniest sound. There was no shout of discovery or demand for him to stop from any direction. Presumably the two rish and the harch must have been sent down on their own to fetch him. Still, he did not want to wait for them to break down the door and raise the alarm.

He moved forwards as quickly as he could. All of his experience and instinct were now focused on one thing – escape. As each second went by he began to feel more alert. His hunger, pain and thirst – whilst not yet completely gone – were fading rapidly. The liquid in the bottle must have had magical properties. He thanked his rescuer under his breath once more as he ran on. But how had he managed to find him in such a place?

The long corridor was lit by an unnatural glow that seemed to be coming from the very stones themselves. It was an eerie, yellow light that pulsed slightly brighter just ahead as he made his way up the incline which began to curve away in front of him. He turned for a moment and saw how the light faded again behind him almost as soon as he had passed. He realised that it was his own footsteps as he made his way up the corridor that was somehow triggering this yellow light.

'This place must have deep magic rooted in the very rocks and stones,' he thought to himself.

As he set off again he saw another yellow glow suddenly light up ahead of him, just around the corner. Someone, or some*thing*, was coming towards him.

A moment later he heard the soft padding of feet. Then, before Vishan could do anything, a rish appeared around the bend. It gave a harsh rasp, its thin mouth opening to show the rows of sharp teeth. Vishan didn't give it time to draw the thin, jagged blade from its belt. In one movement, without dropping his stride, he moved in towards it on one side and ducked low under the rish's upper arms. At the same time, the dagger in his own hand moved upwards to stab under the creature's jaw. Vishan knew that the rish could call out an alarm and he needed to silence it quickly. He did not want others to come running in response to its cries for help.

The blade sliced through the rish's neck and Vishan cut downwards to sever the vocal cords. The beast tried to bellow in pain and anger, but only a hiss of escaping air could be heard. Its narrow eyes were black with fury and an instant later the hissing was joined by the bubbling sound of blood spouting from the wound.

He still hadn't killed it though. Such fell creatures as this could rarely be defeated by a single blow from a small dagger. Vishan knew this from experience, which is why his first strike had been merely to silence it. Using its two lower arms, the rish was still struggling to release the clasp that held the knife in its belt. Vishan pulled back his dagger hand to strike again but the upper arms of the rish now grabbed hold of him. He felt its immense strength as the beast lifted him completely off the floor. Another slice of Vishan's knife raked across its egg shaped face, and his feet kicked wildly into the creature's stomach as he tried to make it let go of him.

The rish raised Vishan above its head and pinned him to the ceiling of the tunnel. He struggled to slash at it again, but the beast had finally managed to release its own dagger.

Blood was still pouring from the wound in its throat, but the rish didn't seem to be weakening at all. Panic engulfed Vishan. He was being forced tighter and tighter against the roof while the horrible creature took its time to bring the knife up and swap it to the claws in its upper right hand.

Vishan's body might have been squeezed against the roof by the beast's strength, but he still had both of his arms free. There was still a way for him to defend himself. As the rish knife came up towards him the pulver parried quickly with his own dagger, knocking the blow to the side. Twice, three times the rish stabbed up at him, but each time he was able to counteract the attack.

At last, by the fourth blow, Vishan sensed that the creature was feeling the effect of the wound in its throat. It was now breathing slowly and each thrust with the knife was becoming more listless. Dark blood was soaking through the rish's tunic front and was pooling on the floor of the corridor. At last its hold on Vishan grew too weak to hold him anymore and he was dropped to the ground.

With what felt like the last of his strength, Vishan turned in the air to land on his feet. He slipped momentarily in the slick blood on the stones, but pushed out his hand to the wall to support himself and quickly stepped out of the way of the rish as it fell towards him.

The creature landed on the ground with a sickening thump. It twitched a couple of times. Then with a final hiss of escaping air from its throat, it lay still.

Vishan leant back against the wall, breathing heavily. Every part of him ached and he felt a nauseous stirring deep in his stomach. He knew it was the adrenalin surging through him, threatening to make him sick. He swallowed down on the feeling, and struggled to stand upright again. There was no time to spend recovering. He still needed to find a way out.

As he concentrated on escape, his ears straining for any other sound, a low vibration began to creep across the floor and up the wall. He felt it shuddering through his feet and up into his back and across his shoulders. 'What now?' he thought to himself. 'I am too weary yet for another battle.'

But even as these thoughts of dismay and fear gnawed at his mind a white column of light sprang up from the ground below him. Vishan threw up a hand to shield his eyes from the blinding flash, the other gripping tighter onto the handle of his dagger. After a few moments the light began to dim again. Vishan's sight was still blurred. As he took his hand away from his face he could only just make out a dim, looming figure in front of him. He raised his dagger defensively.

A stern voice spoke. 'Put your weapon down lad. I've come to get you out.'

Vishan grinned in sudden recognition. It was his rescuer from earlier who had returned.

'About time.' Vishan pointed at the fading light of the pathway. 'If you have the power to do that, why didn't we just use a pathway to make our escape before, from my cell?'

'Your disappearance from these dungeons could not have any taint of magic about it,' his rescuer replied. 'That would lead suspicion to fall upon me.' He gazed at the dead rish on the ground. 'But I see you have created enough of a smokescreen. It will seem that the rish and harch were just too stupid and you escaped using your own wits. That is all to the good. Now come! We must get out of here.'

'You're taking me back?' Vishan asked. 'Back to Beltheron?'

'No,' the figure replied. 'Not to Beltheron. Not yet. I will get you safely out of this castle, but there is more that you have to do here on Atros first...'

A Cloud on the Horizon

A smaller, more intimate funeral service took place on Beltheron the following morning. Now, early rays of sunshine warmed the ground. The puddles of rain from the day before were already beginning to dry and a clear sky promised a hot day ahead.

The sun lit up a solemn procession as it made its way to a secluded spot. Six pulver soldiers carried a plain, wooden bier down the hillside in the same cemetery where Lord Ungolin had been laid to rest only yesterday. All were dressed in the familiar pale blue cloaks that signified their rank in Beltheron's forces.

They were followed closely by a young woman with long, striking, snow white hair. She carried in her arms a carefully folded cloak of the same blue which the rest of the pulver wore. The woman proudly held her head high, but it was easy to see the tears which welled up in her eyes reflecting the morning sun. Orianna Melgardes was paying her last respects to Parenon, the brave young soldier to whom she had given her heart.

Following behind her at a slow, dejected pace came her brother Serrion with Helen at his side. Then came Helen's parents, followed by a host of guards, soldiers and civilians. Each one knew the part that Parenon had played in the defeat of Larena the bird woman. All were keenly aware of the great debt they owed to the young captain for the sacrifice he had made, for saving the life of Orianna, and helping to stop the Andresens from taking over the City of Beltheron.

At last they reached the corner of the cemetery where Parenon was to be laid to rest. As befitting a farewell to a fallen officer, the pulver guards and soldiers all drew their long swords, polished to a dazzling sheen to honour their friend, and raised them in a defiant gesture so they pointed straight up to the cloudless dome of bright blue sky above.

The cry: 'For Mage and Council!' rang loud and clear from one throat, immediately echoed by all the others.

'For Parenon!'

Three more times the cry was repeated. 'For Mage and Council! For Parenon!' The final shout rose above their heads, carried on the light breeze until it could be heard in the streets of Beltheron City, even up to the great hall itself a quarter of a mile away.

A grave had been dug in the soft earth. The guards holding Parenon's coffin held it over the hole on thick ropes spun from the fibres of the hunnokken tree. No formal speeches were made today. Unlike Ungolin's funeral there was little in the way of show or ceremony. This was a farewell to a friend, not a state occasion. After the shouts of the pulver had died away there was silence again. Orianna merely stepped forwards to place the blue cloak over the coffin. On top of that she dropped a single red rose that she had been carrying. She murmured a few brief words in a voice so quiet that only the guards holding the ropes could hear. Some looked up to the sky or away from her, their faces showing the strength of their emotion. One of them, Cannish, who had known both of them well, had tears on his cheeks.

Orianna stepped back, a hand moving quickly up to her face and a sob escaping from her lips. Serrion was by her side immediately. He put his arms around her shoulders to support his sister as they stepped away. Behind them the coffin was slowly lowered into the grave.

More voices were now murmuring their own memories and thoughts of Parenon. In the tradition of Beltheron, these were personal moments of reflection, filled with reverence and honour to mark his passing.

As she blinked back her own tears, Helen thought of how much more meaningful this small ceremony was to her than all the pomposity of the day before. Anger rose in her again at the betrayal she felt at the hands of Ungolin and Cleve Harrow. She was also angry at herself. She still had not been able to summon up the courage, or find the right moment, to tell Serrion the terrible secrets that she had discovered.

Parenon's coffin had now been placed in the ground. The ropes of the hunnokken were then dropped in to curl on top of it. The fibres of the ropes contained seeds from the tree so that they would eventually grow and unfurl their white and gold flowers over the grave every spring.

Soon the figures began to turn away. Again there was no signal, no formal ceremony to the grieving and remembrance.

Serrion turned back towards the grave for a few more moments. This man Parenon had been more than just his protector. Over the two years that he had known him, he had become his friend.

'Thank you,' he whispered. 'Thank you for everything.'

As he began to turn away he saw that Orianna was still standing just behind him. Her attention was focused on the grave. Serrion realised that it was difficult for her to leave this place. Once she had gone from here she would have to begin the next stage of her life without Parenon. She would have to accept that he was really gone. As long as she stood here, by his graveside, that terrible lonely moment could be delayed.

Serrion stepped up closer to Orianna. He felt awkward. He didn't know what to say to her. He knew that he didn't really understand the feelings that his sister and Parenon had for each other. He didn't know what words to use to comfort her and a part of him felt guilty about the embarrassment he now felt.

In the end he just held out his hand towards her. She took it gratefully and squeezed it hard between her own. A simple whispered 'Thank you' was all that was needed between them. She swallowed hard and hugged her brother.

They stood together for a long time. Everyone else had now gone, and they were alone.

At last, Serrion found his voice.

'He'd want us all to carry on, you know,' he said. 'He would want us to be as brave as he was, and carry on fighting the battle against Atros.'

Orianna nodded. She wiped her eyes with the back of her hand and stood up very straight.

'I know,' she said. 'And I will be. I will be as brave as he could wish.'

She looked down once more, briefly. 'Come on, time to go,' she said at last.

Just as they were about to walk back down the hillside towards Beltheron, a familiar sensation began to creep over Serrion. Something about the grave had drawn his attention. It seemed that a faint, red glow was rising up from the coffin. Leaving Orianna's side for a moment he stepped back to the graveside and looked down.

The rose that his sister had dropped on top of the coffin was now glowing brightly. The red colour filled the grave and began spiralling upwards, towards Serrion.

Recently Serrion's visions in the red light had started to become much more distinct and detailed than ever before. He still had no control over when he received these warnings, but at least he didn't have to guess at their meanings any more. Now they were much more specific, like yesterday's vision of the knife hurtling towards him, and the stranger with the odd eyes. The red glow intensified around him and began to take solid shapes like a film unspooling in his head.

There could be no doubt about what he was now seeing. He recognised the high street of Beltheron as it led up towards the main square and the great hall. The vision in his head showed the streets filled with people. It must be a market day for it to be so busy, he thought.

The people began to raise their heads to the sky, pointing amazedly. Serrion saw fear in their eyes. Many opened their mouths in silent screams. A dark shadow sped across their features.

His red-tinged vision swung upwards so that he was now seeing what the people were looking at. For a moment he thought of birds in uncountable thousands flocking to attack. But that had already happened; the attack of the bird army was in the past and Larena the bird woman had been defeated. His visions never showed him the past, only the future. This was something that was *going* to happen. Then he realised that what he was seeing was an immense cloud moving swiftly over the rooftops. It was so large and moving with such intention that Serrion had an immediate sense of a solid roiling mass of evil.

As the shadow of the cloud progressed across the city the people began to fall. Many clutched at their heads as the darkness touched them. Many more ran madly to escape, hurling themselves through doorways or diving behind walls to find shelter.

Serrion cried out and shook his head from side to side to try to clear the horror of the vision.

He felt comforting arms around him. Serrion blinked a couple of times and looked up to see Orianna looking at him with an anxious expression on her face. He had slumped down against the bole of the tree and it was all his sister could do to hold him upright.

'Serrion? Serrion! Are you alright?'

'I've seen something terrible, Orianna,' he began. 'A cloud.'

'Just a cloud? There's nothing so special or terrible about that. Come on, let's go.' The recent sorrow and anguish of the funeral made her speak sharply to him.

'No, wait. This cloud wasn't ordinary. It was thick, like some kind of liquid covering everything, and it's coming this way.'

His fear finally reached her. Orianna felt a quick pang of guilt at being so snappish with him a moment before. She looked all around her quickly, as if she expected to see the cloud about to descend on them even as they stood there under the hunnokken tree.

Serrion shook his head. 'No, it's not here yet,' he told her. 'But it could be coming soon. It's going to happen on a market day. We need to tell Matt.'

Orianna jerked her head once in agreement.

'Come, I'll take you,' she said. 'Can you stand on your own?'

'I think so. It was just the shock of seeing all those people...' he broke off again and shuddered as the memory of his vision came back to him once more.

She let go of his arms and after a moment of wobbling he did feel ok. His legs could support him again.

'Let's go, he said. 'We have to get to the great hall right away.'

* * *

Serrion wasn't the only one with news for the new Lord of Beltheron. Helen was now back at home with her mother and father.

'Mum, Dad,' she began. 'I have something important to tell you.'

Her father had gone straight to his desk after they had returned from Parenon's funeral. His work as the new Lord was keeping him busy. But hearing the tone of his daughter's voice he put down the papers he had been studying and raised his eyes towards her.

'What is it? You look troubled.'

'I don't know how to start,' she said.

'Is it something we can help with?' Jenn asked

Helen shook her head. 'No. I mean, I don't think, I... oh I just don't know.'

Jenn moved quickly towards her. She had seen the fear in her daughter's eyes.

'Don't worry,' she said. 'You know that whatever it is, we will sort it out.'

'You can't,' Helen replied. 'It's too big to sort out, and anyway, it's too late. It's already been done.'

'Now you're beginning to scare me,' her father said. 'What's already been done?' For the first time there was a hint of suspicion in his voice, an extra darkness behind his worried expression.

Even though the new look in her father's eyes scared her she knew that it was too late to turn back now. Helen took a deep breath. She had always been able to trust her parents before, she reasoned with herself. They had always tried to make it easy for her to talk about things. She glanced over to her mother for a moment. Jenn gave a short nod, to encourage her to continue. It gave Helen the extra confidence she needed.

'Please don't be angry,' she began. 'I know where Cleve Harrow is.'

There was total silence in the room for several seconds. Jenn and Matt just stared at their daughter, mouths open, eyes wide with amazement. No reason or explanation had been found for the sudden disappearance of the Cleve over a week ago.

'Have you spoken to him?' Matt asked. 'Has he been in contact with you?'

She shook her head. 'No, or at least not in the way you mean.' She took a gulp of breath. 'Remember when Serrion went to Earth, back to London to search his old house?'

Her mother and father both nodded. Jenn had sunk down onto a chair in the corner of the room. Her eyes fixed on her daughter, intent on her every word. 'Go on,' she whispered.

'There was a missing book on Piotre and Sophia's shelves,' Helen went on.

'And what about this missing book?' Matt asked.

'Orianna seemed to think that it was important.'

Her mother nodded. 'It was. Those books contained vital information about magical lore and new spells that the Andresens were developing.'

Matthias leaned forward eagerly. 'Helen, do you know where that missing book is?'

Helen glanced from one to the other of them. This was it, she had to tell them everything, she had to trust in her mother and father and believe that they would know what to do.

'When I went with the Cleve, I saw the missing book on his desk,' she began. 'I recognised it straight away because it had a purple cover and the same silvery writing as all the others.'

'But why did the Cleve...' Matt's question was stopped by his wife putting her hand firmly on his arm. She looked at him and shook her head, guessing how important it was for her daughter to be allowed time to tell her story in her own way.

'I glanced down at the book and he saw me looking,' Helen continued. 'He must have realised straight away that I recognised it and knew that he had been discovered. I suppose he didn't think there was any reason to hide anymore, and so he told me that there was an inscription in the front of the book.'

'An inscription? What kind of inscription, some kind of spell?'

Helen shook her head. 'No, it was a message. A greeting from him to the Andresens.'

Cold fear filled Matthias at what his daughter was about to say.

'A message?'

Helen nodded. 'Something he didn't want any of us to see.'

'He was a traitor?' Matt asked under his breath. 'You're telling me that Cleve Harrow was the one who betrayed us to the Andresens – and to the Wild Lord himself?'

Helen shook her head. 'Not in the way you mean,' she said. 'He confessed that he and Ungolin had taken advice from the Seer of Beltheron; he told me that the two of them had plotted to convince Piotre and Sophia that their own son should be taken to Atros, to become the pupil of the Wild Lord, and that an unknown child – a child from an ordinary family like Serrion – should be kidnapped from his own home to take his place.'

Jenn was shaking her head in disbelief. 'It can't be,' she murmured. 'I don't believe it.'

'Sorry Mum, but the Cleve told me himself.'

'But why in the three worlds would he do that?' Jenn asked.'

'He must have had a good reason,' Matt said. 'The Cleve never did anything without a good reason.' He turned back to Helen. 'Did he tell you what that reason was my dear?' he asked her in a gentler voice.

She nodded. 'He told me that he and Lord Ungolin had been convinced by the Seer that this was the best way to eventually defeat the Andresens and win the battle against Atros.'

'Even though it has caused so much pain, so much destruction?' Matthias breathed.

Helen nodded again.

There was a long silence in the room. Helen felt a huge relief that she had at last been able to tell her secret. In fact, the relief was so great, that she almost giggled. No one dared speak, or even look at each other for several moments. Finally, Matthias cleared his throat.

'I still do not see all the whys and wherefores of this,' he said. 'No doubt they will be revealed in due course. I will have to question the Seer, T'yuq Tinyaz myself.

'The most important thing now is Harrow,' he decided. 'You said you know where he is, Helen?'

Helen nodded, dumbly. She began to speak, but the words caught in her throat. She tried again.

'After he had told me this, I suppose he realised he was going to have to get rid of me. So that I didn't spoil his plans. He attacked me, and I panicked. I managed to get away from him and back home, back here. You were both out. You were in the great hall I think.

'I managed to get in here, even though he – Cleve Harrow I mean – he had already put pulver guards around the house by the time I arrived. I managed to sneak in and reach my bedroom. I created a pathway and disappeared to Earth.'

'Did he follow you?' her mother asked, concern etched on her face.

'Yes,' she said. 'But I managed to get away again. I took one of the horses from the stables where I used to go riding and he followed me up Roseberry Topping.' She paused for a moment, thinking about the ride up the steep hillside of Roseberry close to their home on Earth.

'There was a struggle near the edge,' she continued at last. 'Harrow fell over the edge. I didn't stop to look but I think...I think I killed him'

'Matt stepped forwards and put his arms around his daughter to comfort her. 'It was not your fault,' he began. 'You could not have done anything else. It sounds as if he would have killed you if he had the chance.'

He squeezed her tightly, and kissed the top of her hair. It felt so good to have her dad there that she hugged him for a long time. But she knew that she hadn't finished yet. There was one more thing she had to tell them both.

'There's something else,' she said slowly. 'I... I wasn't alone on the hill. Someone else went up Roseberry with me.'

She felt Matt's arms go loose around her shoulders. He took a step back to look her in the eye.

'Someone else?' he whispered.

'Someone from Earth?' Jenn added.

'Megan Thomas, one of the girls I used to ride with,' she told them. 'Megan saw everything. Harrow, the pathway, she saw it all.'

There was silence for several moments. All three considered the implications of an Earthbound human becoming aware of the pathways, and the possibilities of the other worlds.

Finally Matt spoke.

'Well, it is done,' he said simply. 'We cannot go back and change it. We must now go forwards and deal with what follows as best we can.'

Jenn was still gazing blankly into the middle distance. 'He must be told,' she said quietly, almost to herself. 'Serrion must be told.'

'I know,' Helen replied. 'But I just couldn't bring myself to do it.'

Her mother nodded in understanding. 'I can appreciate that,' she said. 'You must not blame yourself my love. I do not think that I would have known how to tell him either.'

'I will do it,' Matthias said firmly. 'I will tell Serrion the truth about the Cleve. And I must do it straight away.'

Pictures from the Past

Matthias made his way immediately to the great hall. He was just about to send Cannish out into Beltheron to bring Serrion to him when Cannish interrupted him.

'But Lord Matthias, there is no need. Young Serrion is already here.'

'What? Here in the great hall?

'Yes my Lord,' Cannish answered. 'He arrived a short while ago with his sister and asked to see you. He said it was most urgent.'

Matthias's brow furrowed.

'Thank you, Cannish. Send the boy to me right away.'

Cannish gave a short bow before turning on his heel to find Serrion. As he left the great hall he did not notice the lines of worry on the face of Lord Matthias.

Serrion was waiting with Orianna at the bottom of a wide staircase. It led through a huge tapestry at the top and into the long corridor up to the Great hall. They had passed the time waiting for Cannish to come for him by looking at the pictures woven into the tapestry. He remembered seeing it for the first time, when he had first visited Beltheron with Cleve Harrow.

The tapestry showed images of great battles from Beltheron's past history. Brave riders dressed in the now familiar pale blue of the pulver rode tall horses into a horde of rish. In one corner of the picture he could make out a looming figure in a dark cloak brandishing a long black staff. Flames flickered from its tip. Serrion recognised it as the magical black staff of Atros. He shivered to think that he had faced that weapon himself, and that he had killed Jacques Andresen in a fight by pushing him onto one of its broken shards. He forced the memory back and tried to think of happier things.

'Do you remember when I first came here and you told me about all the millions of stitches in these tapestries?' he asked Orianna.

She smiled. 'Seventeen million, four hundred and eighty three thousand, six hundred and ninety one,' she said. 'How could I forget that day? It was most special to me, it was the day we met, and I didn't even know then that you were my brother.'

They both gazed up at the tapestry again, lost in their memories. Then, the figures in the embroidered picture moved and shimmered as the drapes parted and Cannish stepped through.

Serrion got to his feet from the old wooden bench where they had been sitting as Cannish beckoned to him. He turned and looked back at his sister.

'Will you be alright?' she asked him.

He nodded and climbed the steps to follow the pulver through the tapestry and into the long corridor beyond.

Old statues lined the walls of this corridor but Serrion had never really noticed them before. Today however, perhaps because he had just been thinking of the history of Beltheron, he studied them one by one as he followed Cannish. He felt inspired by the pictures of ancient battles and images from the past that surrounded him.

The lines of statues told the story of the heritage of the land. The lords and rulers of the city were set out one after the other leading all the way up to where the corridor opened out into the wide space of the great hall. Many were ancient, cracked and worn in spite of the care they had received over centuries, but the most recent one closest to the hall shone with newness. Serrion glanced up at this new statue. The familiar features of Lord Ungolin gazed back at him. The sculptor had cleverly worked a friendly gleam into the eyes of Ungolin's stone face.

There was no comfort in that gleam for Serrion though. As he was about to go past the statue and approach the raised dais where Matthias was sitting, he felt a chill wind blow through the corridor behind him. The wind seemed to carry the echoing voices of all the past lords of Beltheron. For a moment it felt like the statues were talking to him, reminding him of all that had happened in that great land, and all that was still to be done. Serrion shivered, though whether it was from the cold of the sudden breeze, or the voices in his head, he couldn't be sure.

Matthias was gesturing for him to step forwards. He made his way to the dais and high throne. Serrion shook his head to clear it and concentrate on the things he had come here to say.

'Matt, I mean, Lord Matthias,' Serrion began. The new Lord of Beltheron waved away the formality dismissively.

'Forget about that title between the two of us my boy. Just plain old Matt will do,' he said. 'Or *Uncle* Matt, if you still prefer it?' He smiled at Serrion. He wanted to give him as much friendship and support as he could before he told him Helen's news.

Serrion nodded gratefully. Then they both started talking at once.

'Serrion, I have something very impor...'

'Uncle Matt, I need to...'

Matt's face grew dark as he looked at the boy's expression. He had been so preoccupied with what he was about to say that he hadn't really noticed the other's mood until this moment. However, he could now see that Serrion himself was also extremely concerned about something. He decided to let the boy speak about what was already on his mind, before he added to his burden.

'Sorry my boy, you go first.'

Serrion began, haltingly at first, but then adding more and more detail about his vision of the dark cloud. As he spoke, Matthias leaned further and further forward, his hands gripping the arms of the high throne until his knuckles were white.

'And you think that this could happen at any time?' he asked when Serrion had finished.

He shook his head in reply.

'The visions are becoming fuller, more complete,' Serrion told him. 'Not like before where we all had to just keep our eyes open and be careful whenever I saw red lights in front of me. Now I'm seeing whole scenes. They're more like proper clues. I still don't know *exactly* when this will happen, but it is on a market day.'

Matthias's eyebrows knit into a ragged line of concentration. 'Well done, Serrion,' he said quietly. 'We can use this information. There are two market days in the next week. I will send out an order for them to be postponed until we can learn more.'

The decision made, the Lord of Beltheron sank back into his chair. He looked exhausted.

The weight of Matthias's new responsibilities were obviously weighing very heavily upon him. Serrion thought that he looked much older. His usual cheerful demeanour had darkened over the last weeks. The usual wide smile on Matt's friendly face had gone and his expression was now grave. He had lines of worry and care creased around his eyes. Serrion also noticed that Matt's hair had begun to sprout several fine strands of grey and silver at the temples.

Matthias stared hard at Serrion for several moments without speaking. Serrion found it hard to meet the new Lord of Beltheron's gaze. At long last Matthias broke the silence.

'This warning you have had is very timely,' he began. 'However it is not the first worrying news I have received today, and I feel that the two things may be linked. This other piece of information concerns you closely, Serrion,' he continued. 'It will come as a harsh shock, so I am afraid you must prepare yourself.

Serrion felt a numbing sensation of dread begin in the pit of his stomach.

'Go on,' he murmured. 'Whatever it is, tell me.'

'This morning Helen came to me with news of Cleve Harrow.'

'Harrow? She knows where he is?'

'No, not quite,' Matt was struggling to find a way to pass on the things that his daughter had told him. He began to understand the difficulty she must have felt in trying to speak to Serrion about it herself.

'So what did she tell you? What news has she got about him?' Serrion was insistent, moving up onto the first step of the dais.

'She wanted to tell you herself,' Matthias continued. 'But she couldn't find a way to begin.'

Serrion stared at him hard for a few moments.

'So please don't blame her for not telling you before,' Matthias went on.

Now Serrion could sense the importance of what was going on. 'What,' he said again. 'What did she tell you? Come on, you're making me nervous.'

'We know that Ungolin and Harrow took advice from

the Seer,' Matthias said.

'Seer?' Serrion didn't know what he meant. 'What is the Seer?'

Matthias leaned forwards in his chair. His gaze held Serrion's. There was a respect there in that gaze that the boy hadn't noticed before. That respect would probably also lead to him having to take more responsibility, he guessed. It made him feel strangely uncomfortable, for he knew that it meant even more dangers would be facing him soon.

'T'yuq Tinyaz, the Seer of Beltheron is hard to explain,' Matt said. 'It's difficult to know where to start.'

He made his decision. He would tell Serrion the truth about Harrow and Ungolin, but it would be easier for Serrion to understand its importance if he himself had met T'yuq Tinyaz face to face. Pushing himself up from the chair by his arms he stepped down from the high dais. He held his hand out towards Serrion.

'It will be better if I show you. Come my boy, follow me. It is high time that the two of you met.'

The Mind of Hethaloner Rasp

Piotre and Sophia Andresen sat together at the head of the long table. They were in the banqueting hall on the first floor of the rebuilt castle in Atros City. Ranged around them down either side of the table were a number of human guards, ministers and advisors. Small groups of rish and harch stood around near the doors at the far end of the hall. Food and drink was in abundance.

The Andresens were both in a foul mood. Vishan's escape from their dungeons two days ago had humiliated them, and robbed them of a vital source of information. Their rage made them push forwards hurriedly with this meeting.

'It is necessary to create a series of distractions on Beltheron,' Piotre was saying. 'Our plans,' he gestured to include his wife in this, 'our plans to destroy the Select Family and the people of Beltheron are about to come to fruition.'

'That is why we have enlisted the services of a great and powerful mage, Hethaloner Rasp,' Sophia added. 'He studied under the tutelage of the mighty Gretton Tur himself, deep in the caverns below Gendrell.'

'Hethaloner Rasp escaped the destruction of the castle two years ago,' Piotre continued. 'He has spent the time between then and now recreating the equipment that was destroyed on that terrible day. He has devoted his every waking hour to writing out the old texts that were lost from Tur's library. Working from memory and experiment he has recorded much knowledge of great value that was thought to be gone forever.'

'My husband and I are proud and delighted to welcome him here to our table tonight,' Sophia said. She raised her hand towards a figure sitting next to her on the left hand side of the table.

'Gentlemen,' Piotre concluded, 'raise your glasses and drink a toast to the worthy Hethaloner Rasp. He is the man who will help us to triumph once and for all over Beltheron.'

All around the table the gathering stood and raised their glasses as they had been bidden to do. Some of them did not look as delighted to see Hethaloner Rasp as Piotre and Sophia were. In fact, some of them looked downright terrified. Even so, Piotre's toast was followed by a series of loud cheers from everyone. No one dared to defy Piotre's word, or wanted to displease his chief guest in any way.

All knew about this man. Rasp's experiments and 'interviews' deep in the laboratories and dungeons of Gendrel were often accompanied by screams of fear and groans of pain. No one knew for certain how he came upon his knowledge, but there were rumours that he was a noetic. The noetics were a group of genius mages and brilliant thinkers that Gretton Tur had gathered around him. Their job had been to experiment with new ways of extracting information and knowledge from the memories and thoughts of others. It was said that Rasp had been one of Tur's most able noetics and that he had learnt how to read minds.

Hethaloner Rasp sat impassively. His gaze wandered slowly around the whole table, observing each and every one of those gathered there. His huge brain and inexhaustible memory took in details of all their faces, assessing strengths and loyalties, but his expression never once gave away anything that he might be feeling. Rasp's right eye was pale grey, almost colourless, but if you looked closely there was a tiny flicker of red and yellow deep in the iris of the other one. This left eye glittered evilly. A pair of wire framed spectacles hung at the end of his thin nose which drooped over a pair of wide, wet lips.

The three cheers echoed around the stone walls of the banqueting chamber and began to fade. When the sound had subsided Hethaloner Rasp slowly got to his feet. He was not a large man, in fact he was shorter than average, but the intensity of his eyes as he gazed around the table was so great that everyone's attention was riveted on him. They all feared him, and none could look away.

He looked around once more, peering into faces over the top of his glasses. Even those veteran soldiers who had faced battle and violent death numerous times now felt a little part of themselves quail with fear as his odd eyes met theirs. None could explain it, but each felt as if the noetic was looking into the most secret corners of their minds as his glance passed over them.

Then Rasp spoke. When he did it felt as if the energy was somehow being drained from the room, and all felt a cold breath upon their faces. Several shivered. Others now turned away in despair.

'The attack upon Beltheron that I am about to propose will be sudden and lethal,' Rasp began. 'We will strike them in the very heart of their city, and in a way that they will least expect.'

There were cheers and loud grunts of approval from all around the table.

'Our attack will use ancient knowledge that I have worked hard to salvage from the wreckage of our libraries. After long searching I found the spell that Gretton Tur was perfecting when he was assassinated by that brattish pulver Parenon and the other Belthronic scum. It is an incantation that we have used once before against Beltheron, many years ago. Its power was great even then, and caused great distress and destruction. Tur was near to finishing his studies to increase the spell's force. Now, I am proud to announce that after months of research I have found the missing links to complete that spell. We are now ready to unleash it upon the unsuspecting masses.'

All were now leaning forward, hanging on Rasp's every word. There were low murmurs of anticipation and excitement.

'There will be no escape. No reprieve. A dark cloud will descend on that city.'

Piotre and Sophia smiled wickedly at his side. This is what they had been waiting for. This was the plan they had discussed with Rasp.

'All will quail and fall before this cloud. Many will droop into sickness, while others will wither with depressed thought. For some it will mean death.'

Rasp felt his audience's attention. Some rose up slightly in their chairs in anticipation of what was coming next. There were glints of malicious glee in many of their expressions.

A nervous hand was lifted halfway down the table. One of the most respected soldiers of Atros had a question. Rasp raised his eyebrows at the thin, grey haired man. 'Yes, Rancid? You wish to ask something?'

Rancid Lure was the captain of great armies, the veteran of many battles, and the brutal killer of his enemies. But like the others, even he was fearful when under the gaze of the noetic. He slowly rose to his feet to speak.

'I am as eager as anyone at this table to support your ideas, Hethaloner,' he said in a deep voice. 'But I am a soldier. I depend upon strategy for success and I need to know your plans in detail.'

Hethaloner's eyes narrowed. Was this old soldier defying him? Was he questioning his authority? He looked deep into Lure's face, focusing on his inner thoughts. Rancid Lure felt the intrusion and almost sat back again in his chair as he felt the power drain from him and into Rasp's mind. It only lasted a few moments though. It seemed that Rasp was satisfied by what he had seen, and convinced that Lure was trustworthy.

'Go on, Rancid,' he spoke softly and warmly. 'We have great faith in your stratagems and knowledge of tactics in matters such as these. Tell us what you need to know.'

Rancid Lure cleared his throat. 'I meant no offence,' he began. 'We simply need to hear the details of how, where and when this spell, this...this *darkness,* is to be created.'

'A good question, and one that I was coming to if you had not been so impatient to interrupt,' Rasp answered. The calming, friendly tone in his voice had gone again. He now spoke in a way that made Lure sit down quickly, his face growing red with embarrassment.

'There is now a way to deliver this threat that will strike at the very core of Beltheron. The illness begins with the poisoning of just one individual. The darkness then spreads quickly, growing from the very breath of the infected one. It multiplies and grows like choking smoke from a wood fire. Within five days the sickness, weakness and death that I have described will cover the whole city.'

'And who will you poison?' asked another of the generals sitting opposite Lure. 'Where exactly will our attack begin?'

Piotre answered. 'It begins with revenge,' he said. 'You all know that our own son, Jacques, was murdered in the recent attack upon Beltheron City.' Everyone lowered their heads in respect. Piotre continued 'My wife and I have suffered the loss of our child. It is a pain and grief that no one can describe. We intend to show the new Lord of Beltheron that same grief. Our target is Helen, the daughter of Matthias and Jenia. She is the one who will be poisoned, and they will see their daughter wither and die before the darkness enfolds them all.'

There was silence around the table. Even the battle-hardened soldiers of Atros were taken aback by the thought of a deliberate attack on an innocent child. Rasp was immediately aware of their thoughts and knew he had to take control of the meeting again.

'But before our main attack we need to cause a diversion to distract our enemy,' he called out in a loud, commanding voice. 'We will set in motion a series of events to confuse and fluster the new Lord of Beltheron and his pathetic soldiery.'

He knew he had recovered their attention. 'Matthias and his wife will soon weep for mercy. They will be so busy running around trying to protect their citizens and loved ones from this diversion, that no one will notice our main attack until it is too late.'

He glowered around the table. Even the rish guards who lined the walls of the chamber leaned forward in expectation of what Rasp was going to say next.

'Rancid Lure, you must prepare your army for travel,' he announced. The diversion will begin in two days. This is what we are going to do...'

Everyone around the table held their breath as Hethaloner Rasp began to tell them his plan.

Serrion and the Seer

Matt led Serrion down a long, dim corridor. They were somewhere in a maze of tunnels below the great hall. A spiral stair leading from the pulver's quarters at the side of the hall had taken them deep below the very foundations of Beltheron City. Serrion followed close behind the older man, fearing that he would not be able to find his way out of this network of passages alone.

In the flickering light which came from the torch in Matt's hand, Serrion could make out torn, dusty tapestries and other, more ancient art sketched roughly into the flaking plaster of the walls. This place must be even older than the great hall itself, Serrion mused to himself. They walked for several minutes without speaking. By now Serrion had stopped trying to work out exactly how far they had come, or what part of Beltheron City might now be above them.

At last they came to a large room. The walls were filled with paintings of former Select Family members, family trees and coats of arms. Several rusting suits of armour peered down at him with their blank visors like silent guardians of age old secrets. He imagined that he recognised features on the cracked, oil-painted faces that had been passed down through the Select generations; he saw Jenn's nose there, on the picture of a young girl in a flowing party robe; Matt's wide mouth over there on the grim-looking face of an old general with a chest full of medals; and surely that was Piotre's evil leer staring down at him from a faded picture of an old man enveloped in a mage's black cloak. And everywhere, in picture after picture, Helen's glittering eyes shone down at him through the years from ancestors long forgotten.

Serrion slowed down to look more closely at some of these portraits. His eyes scanned the dim room. At the far end, near to a doorway that Matt was about to walk through, one particular picture caught his eye. He stepped more quickly towards it. As he drew near and looked up Serrion felt a sudden lurch in his stomach. This painting was a huge full-length portrait of a strikingly beautiful woman. She was very familiar. Dark hair flowed to her shoulders and her thin mouth was stretched into a friendly smile, but her posture was aloof and defiant. She had been painted in the bright flush of youth, only about nineteen years of age, he guessed. The woman stood beneath a tree with open fields behind her leading to a large house in the distance.

The artist had skilfully filled the painting with shafts of sunlight lancing through the branches to shine on her upturned face. As Serrion stood, transfixed, in front of the painting, this sunlight began to glow bright red. The expression on the painted woman's face began to change. From a friendly smile, filled with the promise of a happy life stretching before her, her mouth began to twist in fear. Regret now filled her eyes. As the red of Serrion's vision grew deeper, he saw flames begin to flicker in the windows of the house. 'No, this isn't happening,' he muttered to himself. 'It *can't* be happening. It's just a picture.'

But the image kept changing. The red tints became deeper still and now he could hear the crackling of flames as the fire raged more furiously inside the house. He looked back at the woman and saw that her eyes were filled with tears. The edges of the canvas were beginning to turn brown. An instant later the whole painting erupted in a blaze of flame. Serrion couldn't breathe. He felt a wave of heat blast over him. Just before he blacked out, Serrion thought he saw the young woman raise her arms to defend herself. Her face was charred now and a terrified scream rang in his ears...

The next thing he knew, he was lying on the ground and Matt was crouching down next to him.

'Don't worry boy,' Matt said. 'It's over now, whatever it was.'

'Did you see it?' Serrion asked him. 'The fire in the picture?'

Matt shook his head briefly. 'I saw nothing.'

Serrion looked up at the painting once more. But now there was no sign of the carnage that he had seen moments before. There was the young woman, smiling out at them from the middle of the picture, the sunlight dappling her face, the house peaceful and welcoming in the background.

He struggled up to a sitting position, feeling very embarrassed. He had fainted like this in front of Matthias before, but he had been younger then, still just a boy. With a shiver he remembered the image in his mind had been the same then – flames flickering through the windows of a burning building – on that evening over two years ago which had started this whole new life for him at Matt and Jenn's house on Earth.

As he was helped to his feet, the questions began to come to him.

'The woman in the picture, who was she?'

'You don't recognise her?' Matt's voice had a note of trepidation in it as he asked the question.

Serrion nodded. 'I do,' he murmured. 'Or at least I think so. It made me think of Sophia.'

It was Matt's turn to nod. 'It's a portrait of Sophia's and Jenia's mother,' he stated simply. 'The family resemblance was always very close.'

'I never met my gra...' Serrion stopped himself. He had been about to call the woman in the portrait his grandmother. Of course she wasn't. Why, after all this time, did he still have to keep reminding himself that Sophia was not, had *never* been, his real mother. He clenched his teeth together angrily.

'What happened to her, to...to Sophia's mother?' he asked.

Matt glanced away for a moment. Then he looked back at Serrion firmly and directly.

'It seemed like a terrible accident,' he began. 'Sophia and her mother were alone in the house. 'Jenn and I had recently married and Jenn had moved out of the family home.'

'Is that the house there, the one in the picture?'

'Yes, that is where Jenn and Sophia grew up,' Matt nodded. 'No one knows exactly what happened, but it at the time it was thought that an unguarded fire in the kitchen got out of control. Jenn told me the tale years later, it was clear that she was still very distressed. She said it was almost as if she blamed herself for not being there that day, for not being able to do anything to help.'

Serrion understood this perfectly. He too had felt guilt when his own mother, Korellia, had been killed by Larena the bird woman. Why had he not been there to save her? There had been many nights when he had lain awake, turning that day over and over in his mind.

Matt had stopped talking. He was looking down at the ground, lost in his own memories of what that day had meant to Jenn, maybe even feeling a little of that same guilt himself, at not being able to ease his wife's mind about it after so many years.

'Go on,' Serrion urged. 'What happened?

'Jenn and I were due to visit them,' Matt began. 'In fact, we were just about to set off. Her mother had written to us telling us there was something important that she wanted to talk to us about. She sounded upset in her letter. Jenn knew that she had been arguing a lot with Sophia recently. We thought at the time that it was something to do with that.'

'But now you think perhaps it could have been something more?' Serrion suggested.

Matt nodded. 'Yes, perhaps so. After all we have learned in recent years about Sophia and Piotre's actions, I would not be surprised if her mother had not discovered some terrible secret that she wanted to tell us about. We can't know for certain, but maybe she suspected the truth about her daughter's connection with Gretton Tur. If that is the case then perhaps Sophia needed to silence her mother before she could talk to anyone else about her discovery. It is horrible to think of it, but maybe that fire *wasn't* an accident. Although Jenn and I have never really spoken of it, I know that we both suspect the same thing. Sophia caused that fire. Sophia killed her own mother.'

Serrion did not know what to say. This woman Sophia was expert in all kinds of lies, tricks and cruelty. He knew that from personal experience. Even now, after two years of knowing the truth about his own past, it still hurt when he thought of the deception that Sophia and Piotre had gone through, the way they had used him all through his life.

They turned away from the picture and continued along in silence for another minute or so. Then Matt took a turning to the left. He gestured towards a long, thin corridor ahead of them. Serrion thought he smelt a faint waft of fresh, cool air on his face as he peered down into the darkness. Then, as Matt pushed him gently onwards, and as his eyes began to grow accustomed to the dark, Serrion could make out a dim, yellowy light further down the corridor in front of them.

'On your own from here, boy,' Matt murmured. 'The Seer is through there. She doesn't like crowds.'

'Just the two of us, a crowd?' Serrion thought to himself. He swallowed hard, and started to walk carefully down the corridor, leaving Matt standing alone. With every step he took he was remembering the dangers he had faced before when he had made his way through dark, underground caverns. But that had been on Atros, he reminded himself, not under the great hall of Beltheron, and not with Lord Matthias behind him for protection.

His footfalls echoed on the stone floor. As he walked the light seemed to grow brighter, until he was no longer feeling his way slowly, but stepping with more determination and courage. After some fifty metres, the corridor finally bent around one last time and Serrion found himself in a wide circular cavern. It curved upwards into an immense space over his head that seemed to go up and up without stopping. 'Did we really come down so many steps under the earth?' he wondered. A still pool of milky liquid filled the middle of this huge hall. Yellow, flickering light glowed under the surface. It looked to Serrion as if this was the source of the light that had been guiding him down the corridor.

There, in the centre of the pool rose a small island of bare, white rock and on top of it stood the Seer of Beltheron, T'yuq Tinyaz. Serrion gave an involuntary gasp. She looked unlike anything else he had ever seen. Even his extraordinary adventures in the two years since he had first travelled the pathways were nothing compared to what he now saw.

She was dressed in a long flowing robe of pale green. Although the breeze rippled the fabric, she herself stood perfectly immobile. She had cascading hair which was the same colour as the yellow light, almost as if it had been dyed by the waters of the pool itself. It was her eyes that struck him most. They were white and blank, and as Serrion stared at her he realised she didn't once blink, but stared ahead impassively.

He continued staring until he thought he must have been there for over a minute. He was just considering whether to clear his throat, or introduce himself in some way, when the Seer spoke. Her voice was clear and strong, and had a hint of melody in it.

'Welcome Serrion Melgardes, hero of the future.'

His throat closed as if he were choking, and no words, no sound, would come from his lips to reply to her. He remained staring at her eyes and realised that the whites had gone from them. They now glared out at him in a vivid, bright red. He gasped and clutched at his dry throat. As she fixed her hypnotic stare at Serrion a crimson mist engulfed him. It swirled through the cavern, twisting around him in bright, rapid currents. He felt himself being lifted up into the air by it, and gasped in shock as he realised that he was being carried over the lake by the force of the Seer and his connection with her. He felt the light touch him like questing fingers as it curled around his body. Then the grip of the red tendrils grew tighter and it clutched at him like ropes, pulling him closer to the centre of the lake.

T'yuq Tinyaz's hands were now stretched out towards him in a strange, unsettling welcome. Shafts of light an even brighter crimson than that surrounding them shot from her fingers. He couldn't struggle, even though he felt a wild panic rising up in his chest. He could only wait, until he felt himself being drawn down onto the island to stand next to the waiting figure.

His toes touched down on the rock of the island. Serrion stretched out his arms to balance as he felt himself begin to topple over after his strange descent.

T'yuq Tinyaz, the Seer of Beltheron, reached out her own arms to the boy. Her fingers gripped his shoulders tightly, steadying him. Her grasp felt icy cold and a numbness began to spread through Serrion's body.

'There is a reason you are here,' she whispered. 'Can you see it? *Have* you seen it?'

He gulped painfully, but then found the dryness in his mouth and throat receding. He took a breath and shook his head.

'I don't think so. Not yet anyway. But what is it... what am I supposed to see?'

Her eyes bored into him. He felt it as a physical connection. It was as if her gaze was holding him as firmly as strong arms could. He forced himself to match her stare. Up close he could see a sequence of tiny, moving images in the red of her eyes.

Harrow, the golden staff, followed by Helen's sleeping face, then an image of a small bright flower. And then he saw a whirling figure, spinning swords effortlessly in his hands. Then, finally, another figure, throwing a hidden dagger towards him, far too swiftly for him to avoid. He saw the dagger speed towards his chest.

This last image made him cry out aloud and he staggered backwards from the Seer. Thankfully his mind began to clear and after a few moments, his visions had gone.

'He is quick, is he not?' she asked him. It was immediately obvious to Serrion that, whatever he was seeing, T'yuq Tinyaz was seeing it too. 'And his blades flash like fire with their frightening speed as they come towards you.'

Serrion nodded. 'But I don't know what this is supposed to mean. How can these images be any good to me if it's all just a mystery?'

'Do not try to solve this as if it were a riddle,' she answered. 'Remember that answering a question is not always about finding one solid meaning. Proper understanding, *real* knowledge, never comes from just one answer Serrion. So don't expect your visions to give you one decision, or point you in the direction of only one path. There are many paths. Sometimes your visions will only leave you with an awareness of a possibility of some of those paths.'

An *awareness* of a *possibility*? What did that mean? This was worse than the maths lessons he had struggled with in school. His head spun with even more confusion.

'I still don't know how...' he began.

'These images that we see are not always visions of what *will definitely* be, but only hints of one of many *possible* futures. With awareness, with knowledge of these possible futures, we can then choose how we act to change the outcomes, how we might alter the path to create a different future.' T'yuq Tinyaz paused. Her strange eyes flickered for a moment. Serrion imagined that there was a terrible grief in her expression as she continued. 'Different futures for others... and for ourselves.'

This was by now far too much for Serrion to take in.

'But what if I don't want it,' he butted in. 'What if this gift, this ability to see the future is something I can't cope with. Something I don't *want* to deal with?'

'It is too much for some,' she answered him kindly. She opened her arms in a gesture that took in the cavern and milky lake surrounding them. 'This was the path that I chose, to come here, to give in completely to my visions. And, by doing that, to serve Beltheron. But it does not have to be your path too. Remember that you have a choice in this as well Serrion.'

'So can I...can I stop my visions,' he asked. 'Can I do that?'

She shook her head and, for just a moment, Serrion thought he saw a deep regret in her eyes. Then it was gone again and her strength returned.

'No Serrion, they cannot be stopped. You cannot simply turn off your Seering like turning a tap to stop a flow of water. Your visions are part of who you are, you can no more stop them than you can stop yourself dreaming when you are asleep, or drinking when you feel thirst.'

'In that case, what you said a minute ago was just a lie.' His voice had become angry now. He had hoped for clear answers from T'yuq Tinyaz. Instead he was left feeling more frustrated and confused than ever. 'I don't have a choice in all this, I can't choose my own path at all.'

'It is hard, I know,' she spoke soothingly, ignoring his growing frustration. 'As so often happens when the answers are not what we want to hear, they are difficult to accept. But believe me when I say that you *do* have a choice. You cannot *stop* these visions, but you can *control* them.'

'How do I do that?' he asked.

'Try to put them in a part of your mind where they can be ignored for a while. That will give you time to think more clearly about how you are going to respond to your visions, and what they will inspire you to do.'

Serrion considered this deeply for several moments. He realised that he had never really acted on his visions before. He had merely seen them as warnings of definite danger, something that was bound to happen no matter what he did. Now it seemed that T'yuq Tinyaz was telling him that he had the power to change the things he had seen.

The Seer began speaking to him again.

'Don't just let the visions happen to you,' she said, almost as if she knew what he had just been thinking. 'Summon them yourself. The very act of taking control of your premonitions shapes them, dictates which things you actually see.'

'But how can I do *that*?' he asked again. Serrion was getting impatient at T'yuq Tinyaz's incomprehensible words. 'It sounds like you're asking me to knit fog.'

'It can feel like that,' she replied. 'So focus on something solid. Something you know to be real, and of the earth.'

'Like what?' '

A stone, or a rock will do. They are older than imagination, and can be a source of opening.'

There she goes again, he thought, talking madness. '*Opening*?' he asked. 'What's that?'

'The opening is the red light that you see. The herald of your visions. So far you have seen these openings in many things, random objects and places. As I have just told you, now you must control the openings, direct the light to show you specific things.'

'So I stare at a *rock*?'

'A rock is a good place to start. An easy object to begin practising upon. But a rock is a dead thing. Much better – when you are ready – is something living and ancient.'

'Like a tree?'

'Ahh, now you begin to understand. A tree is perfect. Think of all it has seen, its long life. Think of roots going down into the earth and branches shooting high into the air, with a view over miles and miles...'

Serrion was reluctant to believe that this made any sense. It sounded crazy. And yet, crazier things had happened to him – frequently. Harrow and Ungolin had trusted this strange woman, and – it seemed – so did Matt.

T'yuq Tinyaz continued. 'Let the world around you

fade, and let the tree, or the rock, become your whole world. Stare into it. Try to see inside it. Let the opening show you... show you...'

Her voice drifted off, and her eyes which had held his with such fixity began to flicker. Serrion realised that another of her visions had suddenly begun.

As if he had been told to do it, Serrion closed his own eyes as well. Immediately he felt the Seer's grip on him tighten and there sprang up between them the image of a long, cold looking hallway of carved stone. He knew at once that he and T'yuq Tinyaz were both seeing the same thing. He concentrated along with her.

> At one end of the hallway was a high throne of hard obsidian and seated on it was Piotre Andresen – the new Lord of Atros.
>
> Another figure bowed down to Andresen from the floor in front of the throne. A large, bearded man with yellowy green eyes, dressed in a long black cloak.

'Cleve Harrow!' Serrion breathed.

Serrion could see that Harrow was speaking, but at first it was hard to make out the words. Then, like a zoom lens on a camera bringing everything closer and into sharp focus, Harrow's face filled Serrion's sight. He could see the Cleve's lips move quickly, urgently, secretively.

What Serrion heard next made him feel as if everything he thought he knew had been snatched away from him. The words that came to him in the vision took away all of the things he believed in, and for the second time in his life, he felt himself losing everything he thought he could trust.

'Trust me Lord,' Harrow was saying. 'I can help you in this and then we can bring a dreadful end to all your enemies.'

'You will do this?' The Lord of Atros replied. His voice was a hiss of excitement. 'You will aid me once more?'

'Yes, Master,' Harrow continued. 'I will bring you what you seek. I will bring you the Melgardes boy.'

Serrion staggered back with the shock of what he was seeing. If T'yuq Tinyaz had not been holding onto him so tightly, he would surely have fallen to the ground.

'Harrow,' he gasped. 'Harrow is working for the Andresens? He is a spy?'

'Remember, this is just one possible future,' she whispered in his ear. 'But keep concentrating, for there is more yet.'

A swirl of images then followed in quick succession for Serrion. They seemed disconnected, and he couldn't make any sense of what they might mean.

...There was the figure of another man, a stranger whom he did not recognise. He was old but powerful. Serrion caught a sudden close up view of his face and saw something strange about the man's eyes. One of them was pale, almost without colour, but the other flickered with a gleam of red and yellow over wire framed spectacles...

This was the vision that had first come to him at the funeral.

...He saw the evil deep in this flickering red and yellow eye as it now looked directly into Serrion's own.

'You are with us then?' a cruel voice whispered into his ear. 'You will serve us on Atros after all?'

A wicked smile spread across thin lips as Serrion realised that this stranger with the odd eyes was reading his mind...

This couldn't be! He would never serve the Lord of Atros. Never!

But now the vision shifted once more.

...He saw a dagger flying towards his chest. He was hiding behind a curtain...

...Next he could see a familiar room. A broken jug of water lay on the ground and he saw an outstretched arm nearby, a glass still clutched in its hand. He tried to look at the person the arm belonged to and struggled to remember which room it was but his vision quickly changed again...

...Now his sister Orianna was bending over him. She was holding his hand and there were tears in her eyes. Orianna was saying something over and over again but he couldn't hear it...

Then his visions disappeared. Without warning the Seer of Beltheron released him from her clasp. She gave a sharp cry of pain.

Serrion tumbled back onto the rock. The Seer was gasping for breath as if she had been underwater. One hand was clutching at her throat. The red light all around them began to fade. Serrion struggled to his knees.

'Is it... Is it like that for you all the time?' he asked her. 'Can you ever get away from it? From seeing all those things I mean?' He was terrified at what her answer might be, for he had begun to realise that this could become his fate as well.

She nodded and replied quickly. 'What is our gift, Serrion, is also our curse.' She was still gasping for breath and Serrion sensed a new panic about her.

'Remember we Seers have the power to see all possible futures. We cannot intervene in them all. That is our sadness, Serrion.

'There will always be mistakes,' she continued. Her head had now started to jerk briefly from side to side as if searching for something nearby. 'Always mistakes – we cannot see it all in time – there is always something – or someone – we miss; someone's future we cannot help.' The Seer's voice had now dropped to almost a whisper. Her shoulders sagged with defeat. 'I am sorry, Serrion, if I have made mistakes concerning you.'

'So what if...' he began to ask her.

Without warning her head shot up and she gave a quick gasp. Serrion wondered if she had been injured in some way.

'No time now,' she hissed as if she were angry at him all of a sudden. 'You must leave.'

'Leave? Now? Why do I have to...'

Then Serrion realised why T'yuq's behaviour had changed so quickly. The knowledge struck him like a fist in his solar plexus; T'yuq had just seen something else, another vision that he had not witnessed. That was why she had released him from her grip a few moments ago; that was why she had cried out and clutched at her throat.

The things she *had* shown him were terrible enough, so how horrible must this one be if she was *not* willing to share it with him? He shuddered. He felt terrified, but he had to know. He had to ask her what this new danger was.

'Tell me,' he said slowly, trying to fight back the panic that he felt rise in him. 'What have you just seen?'

T'yuq Tinyaz didn't answer. She was still reeling with the repercussions and consequences of this new vision.

Instead she turned on him. 'Remember what I have told you. Think on it!' she pushed him away from her. 'Now you MUST GO!'

There was now a terror in her voice as well. It was the first time that Serrion had sensed any fear in her, and it was this that drove him away. Turning away from the Seer he began to run. In his haste he slipped on the wet stones at the side of the pool and staggered through the milky water. It came to his waist, slowing him down as he dragged himself forwards. Behind him he heard T'yuq Tinyaz call out to him once more.

'*Remember. Whatever you see is only one of many possible futures Serrion.*'

There was a tone in her voice that made Serrion think she was trying to comfort herself, as well as him.

As he disappeared around the bend in the corridor T'yuq Tinyaz finally slumped down onto the rock.

Left alone, the exhausted Seer began to ask herself questions. Was she right in sending him away like that without telling him what she had just seen? Had she used her visions over the years to push events in the right direction? But most importantly of all, was Serrion ready for what was about to happen to him?

Tomorrow would decide. The new vision that she had just decided to keep secret had told her that. But had she made a mistake? Would Serrion behave in the way she had predicted? She shook her head.

Whatever happened now, she realised, *her* time was about to end. T'yuq knew that she had made her decision and it was pointless thinking about it any further. It was out of her hands now. Tomorrow would decide.

From tomorrow it would be the visions and actions of Serrion Melgardes which steered the destiny of Beltheron.

*   *   *

Matt met him further up the corridor. They walked back past the pictures in the gallery in silence. Matt guessed that Serrion was not ready to talk about what had happened to him. He left the boy to himself and returned to his work.

As soon as he was safely out of the corridors and on his own in the familiar rooms of the great hall, Serrion began thinking once more about T'yuq's final vision. Why had she not shared it with him he wondered? He crept into one of the anterooms close to the great hall and sat down on a long couch in the corner by the window.

Serrion looked out of the window and focused hard on a tree swaying in the wind. He waited for an opening, just as she had told him. He concentrated so hard that his vision began to blur and the tree lost its shape in front of him. A familiar red glow started to spread out from its branches. 'It's working,' he thought to himself. Sure enough, after just a few moments a new vision began to take shape. What he saw stunned him.

> *He himself stood alongside Cleve Harrow now.*
> *Piotre and Sophia were standing in front of*
> *them. They were in a dark room with only one*
> *small, murky window high up on the wall. Both*
> *he and Harrow fell to their knees. Serrion spoke*

three words: 'For you, Master.' He was holding
the golden staff of Beltheron out towards Piotre
who grasped at it eagerly...

'No!' Serrion screamed. He shook his head to clear the vision from his mind. 'No,' he repeated to himself over and over. He staggered to his feet and ran from the room. His eyes were still not focusing properly, but it was only after he had escaped outside into the sunlight that he realised this was because tears were now streaming down his face.

All Change

In the weeks after the death of a Lord of Beltheron, it was traditional that the funereal period of mourning was followed by one of celebration and renewal. As part of this, a carnival was being held on the fields just outside the eastern walls of Beltheron City. Strains of music drifted over the field. The sound of trumpets built to a crescendo followed by applause and cheering carried on the warm breeze.

Orianna could smell the tang of roasting meat from the spits over the barbecue fires that had been erected at several places across the field. She made her way through a variety of stalls, huge marquees and smaller tents, looking around her excitedly.

Today, in the midst of all this excitement, she had forgotten her sadness for the first time in many days. She was able to put the memory of Parenon into a corner of her mind for whole minutes at a time.

A high grassy bank ran down one side of the field. Beyond it, the tops of the masts and rigging from passing yachts and merchant ships could be seen moving slowly as they sailed down the long, wide estuary and out towards the open sea just over a kilometre away. A row of benches had been erected at the top of the grassy bank. The benches looked out onto the estuary so that people could sit, relax and watch the boats. It was a popular spot, particularly on warm, fine days like this one, and there were always several people gathered there, gazing out with telescopes, or waving to the seafarers working on the decks of the boats as the vessels went by.

This afternoon however, all eyes were turned inwards, towards the carnival field itself.

Huge white marquees and brightly coloured gazebos had been growing in number on every spare patch of lawn throughout the week. For days children had peered excitedly though the railings for a glimpse of the attractions which would soon appear. Now the festival was about to begin. The feeling of expectation had grown to fever pitch – not only amongst the young people of Beltheron, but with their parents and other adults too. Crowds had been growing by the entrances to the field since first light had glimmered on the horizon, promising a bright, sun-filled day ahead.

Serrion had not been sure whether or not he wanted to go to the carnival that day.

'Come with me,' his sister had pleaded. 'It will cheer us both up and help us to forget our sorrows for a time.'

He knew that she was right, but he didn't want to admit it. Not to her, and not to himself.

There were two reasons why he did not want to go with her. It was partly was because he knew there would be a lot of people there at the festival. He still felt nervous at times, especially when he was in crowded or noisy places. The memories of the battles he had been involved in came back to his imagination more vividly when he was surrounded by jostling people, and noisy yelling and nearby shouts reminded him of the many dangers he had faced.

That was why he had told her he would rather stay at home, where it would be quiet and peaceful. His sister was beginning to recognise and understand his moods more and more, and so she had soon given up trying to persuade him and had set out for the festival on her own.

The main reason, however, was the memory of his vision from the day before.

Kneeling with Harrow before Piotre, offering him the golden staff, betraying Beltheron!

The very thought that he could do such a thing filled him with disgust. Piotre had tried to take the golden staff before, to try to master its powers for his own uses, and people had died trying to protect it. Serrion could not understand how he could ever offer it up to Beltheron's enemy like that. He knew that he could not face those who had helped him so much while such thoughts filled his head. He needed to be alone.

In memory of Parenon, Orianna had decided to write about the history of the pulver and Serrion thought he would use this opportunity of being on his own to help his sister with her research for the book. She would be pleased to see he had made progress on it when she returned from the carnival. It was not peaceful though, even in the house. He could hear the noisy crowds making their way to the carnival fields.

He glanced out of the window from where he was sitting at Orianna's desk and saw the huge groups of people jostling past. Many wore brightly coloured jesters' party hats with bells and ribbons fastened to the fabric. A boy of about eleven years old hurried past. The hat he wore was a vivid red. As Serrion watched the boy the colour of the hat seemed to grow brighter and brighter until it made his head ache. He recognised the signal immediately of course. He was about to have one of his visions. 'Here it comes,' Serrion thought to himself. 'The hat is acting like an opening. But what is it going to open *onto*?'

He tried to concentrate hard on the red hat as the boy scurried away down the road. He remembered what T'yuq Tinyaz had told him the day before.

'Don't just let the visions happen to you. Summon them yourself. The very act of taking control of your premonitions shapes them, dictates what visions you actually see.'

Serrion pushed his chair back and stood up. He craned his neck to focus on the boy. Just as he disappeared around the corner, Serrion caught one last glimpse of the red hat bouncing on his head. He closed his eyes and fixed it in his imagination. Sure enough, an image sprang to him as clear as day.

The streets were filled with people...

Just like today, he thought.

...The people began to raise their heads to the sky, pointing amazedly. Serrion saw fear in their eyes. Many opened their mouths in silent screams. A dark shadow sped across their features...

It looked the same as the vision that he had seen during Parenon's funeral. But then he saw a new detail. Something that had not been there in his premonition before.

...A boy of about eleven years old, running happily in the crowds. On his head was a bright red hat...

'It's today!' Serrion realised with a jolt. His prediction was going to happen today! When the vision first came to him, he thought it must be a market day because of the crowds. But it wasn't. It was the festival crowd that he had seen instead.

He steered his vision upwards, taking control of it again just as T'yuq had shown him, so that he could look at what the crowds were seeing.

...A huge dark shape, like a solid cloud, floated above their heads. It was coming from the carnival field.

As the shadow progressed across the city the people began to fall. Many clutched at their heads as the darkness touched them. Many more ran madly to escape, hurling themselves through doorways or diving behind walls to find shelter...

Once again Serrion focused his mind on the memory of the red hat as it disappeared around the corner. 'Show me the time tower!' he screamed at himself. 'Let me see the time tower!'

...The red vision shifted, like a tilting camera shot in a film. There it was in front of him. Beltheron's time tower, the central piece of the intricate system of mirrors and sundials which showed the correct time all around the city. As he looked at the shadow falling over the clock face he noticed the time. 12.17...

He shook his head to clear it and looked down at his own watch. It was already 11.46. This deadly cloud, whatever it was, would fall across the city in thirty one minutes.

Serrion dashed to the door and ran at full pelt down the street. He had just over half an hour to stop it.

In the largest tent on the carnival field a group of actors were finishing their make-up and warming up their voices. They were going to perform a brand new play – with songs and 'special fire effects' – about the victory over Gretton Tur, the Wild Lord of Atros. Carvel Braggart, the lead actor, was squeezing himself into a leotard that looked at least three sizes too small for him. Over the top of this he then draped a billowing robe with a flowing black cape. He was playing the role of Gretton Tur himself, and his stage make up included deep, dark grey circles of weariness under his eyes and savage cruel lines curling about his mouth.

'This, my loves, will be my greatest triumph,' he crowed to the other actors in the tent. 'Today, on this field, I will re-imagine the rules of Thespis, and create a performance to stagger, to enthral, to, to...'

'...to bore us all to death?' murmured one of the younger actors under his breath. A few others, sitting nearby choked back laughter and stifled their giggles as they concentrated on their own costume and make-up.

'...to OBLITERATE the memory of any other performance,' continued Carvel, who hadn't heard the interruption. 'This afternoon dears, you will see me not only PLAY the evil Lord of Atros, you will see me BECOME him.'

Eyes rolled, lips were bitten to stop smiles, heads were turned away to avoid catching Carvel's glance. None of this mattered. He didn't care what they thought. He, the great Carvel Braggart, was on a roll.

'Observe, my young friends,' he spread his arms wide to include them all as he spoke. 'You will learn the most valuable lessons of your fledgling acting careers today. Just watch the great Carvel Braggart in action and weep!'

'I'll be weeping if he doesn't shut up soon,' another of the actors whispered to her companion, who gave such an uncontrolled 'PAH!' of laughter that her make-up powder erupted in a pink cloud around the tent, making several of them cough and choke.

This distraction was very welcome for two reasons. Firstly, because it gave the rest of them an excuse to laugh out loud, and secondly because it finally stopped Carvel Braggart talking about himself.

'Oh my loves, my dear LOVES!' he crooned at them. 'Do be careful. We don't have much longer to get ready. Look - it is already ten minutes to twelve. Our performance begins at noon.'

He busied himself once more with the finishing touches to his appearance, which he felt sure would result in him giving the performance of a lifetime, as if he really *were* the Wild Lord of Atros...

There seemed to be thousands more people on the streets than usual. Every one of them was making their way to the festival ground in the distance. Serrion was angry at himself. He should have thought of this before! What was the use of his visions if he did not think them through? 'I should have worked it out as soon as I found out about the festival,' he thought. His conscience stung him.

The streets were so busy that Serrion knew he would never be able to get to the festival in time. Not on foot anyway. An idea came to him and he began casting his eyes around urgently.

Up ahead he saw what he had been looking for. A pale blue flycar hovered a metre above the ground, piloted by a young pulver who was directing the crowds down one of the main streets. The pulver was trying to give out instructions so that the other flying machines could move around safely. Serrion had always loved seeing these flycars and other buggies shooting around in the air above Beltheron's streets. Today, on such a celebratory occasion, there was an even wider variety of flycars than usual. All kinds of shapes, sizes and colours whizzed around as people took pleasure rides, or rose up into the skies to get a better view of the festival field.

As Serrion raced towards him the pulver turned to point his machine towards a small, zippy sports flyer covered in gleaming silver and chrome and with large, curving handlebars like a motor bike. It was being driven by a young man who had swooped just a little too close over the heads of the passers-by on the street. The pulver was about to give chase, when he saw Serrion frantically waving up at him. The young pilot instantly recognised this boy. He knew that he had been a friend to his colleague Parenon, and that he had already done so much for the city. If this young man needed him then he wouldn't have to ask twice. The pulver pilot forgot any idea of pursuing the reckless bike-flyer and swung back down towards street level.

'Master Melgardes, can I assist you sir?'

'We have to get to the festival ground,' Serrion replied breathlessly. 'As quickly as we can.'

The anguish and urgency in Serrion's eyes was enough for the pulver. He made a brief turn of the steering handle and the flycar dropped down to hover immediately next to him.

'Jump on,' he said. He held his hand out to help Serrion climb aboard. Serrion jumped up and swung his leg over the back of the vehicle.

'Hang on!' yelled the pulver pilot.

Serrion grabbed the pulver's shoulders. In another moment Serrion felt his stomach turn sickeningly as the pilot quickly rotated a small wheel on the control panel in front of him. The flycar spun rapidly through 180 degrees. Then, to escape the heavier traffic on the streets, it shot up towards the rooftops...

Orianna wandered slowly down one of the long rows of marquees. She looked from side to side, enjoying the variety of things going on, and the different attractions and food that were brightly painted on the sides.

'Hot sausage, pies and stews!'

'Face painting –amuse and surprise your friends,'

'Dance competition, choose your partners!'

'Ice cream and candy floss – new flavours and every colour you can think of.'

Two blonde haired girls of about eight or nine years old – obviously sisters – ran out of one of the tents occupied by an elderly woman who was painting faces and decorating skin with light touches of her brushes and pens. The sisters' faces had been transformed into bright patterns – one depicting a tiger-like creature called a pedjiaar, with vivid red and grey stripes. The other girl's face had been painted like a fantastic bird of paradise, with yellow and golden circles around her eyes. The blonde of the girls' hair was also streaked with colours similar to these beasts, and their fingernails glinted with sparkly lights. They both giggled at each other, waving their hands in front of their faces, delighted with their new look. Orianna watched with amusement as the two girls ran off, growling and twittering at each other.

There was a very different kind of tent at the end of the row. While all the others were pure white, or brightly coloured, this one was made of an untreated canvas of dull grey. No flags fluttered above it. There was no painted sign to tell what this tent offered. There were no decorations on this tent at all. It was much smaller than the others too, not much more than an average person's height. You would have to duck down low to enter through the flap of material that was lifted at one corner to make an entrance.

As Orianna approached she noticed the two little girls again. They were still giggling madly at each other's faces and showing off their glittering finger nails to each other. One growled like the pedjiaar tiger she was pretending to be, the other played at being a scared bird, flapping her arms as if to fly away from the hunting big cat.

The girls stopped their antics at the flap of the dark tent. Orianna thought it was strange that their laughter should die away so quickly, but she put it down to the idea that they had seen some new attraction inside that had grabbed all of their attention. Whatever it was, the two girls stood motionless together, staring into the tent for a moment. Then, without a word, or even a glance at each other, the girls stepped inside.

Orianna would have thought no more about it, if she had not heard the whispering voice as she walked past.

'Transiform in toto, alterium in ultimus...'

These strange words stopped Orianna in her tracks. Someone was casting a spell! Not only that, but it was one which she was sure she had heard before! She struggled to remember, but while she was still trying to work out its meaning there was a terrible scream from the within the dark shadows of the tent.

The next moment the tent flap was torn violently to one side. Before Orianna could step back, a brightly coloured bird flew out, screeching into the sky. Maybe it was a trick of the light, but Orianna was certain that she saw the bird's claws glittering with sparkling lights as it shot into the air. Blonde feathers fluttered down around her.

Suddenly the spell that she had overheard made sense. *'Transiform in toto, alterium in ultimus...'*

The child had been transformed! Someone in the tent had changed the little girl into the creature she had been dressed as!

As the awful truth began to dawn on her, Orianna heard the cry of the other little girl inside the tent – the one who had been painted like the pedjiaar big cat. In one long, drawn out wail the girl's cry turned from a high pitch into a terrifying low growl. Orianna spun around to look at the tent flap. There, crouched down in the opening was a pedjiaar. She saw it just as it finished growing from child size to that of a fully grown tiger. Its teeth were bared in a savage grin and its tongue lolled hungrily out of its mouth. All of the creature's attention was fixed on Orianna.

What shocked her most though, were the remains of the little girl's clothes that still clung to the pedjiaar's shoulders. The pedjiaar shook its head from side to side and the last blonde hairs dropped away from its cheeks leaving just the red and grey stripes.

'Oh you poor things,' Orianna whispered to herself pitifully. Then with growing anger and outrage 'Who could do such a thing to children?'

The pedjiaar was readying itself to attack. It crouched down further on its haunches, hard eyes still fixed on Orianna who was only a short distance away. The predator's tail flicked once, and then with an avid howl of excitement, it leapt at her...

There was commotion inside the actors' tent. The excitement and pre-show nerves had reached a crescendo. The actors had all changed into their costumes as rish and harch warriors from Atros. Their faces had been painted grey and many had even shaved their heads to make their appearance even more realistic and frightening.

'What dedication to the theatrical craft, my loves. What METHOD!' enthused Carvel Braggart.

He himself stood in their midst about to take control of the humming and singing that warmed up their voices before every show. His own costume and make up were also complete. The very image of Gretton Tur, the wild Lord of Atros, stood before them. 'Oh my dears, this could be the performance of a lifetime!'

He was sure that this year his talent would be recognised and that he would be awarded with a BAFTA. This was a golden statuette which was the highest honour that could be bestowed upon an actor. (BAFTA was short for The Beltheron Actors' Favourite Theatrical Award, although the younger actors joked that it also stood for Braggart's Annoying and Fearfully Tiresome Attitude).

As they began readying their vocal chords with humming and aahhing sounds, their voices began to change. From beautiful fluting songs they turned to guttural grunts and snarls. The extra pair of fake arms that had been fastened around their waists as part of their rish costumes now fell away, as real limbs grew in their place, ripping away the fastenings that held them to the cloth. Soon the actors' costumes hung in rags about them as their figures grew into the shape of huge, fearsome beings.

Underneath the growling you could hear the howls of protest, pain and horror from the actors at what was happening to them.

Braggart himself grew in size, filling his billowing robes until they stretched at the seams. The cheap, painted metal staff which he had held in his hand extended and flared with magical light.

Braggart had been right in his boasting, He was about to give the performance of a lifetime. The magic of the *transiform* spell had spread across the field and turned him into the very ghost of Gretton Tur himself. Instead of a troupe of actors, he now commanded a mighty following of rish and harch. Carvel Braggart and his company of rag tag performers leapt out onto the field fully transformed. With a cry from Braggart of 'Atros undefeated!' they swept though the field swinging their ugly, lethal weapons....

*   *   *

Helen had been working with her mother at a stall in the very middle of the carnival ground. All morning they had been preparing dishes of the magnificent, mouth-watering food for which Jenn was famous. She had used her great knowledge of herbs and spells, and her abilities to mix potions and cures in the kitchen at home for as long as Helen could remember. It was always Jenn that people came to for advice on medicine, and also for recipes or ideas for special meals and celebrations.

Therefore it had been decided that Jenn, helped by her daughter, would set up a stall to sell food to the revellers and partygoers at the festival. Any money that they made was to be donated to a number of charities to help people in Beltheron City.

So far they had had a very busy morning. Tasty cakes and sandwiches had been devoured by hungry children from the plates on the stall. Gallons of steaming soup had been bought up and gulped down as quickly as Jenn could ladle them out into bowls from the large pans that bubbled away on a portable stove behind the counter.

Now it was almost noon and Jenn and Helen were ready for their own lunch.

'We have done well this morning,' beamed Jenn. 'We are almost out of pastries.'

'I'm not surprised,' her daughter replied. 'The smell of them alone has been bringing everyone running from all over the field.'

Jenn laughed. 'And think of all the money we've made for the city. People have been so generous.'

Indeed they had. Many had told Helen and her mum to 'keep the change!' as they sauntered off, happily tucking into their food.

As they began to discuss the projects that the money could be used for they heard angry shouts and scared screams from another corner of the field. Both of them turned in the direction of the noise.

'It's coming from outside the actors' tent,' Helen said, craning her neck to see.

Her mother grinned. 'Probably that old ham, Carvel Braggart, getting everyone worked up into a frenzy before his grand performance.'

'Oh him,' Helen replied. 'He's funny. I remember when I was six and we came back to Beltheron from Earth for my birthday. He performed at my... Oh!'

Helen's memories were suddenly interrupted by the sight of a group of children, racing towards them. They were obviously terrified, their faces wide in astonishment and fear as they ran as fast as they could away from the direction of the noise. At the same instant, the roars of the actors and dismayed cries of their audience reached their ears even louder than before.

'Yes, funny he may be,' Jenn said, her eyes narrowing with anger. 'But we can't have the little ones being terrified like this by his performance. Sometimes he goes a little too far looking for his "artistic perfection".'

She was already wiping her hands on her apron, and moving around to the front of their stall. 'I don't want to spoil the fun,' she continued. 'But this is a family carnival, and he has to remember that we...'

She didn't have time to finish her sentence before a rish guard came hurtling around the corner of a nearby tent. He wielded a heavy mace in one of his upper arms, while the lower pair ripped at the guy ropes, bringing the tent down in billows of canvas.

'Wow,' thought Helen. 'The costumes are brilliant! He looks just like a real rish! Much better than the carnivals I remember when I was little.'

Her mother wasn't so impressed. She had seen the

hard glint in the eye of the creature, and knew immediately that this was no costume. Somehow, the soldiers of Atros had appeared in the middle of the festival!

The rish had spotted Helen, who was watching it, fascinated by what she still believed was just an actor's performance. It snarled, showing rows of small jagged teeth in its puckered mouth.

'Amazing,' Helen said to it. 'You really have done well this year. That has to be the best make-up I've ever seen.'

The rish seemed puzzled that this young Belthronian female was not running from it in terror. It hesitated for a moment, then came rapidly towards her with another growl of rage.

'Helen, step back!' Jenn yelled out at her daughter. 'Come away from it now.'

Helen heard the fear and panic in her mother's voice and in the same instant realised the danger she was in. This was no actor standing in front of her and raising his pretend weapon to strike in a mock battle; at last she understood that this was a genuine rish, and it meant to kill her...

Serrion held on to the pulver's shoulders, and gripped the side of the flycar harder than ever with his legs. They had shot up almost vertically into the air above the streets to avoid the crowds. But even higher up, many more celebratory flycars, buggies and oddly shaped rockets moved haphazardly in the sky ahead of them. Serrion risked a glance down and immediately wished he hadn't. A lurch of vertigo made the ground seem to rush up towards him as the flycar suddenly dipped under a floating buggy in the shape of a dolphin. The family riding it gave whoops of delight and waved frantically at them as they shot past.

The pulver made a slight adjustment to one of the switches on the control panel at the front of his flycar. It careered forwards again at even greater speed. Serrion shifted his gaze to look ahead.

There, less than half a kilometre away, he saw the festival ground. With the sea twinkling beyond it, and the flags above the tents fluttering in the wind all still looked peaceful. Rising up at the gates to the field an enormous balloon in the shape of a dark grey dragon was being inflated. As they got closer Serrion saw it begin to climb into the air. More gas was pumped into it and the head – the last part to be filled – had almost reached the perfect shape. As the wind buffeted it, its canvas wings fluttered realistically and it turned towards them, the mouth opening up and showing sharp rows of teeth as it was finally completed.

Over and over again the same thought churned away in Serrion's mind. Why hadn't he foreseen this? Why hadn't he guessed? At least there was still no sign of the smoky cloud from his vision.

They were closer to the dragon balloon now. Serrion was trying to see beyond it, down to the field itself, but it suddenly seemed to lurch sideways, blocking his view of the people below on the field. There was something odd about the movement he thought, something not quite right about the way the balloon had suddenly shifted sideways, against the direction of the wind that he could feel against his face.

BANG!

The flycar lurched around violently as something struck it just behind Serrion's right leg. The pulver gave a cry of shock and struggled with the controls. Serrion felt himself begin to slide sideways, out of the seat.

'Hang on!' the pulver yelled at him as he twisted both hands rapidly on the steering shift, and the flycar staggered in the air to regain its balance and direction.

SLAM!

The vehicle flew around the other way with a bone-jarring jolt that forced Serrion's jaws closed and set his teeth hammering together painfully as his head shook with the impact. He managed to scramble back into a more secure sitting position.

The flycar had now been turned around again so that they were looking back at the dragon balloon they had just been passing.

Serrion's mouth opened wide once more in astonishment. For there, flapping its wings just a few metres away from them and readying itself for a third blow, the balloon that he expected to see had turned into a real dragon...

Orianna ducked at the last moment. She threw herself sideways to the ground as the pedjiaar leapt towards her. It realised it had missed its prey and tried to twist in mid-air to rake her with its talons. Snapping fiercely and angrily with its jaws it landed, and turned immediately to pounce on her again. Orianna was already rolling away from it over the grass, trying to get behind the tent and give herself a few moments to think.

She had recognised the spell at the last moment. Her mind raced to remember the antidote words, the incantation that would cause a reversal and change the girls back into their real selves.

Reversium in... NO! She yelled at herself. THINK!

The pedjiaar's claws raked the ground next to her leg

as it tried to scrabble around the guy ropes holding the tent to the lawn.

Alterium reversa... NO! COME ON ORIANNA, CONCENTRATE!

Still on the ground, Orianna scrambled backwards with her hands and heels digging into the earth.

Correctior....Correctius... NO!

The pedjiaar's head shot forward and she felt hot, rancid breath on her cheek. Slaver from its clashing teeth splashed her face. It was almost on top of her. Luckily, in its last lunge towards her it had managed to get its back foot caught in the one of the metal pegs that held the ropes of the tent. Orianna had an extra few seconds as the pedjiaar pulled furiously with its back leg and snapped at the rope behind it in maddened frustration.

Mutantor? Mutantor omnis? Why couldn't she remember the antidote spell?

Then, finally, it came to her. She had it at last, dredged up from a corner of her memory, the spell she needed. Just as the pedjiaar managed to slice through the rope with its jaws, Orianna pointed her finger at it and spoke in a clear, steady voice:

'Omnia mutantor, sed nosce te ipsum.'

With a howl the pedjiaar began to shrink in size. The colours began to fade and soon it was possible to see the little girl's own complexion underneath. Her shape started to reform and Orianna threw her cloak over the girl to protect her from the sudden cold wind that had begun to blow.

Orianna didn't even have time to breathe a sigh of relief about the girl. Behind her, in the mouth of the tent, she caught sight of a sudden movement.

She spun around to see the old woman who had transformed the children. Already her bony hand was stretching out towards Orianna and the words of another incantation were forming on her lips. Before she had chance to cast her spell however, Orianna launched herself at her attacker. Driven on by her anger at what she had just seen happen, she moved much faster than the witch anticipated. Orianna struck the old hag on the shoulders with such force that she was knocked off her feet and both of them tumbled inside the tent.

Their limbs tangled together on the ground as each fought to get the upper hand. Orianna had been winded by the impact and felt dizzy for a few seconds. She came to her senses to feel the witch's hot breath on her neck and hear her hissing venomously.

The witch's mouth was open and she was trying to sink her teeth into Orianna's neck.

'First the pedjiaar, and now you,' she thought. 'I must look tasty.'

Orianna twisted her head backwards painfully. She reached up with her hand and grasped at the witch's hair. She tugged sharply, pulling the hag's head away from her own.

In response the witch screamed out in pain and tried to pull away from Orianna. She had not suspected this young waif of a woman to be so strong, so determined. Orianna took the opportunity to pull even harder at her adversary's hair. A clump of it came away in her hand. The witch screamed again and leapt away.

Raising her arms above her she whispered something that Orianna could not hear. In an eruption of flame, the witch vanished, igniting the tent as she did so. Fire flickered up the sides of the canvas, and heavy smoke began to fill the interior.

Still clutching the tufts of hair, Orianna struggled to her feet. The fumes made her cough violently. Her eyes were already streaming. They stung and it was difficult to keep them open. She knew that if she didn't get out straight away she was done for.

The tent flaps were already burning brightly, the heat scorching her skin. She threw one arm in front of her face, to protect her head from the heat and the falling embers. Gripping even more tightly onto the witch's hair with the other hand, she curled it up protectively in front of her body. She needed that hair. Orianna made a dive towards the opening.

Outside there was even more commotion. Several figures were approaching the tent with buckets of water as Orianna burst from within, her clothes smouldering. One quick-witted woman threw the cloak from her own shoulders and wrapped it around her tightly to smother the threat of flames.

Orianna Melgardes sank to her knees. Her harsh, hacking coughs choked her for several moments.

Matt came running towards her.

'Are you alright?' he asked desperately.

She nodded in reply, still unable to speak.

'Thank the Three Worlds.' He turned and began calling to the other people nearby.

'Who was she?' he asked.

Everyone shook their heads in apology, no one knew.

'The woman inside this tent; did anyone see where she came from, did anyone know her?' he repeated.

Still there was no answer. No one had any idea who this woman had been. Cursing in frustration, Matt knelt down next to Orianna.

She opened her palm. Curled around in her hand were a few wisps of grey hair.

'I never saw her before, but we can find out where she went to...' she began.

'Matt's eyes glittered with fierce excitement as he realised what she meant.

'Yes,' he nodded at her. 'But it must be done straight away, before the trail goes cold. I will call a pulver to...'

'There is no time,' Orianna replied quickly. Everyone else is too busy.'

Orianna had already made her decision. She took a small vial of pale blue glass out of her pocket and uncorked it. The liquid inside it would create a pathway. By pouring this liquid onto an object it was possible to follow its owner wherever they had gone to.

'No!' Matt held onto her arm. 'You cannot go alone.'

'There is no time!' she cried. 'All the others are fighting or helping the wounded.'

'But the danger...'

'...will be greater for everyone the longer I delay!' she continued, speaking quickly, and more urgently now 'You know that every second we waste here means I have less chance of finding this woman, and getting to the bottom of who sent her here, and how she has done this.'

Matt knew she was right. He looked around him at the devastation and confusion of the fairground. All the pulver were preoccupied with fighting off the group of actors on the other side of the field. The whole of the theatre company were now fully transformed into the images of Gretton Tur and hordes of rish.

He nodded briefly to Orianna. 'You are right, of course. Go now, with my blessing, but take this.'

He handed her the dagger from his belt.

'Omnia mutantor, sed nosce te ipsum,' she said to Matt as she took the dagger. She hid it away amongst the folds of her pockets and then held the glass vial over the strands of hair between her fingers.

'What?'

'*Omnia mutantor, sed nosce te ipsum.* It's a spell. It's how to change everything back to normal. Say it after me, quickly!'

She repeated the phrase again until he could recite it back to her without any problem.

'Good,' she nodded. 'Now go. Help the others.'

Orianna tipped the glass vial and sprinkled a few drops of liquid onto the grey hair of the witch. Immediately it began to fizz and sizzle in her hand and a low humming sound began.

'Stand back,' she called out. 'Look after our people, Lord Matthias.'

Matt nodded. 'I will. Go carefully Orianna.'

But already, Orianna Melgardes had disappeared in a swirling column of white light. He turned and ran into the fray of fighting...

...And Change Again

The rish lunged towards Helen. In the same moment, Jenn grabbed a towel from the stall where they had been selling food. She wrapped the towel around her hands and hoisted the heavy pan of soup off the stove where it was still bubbling. Stepping between the rish and her daughter she threw the remainder of the boiling liquid into the rish's face. It gave a piercing cry of anger and pain. There was a horrible stench of hot flesh as it clawed at its face, trying to wipe away the hot soup.

Jenn took her chance. Changing her grip on the pan she swung it around towards the creature, who still could not see. The heavy pan struck the beast across the jaw, and sent it staggering backwards. Making sure she had a firm hold with both hands on the towel and the pan, Jenn moved in once more for another strike. This time the blow sent the rish back into the falling tent, where it tripped on one of the ropes and sprawled on the ground.

Helen thought quickly. She didn't waste a second but jumped to her mother's side. Bending down she reached for one end of the rope that the rish had ripped from the ground. Taking a big piece of canvas in the other hand, she looped it around the rish's legs, winding the rope around it until the bottom half of its body was securely fastened. It struggled on the ground, still hazy from the blows with the pan, but couldn't get back onto its feet.

'Wow Mum,' Helen said, grinning with relief and the excitement of the sudden battle. 'I knew you were a good chef, but I've never seen anyone use a pan like that before!'

Jenn had no time to reply before they heard a familiar, impossible voice behind them.

'Lady Jenia and the young Yelenia of Beltheron,' it hissed. 'How convenient I find you both here together.'

They spun around. It couldn't be. It was unthinkable! Gretton Tur, the Wild Lord of Atros, stood in front of them.

'But... but... You're dead!' Helen cried.

'And now returned to seek revenge,' he rasped back at her in reply.

'It's Braggart,' Jenn breathed. 'Someone has cast an *alteria* spell over the actors.'

'Well done, you've guessed!' said the figure who was now Gretton Tur. 'Hard to pull the wool over the eyes of a Select for long, isn't it?'

He raised the black staff of Atros over his head and began to bring it down towards them...

'Hang on tighter!'

The pulver yelled his warning at Serrion in the same moment as he pulled a daredevil manoeuvre on the controls. The flycar shot vertically upwards with a swooshing sound as the dragon turned on them.

In a quick glance at the creature, Serrion's heart had sunk within him. The beast was huge – at least as large as a whale. The fact that something so large could fly left Serrion slack jawed in amazement. The scales on its wings and the upper part of its body were pale grey. The underside of its softer belly and underneath the wings were pure black. The long sinewy neck grew brighter and paler towards the head. Here the scales of the dragon turned to a bright red colour.

The dragon's head itself was a thing of terror. It was the size of a fully grown man and when it opened its long mouth the stretch was as wide as an eagle's wingspan. Serrion and the pulver caught a glimpse of row after row of sharp, serrated teeth running the full length of its jaw-line. A thin, muscular tongue whipped out at them as they rose above it. The tongue only just managed to make contact with the underside of the flycar but it was enough to jar them in their seats as the vehicle shook and almost bucked out of control.

Higher and higher the pulver pilot took them. The engine of the flycar began to strain and groan with the effort. Serrion's ears popped. He swallowed hard to try to release the pressure.

The dragon flapped its massive wings once, slowly, and curved around in a wide rising arc to come straight at them from below. Its long neck curved and sparks shot from its mouth towards them.

The wind buffeted them and howled in their ears as they shot into a patch of thick cloud. Under them, but unseen now through the cloud, they could hear the pulse of the dragon's wings on the air as it drew nearer. The pilot was straining all his attention on the direction of that sound as he kept them climbing to higher and higher altitudes.

Serrion was aware of the dragon getting closer and closer. It was even more frightening not to be able to see it, or even where they were going. He risked his balance to turn and take another look down.

Through the swirling haze of cloud he could just make out the darker shape of their pursuer. Then it burst out of the clouds underneath them, flames now licking along the sides of its lips as it flew. It seemed impossibly big as it approached. It filled his vision and blocked out any view of the earth or clouds below. The pulver was aware of it too and suddenly levelled the flycar out of their steep ascent. He slowed the engines so that they made much less noise and flew them horizontally for a few moments.

Turning towards Serrion he spoke in short bursts, gasping to get his breath in the thinner air of the high altitude.

'Can't outrace him,' he gulped. 'Can't outmanoeuvre him. Can only trick him.'

'What?' Serrion asked.

'Sorry if this doesn't work,' the pilot replied. 'Hang on again.'

Serrion didn't have time to wonder, or to question him any more. As they shot out of the clouds back into clear blue sky with the dragon mere seconds behind them, the pulver cut the engines. He threw his weight forwards to tilt the vehicle. The flycar began to tumble towards the ground far below...

'Run!'

Her mother's shout broke Helen out of her frozen terror. The sight of Gretton Tur in front of her had rooted her to the spot. She was unable to move at first. But now she turned and raced away with Jenn.

'No escape is possible!' screamed Gretton Tur as he followed them, moving effortlessly between the tents.

A pulver ran towards them, swinging his sword high. As Helen rushed past she saw him bring his weapon down towards their pursuer. She instinctively ducked her head down into her shoulders, turning away to give the pulver more room to fight. There was a flash of light from the black staff in Tur's hand and the pulver evaporated in a mist next to her. The shock almost froze her again and she slowed her running.

'Go right,' she heard her mother yell. In the same instant Jenn pushed her daughter sharply behind a tent to her right, while she herself leapt to the left. Her instinct had been correct. The spot they had been running over burst into a gout of earth and mud as another of Tur's blasts hit it.

Helen scrambled around the tent, trying to keep away from this demon from the past.

'*Revelator!*' the rasping voice of Gretton Tur sounded again and to her astonishment the tent grew transparent in front of her, and then disappeared completely. She was exposed. Tur saw her immediately and his grey face split into a grinning leer.

'You!' he cried. 'The whelp of that Select dog, Matthias. How fortunate! Now I get the chance to put you down – just as the runt of a litter should be,' he hissed at her with venomous hatred.

Tur rose up before her. It seemed he had grown to almost double his height. He lifted his hand to point towards her. There was nowhere to run.

Jenn reappeared from behind the market stalls where she had hidden. She was not going to leave her daughter to face such a horror alone. A crackle of yellow fire shot from her fingers towards him. Tur merely lifted his hand and swatted her magic away. Pointing his own finger at Jenn he twisted her off her feet and sent her crashing down amongst tables laden with fruit and vegetables.

'I'll deal with you next!' he growled at her and turned back towards Helen...

*   *   *

Serrion knew he was going to die. The earth was rushing towards them at an unbelievable speed. He could hear the howl of the dragon only a few metres above them. The pulver had not been able to shake it off by his daredevil tactic of switching off the engines of the flycar and making it plunge towards the earth. The dragon was just too quick.

Closer and closer it came.

Closer and closer to the ground they fell.

'Hang on!' the pulver cried out again.

Then, Serrion realised what the pilot was going to do. He had told him that he wasn't trying to outmanoeuvre the dragon. He knew that it was impossible to do that. No, the pulver had said that he was going to *trick* it!

As Serrion thought this, in the last moments before they hit the ground, the pulver hit the engines again full throttle. There was a roar of sound. The flycar sprang back into life. The pulver pilot lurched backwards, shifting his and Serrion's weight onto the back of the vehicle. The nose of the flycar lifted and it shot forwards horizontally, parallel with the ground. This tactic took it out of the path of the descending dragon. They were only metres from the earth and the dragon was plummeting at a terrific speed. It beat its huge wings frantically, trying to slow its fall. It was no good. There was no way it could possibly stop.

Serrion glanced back just in time to see the beast hit the field. As it did there was an eruption of noise, a huge bang, and the dragon burst outwards. Scraps of it shot in every direction. The dragon had popped like a balloon as it hit the ground, but it was not scraps of rubber that burst out, but real flesh, blood and bone that sped through the air like shrapnel.

People screamed in fear and revulsion as bits of bloody dragon skin slapped against their bodies and faces. Many picked hurriedly at the mangled flesh, trying to get it off themselves as quickly as they could. Others were completely freaked out and stood with arms spread and eyes closed, flicking their hands without success to get rid of the gore. One man was shaking violently and whimpering in a small voice for help. 'Get this horrible stuff off meee!' he yelped.

The flycar sped on over the field.

Jenn was dazed and shaken by her fall onto the tables. She shook her head to clear it and heard Tur's voice.

'I'll deal with you next!' he growled at her as he turned back towards Helen.

'You'll deal with me first,' said a familiar voice. There stood Matthias, both hands outstretched towards the image of Gretton Tur. *'Omnia mutantor, sed nosce te ipsum,'* he cried.

With a scream of rage, the Wild Lord spun to face his new attacker. He raised the black staff of Atros once more. But even as he did his attention was distracted by a massive winged shape hurtling towards the ground on another part of the field. Everyone turned to look. For an instant Helen imagined she had seen a dragon disappearing behind the tops of the distant tents. A second later there was an enormous bang from that part of the field and the ground shook. There was a whooshing sound in the air. A flycar shot past only a dozen metres away, the flash of a pulver's pale blue cloak was clearly visible for an instant. Helen could have sworn that she saw Serrion clinging to the pulver's back.

This distraction had given Matt the time he needed to repeat the incantation. Helen noticed a change beginning. Tur's billowing robe lost its glistening sheen and began to hang more limply around his shoulders. The scream of anger turned to a whimper and the horrible face shimmered and transformed into a mask of make-up and theatrical paint. After only a few brief moments, Carvel Braggart stood in front of them, his performance ruined, his ego crushed, his acting dreams shattered, and his hopes of a BAFTA in tatters.

'Oh my loves, my loves, what have I done!' he cried melodramatically and burst into tears.

Matt leapt up onto one of the nearby tables. He raised both arms to the sky. Taking a deep breath he cried out towards the entire field. *'Omnia mutantor, sed nosce te ipsum!'*

A ripple shot through the air, spreading out from the Lord of Beltheron. Across the field rish and harch dissolved into actors; clowns, princesses and butterflies transformed back into children with painted faces who ran into their parents arms, confused and excited by their adventure. Cries of fear turned to expressions of relief as everything returned to normal.

Matt looked down towards his daughter. His expression was still fearful for her safety. She gave him the thumbs up sign and grinned. Thank the Three Worlds she was alright! He smiled back at her and leapt from the table to help Jenn who was already scrambling to her feet.

Helen looked around the field. People were already beginning to clear up, and attend to the wounded. At first glance it seemed that things could have been much worse, although several tents were still in flames and she was stricken to see several pulver bodies lying on the ground with no sign of movement.

Behind her she heard a whimper. Turning to look she saw a little girl, shivering under a ripped piece of tent canvas. There were smears of bright paint on her face and a scattering of feathers on the ground nearby. Helen immediately guessed what had happened and ran to comfort the child. Noticing that the child's clothes had been ripped to shreds by the transformation, Helen quickly shrugged out of her own coat and wrapped it protectively around the girl.

'Here,' she said. 'Put this on. You'll be alright now. Let's go and find your mum.'

The little girl gratefully allowed herself to be wrapped up. Her shoes were nowhere to be found so she instinctively lifted her arms up towards Helen, in the unmistakable gesture that meant 'carry me.'

Helen smiled down at her and picked her up. Together they made their way across the shattered field.

Serrion climbed down from the flycar and wobbled on his unsteady legs. 'Thanks,' he said to the pulver pilot. 'Next time though, I think I'll do without the rollercoaster ride.'

The pulver grinned back at him. 'You're welcome, master Melgardes. It was an honour, sir.' Then the pulver's face clouded over. 'You must forgive me. I have friends who will need my help.'

'Of course, you must go at once.'

The pulver leant down from the flycar and they shook hands warmly. Then he accelerated away into the air to help his wounded companions.

A thought flashed across Serrion's mind. He glanced down at his watch. The glass face had cracked at some point during the aerial battle with the dragon, but the second hand was still ticking around, showing that it was still working. He looked at the time.

12.17.

The same time that he had seen on the clock in his vision.

Many nearby tents were now no more than smouldering piles of jagged struts and charred wood. Black smoke curled from them and gathered in the air. It joined the smoke higher up from other fires and earlier explosions from the battles. The growing cloud hung like a threat of rain over the whole field. It wasn't like a normal cloud though. This looked solid.

'Just like the smoke I saw in my vision,' thought Serrion to himself. The vision *had* been a warning, but not the kind he had imagined. The people did not fall, or cry out in the way he had seen. 'There must be more danger to come,' he thought.

A gust of cool wind passed through the crowds. The pall of dark smoke over their heads began to move slowly towards the city walls, shading Beltheron like sudden night-time.

Pursuit

Orianna felt the familiar swirling, sickening feeling as she hurtled away from the carnival ground and through the pathway in pursuit of the witch. But where was this pathway taking her? She looked down at the wisps of hair still clutched tightly in her fingers. They were fizzing and sparking like little fireworks.

She spun and twisted until there was a sudden lurch as she was brought up sharply at her destination. She stumbled and almost fell as her feet hit a solid floor. Pain shot through her knees and she struggled to keep her balance. Her stomach was still twisting with sickness and she feared she might throw up.

When her vision started to clear she realised she was inside a house. It was quite dark, as all the curtains in the room were closed. However, she could tell that it was still daylight outside; there was enough light coming through a chink in the curtains for her to make out the features of the room.

She was in some kind of library. Every wall was filled with old books on shelves that reached from floor to ceiling. She was standing on a rug over old wooden floorboards. One corner of the rug had been rolled back and she could see the corner of an old symbol painted on the floor.

With a rush of realisation that made her head spin again, she knew where she was. She had been in this house before and had no desire to be in it again.

The pathway had taken her to Earth. The witch had led her straight to the lair of her master and mistress; Orianna was standing in the London home of Piotre and Sophia Andresen.

Orianna listened intently for any sound. The house was perfectly quiet. It seemed to be empty. But she had followed hot on the heels of the witch, so there was a good chance that she was still hidden away somewhere in one of the rooms. Orianna knew she could not take any risks.

Why had the witch come here? Why had she not just returned to Atros? There must be a good reason. Orianna scanned the bookshelves on the walls, trying to spot anything that seemed odd, or out of place. A book hastily put back in the wrong place, an object or ornament that had been moved recently and left a mark in the dust. It was almost an impossible task of course; she wasn't familiar enough with the layout of the room to really be able to tell if anything was different. But she knew from her long studies that there was almost always a clue somewhere. If only you looked long enough.

Time was not on her side today however. Her most important task was to follow the witch – if she could – and find out how such an attack on Beltheron had been possible.

Above her she heard a slow creak. Gently tilting her head, Orianna raised her eyes to look up. There it was again, a gentle squeak of floorboards as someone moved carefully across the upstairs room directly over her head.

As silently as she could, Orianna moved towards the door. Her feet gently brushed the ground. She made no sound at all, like a gazelle moving through a thicket to avoid a hunting wolf.

When she reached the door she turned the handle slowly. There was a tiny *click* as the catch was released and Orianna froze. Her heart was pounding in her chest. It sounded so loud in her own ears that she worried the woman upstairs might hear. Then she laughed inwardly at herself for being silly. That was impossible of course. There was no way that such a small sound could be heard all the way upstai...

Before she could complete the thought, an unearthly shriek of anger rent the air. The witch began to run across the floor to the top of the staircase. Orianna slammed the door behind her and retreated back into the library. She had been discovered!

The easiest thing – the safest thing – would be to reverse the pathway and disappear back to Beltheron. Orianna knew that if she thought of that for even a moment, her courage would fade and she would run. But there was a part of her which was still more furious than she had ever known. The image of the little girls came back to her again.

'No!' she steeled herself. 'This hag is going to pay for what she did. She is not going to get away with the spell she placed on those two children.' She took the dagger that Matt had given her, and gripped it tightly in her right hand. As she felt the weight of the weapon, the reality of using it struck her. She had been in terrible battles before, and already seen more bloodshed than anyone should. She herself had cast spells to defeat enemies, but the act of using such a weapon as this made her feel faint.

The footsteps had reached the top of the staircase now. Orianna opened the door a fraction. The footsteps stopped abruptly.

The shape of the house and hallway meant that the witch would have to come around a bend in the staircase and descend over half way down before she could see the doorway that Orianna was lurking behind. However she obviously knew instinctively that she was not alone, and who had followed her.

'I know you are there, Dove Hair,' she called down the stairs.

Orianna shuddered at the use of that name. It was what Piotre Andresen and his son Jacques had called her during the battle in which they had killed her beloved Parenon.

'If you stop wasting my time and reveal yourself to me now I will kill you swiftly, and without pain,' the witch continued. 'But if you annoy me more than you have already, and refuse to show yourself, I will make your last experiences dire and dreadful.'

Orianna shivered once more. She knew that the witch meant what she said.

'I can use the revelator spell,' the witch continued. 'There is no escaping that, you know.'

Orianna did know. She had studied the revelator spell herself but had never been able to master it. The spell could be used to call up a damp mist which then spread out to cover everything in the area around you. As soon as it touched any surface the mist made that object completely transparent. It continued working until it reached the object or person you were looking for. There was no use hiding, because the thing you hid behind would just disappear and leave you vulnerable to attack. It was deep, dark magic and if the witch had power to control it then Orianna knew that she was truly lost.

As she thought this through, Orianna realised that the witch had used the last threat to cover her descent down the staircase. She was already past the bend half way down and Orianna could see her pointed shoes and bony ankles through the gap in the banisters. She shrank back into the room again, thinking rapidly.

If the witch really could use the revelator spell then why was she coming downstairs to meet her? Why did she not stay upstairs and release her magic? It was safer, and made more sense than walking downstairs to confront her, risking being seen, or being hit by a shot from a wand.

'She's bluffing,' Orianna thought to herself. 'She can't use the spell at all!'

In her head she went back over the fight in the tent. Although the witch had shown great ferocity and violence towards her, she had not used any magic. The only thing she had done was transform the girls into the bird and the pedjiaar. Orianna considered the possibility that this woman was not even a full witch. There were students of spellcraft who specialised in changing shapes and casting shifting spells on others. Maybe that was all that this one could do. It was a desperate gamble, but Orianna was willing to risk it. She placed the dagger back in her belt. She would fight by pitching her own spellcraft against the witch. She opened the door a crack further and looked out into the hallway again.

'This is your last chance, your final warning!' the witch was saying as she same down two more steps. 'It is hopeless, Dove Hair. Give up now!' She was moving more carefully and slowly now, but still revealing herself more and more to possible attack. Surely she wouldn't do that if she could really send out the revelator spell?

'I bet she can't do anything at all,' Orianna told herself to try to build up her confidence. 'I bet I know more about witchcraft and spells than she does.'

Was she right though? Was she judging the witch's behaviour correctly? Now was the time to put it to the test.

'Go on then!' she shouted up the stairs from behind the door. 'Cast your spell, see if I care!'

There was silence for several long heartbeats. The witch did nothing. She was hesitating on the stairs, more of her thin legs and skirt were now visible as Orianna peeped through the narrow gap in the door.

'You have one last chance,' the witch said, in a voice that sounded nervous. 'I won't give you another.'

'Since when did the vile servants of Atros give anyone a second chance?' Orianna answered.

As she said this she threw herself through the door and into the hallway. Her hand was already outstretched. She had decided upon the spell that she herself would use.

'*Excoriator!*' she yelled as bright light shot from her fingers towards the witch's face.

Her adversary reacted quickly, leaping backwards up several stairs in one bound. Orianna was taken completely by surprise at her speed and agility. It seemed impossible to make such a jump from a standing position. The blast of Orianna's spell missed the witch by centimetres. It hit the banister instead, splintering the wood into twisted shards.

Orianna was frustrated at her wasted shot. The fact that the witch was retreating was good news though. It meant that she was scared. Orianna knew then that she had guessed correctly; the witch *had* been bluffing and didn't have the powers that she claimed.

Orianna was already at the foot of the stairs, her arm raised again for a second attempt. But she was too late. The witch had already disappeared around the corner and onto the upstairs landing.

Cursing her disappointment, Orianna hurtled up the steps two at a time. All fear had gone now, and the exhilaration of gaining the upper hand in the struggle filled her with confidence and courage.

At the top of the steps she slowed and ducked automatically. After all she had done it would be stupid to give the witch a clear shot at her head as she turned the corner.

She had nothing to fear however. By now her quarry had scurried away into one of the bedrooms. Cautiously Orianna checked them one by one, but the witch had gone. In the final room that she came to she thought that she could smell a familiar scent in the air, a bitter aroma that was usually left after a pathway had been created. Sure enough, when she looked down she saw the tell-tale scorch mark burnt into the floor.

'Drat it! She got away,' she thought.

As she made her way back down the staircase she noticed something that she had missed before. She bent to pick it up. It was a small piece of torn paper. It had been folded over two or three times.

This must have dropped from one of her pockets when she leapt back up the stairs, Orianna considered. She opened it out to see what was written on it.

Her eyes grew wide when she read the words on the scrap of paper.

There was nothing but a handful of words scratched down on the paper between her fingers. Just two short sentences.

Attack the carnival. Send the Darkness.

A cold fear fell upon her as she read the words. She had to get back to Beltheron straight away. She had to warn Matthias and the others.

A Scorch of Dragons

Serrion strode furiously down the passageway to T'yuq Tinyaz's lair. It was only an hour after the attack on the festival field. The mortal danger he had so recently found himself in made his legs tremble. He felt a hot anger inside his chest directed at the Seer of Beltheron.

'She knew!' he kept repeating to himself. 'She knew about the attack on the festival. That is what she saw yesterday. That was the vision she wouldn't tell me about just before she sent me away.'

But *why* hadn't she told him? Was *she* using him as well? He felt angrier than he could ever remember at the thought that he was still being kept in the dark and manipulated. 'Even now,' he thought to himself. 'Even now, after everything I've done for them, they still don't trust me. They still have to have their secrets.'

He rounded the long bend in the corridor which led to the lake. In his mind he was forming what he wanted to say to T'yuq Tinyaz. The rage inside him was so strong that he had arrived at the Seer's underground lake without even noticing how he had got there.

T'yuq Tinyaz stood on the island in the middle just as she had the day before. Her head only turned slightly when she saw Serrion. It was obvious from her expression that she had been expecting him. In spite of himself, Serrion smiled. How could she *not* be expecting him? After all, she knew *everything* didn't she?

'Why didn't you warn me?' Serrion shouted across the lake at her.

'Warn you?' she answered. 'As if warning you would have made any difference. I have been warning people for longer than I care to think about. It seldom does any good.'

'But we might have been prepared for the attack...'

'...and the course of the day would have changed,' she yelled back at him. 'Yes, Serrion of course it would. But there would still have been death, there would still have been failure. I saw that as well. I saw four or five different outcomes to this day. And I saw beyond. The decision I made, the choice not to tell you, led to something that could have been far, far worse.'

'What gives you the right to make these decisions for everyone?'

'It is my responsibility to make decisions,' she said. 'I am given these visions and have to decide whether or not to act on them, what to tell people. Sometimes it is best not to tell them at all.'

'So you just sit there on your island and do nothing!' he shouted.

The Seer's bright eyes darkened with anger.

'Nothing?' she spat at him. 'Nothing! You dare to call what I have lived through *nothing?*'

The venom in her voice rocked Serrion.

'One day Serrion Melgardes, that responsibility of making these decisions will be yours.'

'Well I hope I make a better job of it than you!'

As soon as these words were out of his mouth he regretted them. T'yuq Tinyaz's face grew hard. She looked at him sternly and silently for several moments. When she did speak, her voice was cold.

'You say that even after all I told you yesterday; even

after I tried to explain how to live with such a curse as ours. I was trying to help you Serrion, and even now you still have the nerve to speak to me in such a way.'

Serrion dropped his head. Guilt overwhelmed him. He could not look at her. He knew that his own visions – so far – were just pale echoes of what she had lived through day after day, year after year. He had no right to criticise the way she dealt with this gift that they shared.

'Gift?' he thought to himself. 'It's more like a curse.'

And he knew that she had told the truth. She had helped him in the best way she could think of, with all her information and knowledge.

He was lost in these thoughts but then realised that she was speaking to him again. Her voice had changed once more. It was softer now, filled with care and regret.

'I am sorry my boy. I did not mean to get angry with you. You should not have come here today. It is best you leave straight away.'

'No, I'm the one who's sorry, T'yuq,' he began to reply.

'There is no need. Just go.'

'But I don't want to go. There is so much more I want to ask...'

'No time!' she snapped in interruption. 'You should not have come back here today!' Her head suddenly shot up and her eyes moved from him to a place on the wall behind him. Their colour changed and Serrion saw them lose focus.

'Already it is too late,' she murmured.

'T'yuq, What is it?'

She stared blankly at the wall, her eyes still unfocused.

'You need to leave. NOW!'

Serrion spun around in the direction that the Seer had been looking. He couldn't see anything.

'They are coming. I can see it,' she gasped.

'What are coming?'

'For the last time Serrion, GO!'

This time the look in her face was enough to drive him back towards the exit in fear. He turned and started to run. But as he did, his eyes dimmed and the room seemed to fill with red light. He stumbled as he shook his head to try to see the ground in front of him. It was no good. His sight was blocked by the beginning of another premonition.

'Not now,' he thought. 'Not here. I don't have time. I have to get out.'

But the red light of his vision increased. Now he could hardly make out anything of his real surroundings at all. He groped blindly in front of him, tripping and lurching towards the corridor that would take him back up towards the light, and safety.

Then he heard them.

The sound started as a low fluttering at first. It grew rapidly louder. After only a few seconds it sounded more like the hum of a swarm of bees, but this noise was higher pitched, and drier somehow, like the flapping of leathery wings.

'Bloodbats!' he thought, remembering the horrible nipping creatures he had once met in the tunnels beneath Atros City.

He stopped running blindly and dropped down onto all fours. Desperately, still trying to see through the blinding red, he scrabbled around, looking for shelter. He needed a large rock, a curve in the wall, anything that he could hide behind.

T'yuq's advice came back to him. *'You do have a choice, Serrion. You cannot stop these visions, but you can control them, put them in a part of your mind where they can be ignored for a while.'*

He imagined pushing the red into one corner of his

mind. He thought about a rock on the beach and making the bright colour flow into it. With all his might he concentrated on the path in front of him, and struggled to force the visions away. Slowly, the red seeped into the rock in his imagination. It was working!

After another moment his sight cleared. The corridor was in front of him again. The flapping, fluttery noise was still getting louder.

He looked up and saw them come around the corner, flying towards him at great speed. They were not bloodbats as he had feared. These were worse.

Much worse.

As they drew nearer Serrion saw that they must be some breed of small dragon. Their bodies were about thirty centimetres in length, but they had rat-like tails trailing behind them that were almost as long again. Their skin was not scaly like an ordinary dragon's, but hard and leathery. They ranged in colour from dark greys and icy blues to black. Each creature had two sets of thin translucent wings like dragonflies. These flapped rapidly as the creatures sped closer. The beasts' heads were shaped a little bit like that of an alligator. Their snouts were long and narrow, with small eyes on short stalks that rotated to see all around them. Rows of jagged yellow teeth were clearly visible inside their hot mouths, which hung open or snapped with a dry popping sound. The noise of them chilled Serrion to his bones.

He dropped to the ground and rolled behind a large rock. He curled up into a tight ball, pushing himself further into the corner to escape these deadly beasts.

He could hear the sound of them almost over his head now. Many flew straight on, shrieking, towards T'yuq's island in the lake. Others lunged down upon Serrion's huddled form, nipping and grabbing with their teeth.

Serrion thrust back with his right arm and fist. He kept his left arm curled tightly around his head, to try to protect his eyes. He succeeded in knocking several of them away, but the onslaught seemed to be without end. More and more of the small dragons dropped onto him. They were biting and ripping. Serrion felt the slickness of his own blood on his fingers, and running into his hair.

He grabbed hold of one of the creatures in the middle of its body. The dragons were so slender that his fingers and thumb almost met around its torso. The texture of the creature's gristly skin under his fingers made him gag and he thought he would be sick. He felt it writhing and wriggling in his hand. His instinct was to throw it as far away as he could, to get rid of the disgusting thing. He didn't though. Instead he held on to it even more tightly and started to use the captured dragon as a club.

With his eyes still firmly covered Serrion smacked the creature back and forth through the air. Time after time it struck the other dragons as they flew past. He could feel each impact and heard the squeals of anger and pain as his winged attackers began to veer away. Swinging wildly he felt the dragon in his grasp go limp as time after time it hit one, then another of its fellows. He risked uncovering his eyes for a moment to take a look. Sure enough, most of the dragons were now leaving him alone and heading for the lake. He loosened his grip on the dead dragon and took it in both hands by the tail.

There were just five more of the creatures hovering above him. With a loud yell, Serrion swung his makeshift weapon again. He caught one dark grey dragon at the side of the head as it dived down to take a chunk out of his ear, and tipped another end over end as he broke its wing, smashing it heavily into the wall and down to the ground where it limped away. The rest gave up their attack on him and followed the rest in their assault on T'yuq Tinyaz.

She stood on the middle of the island, surrounded by the flying creatures. Her arms were stretched out above her. Then she plunged her hands down towards the water. Flashes of lightning sprang from the Seer of Beltheron's fingertips and hit the lake with a crackling fizz. The sound stopped the dragons in their onslaught for a moment. Their wings flapped idly as they hovered, wondering what this might mean. Their long heads turned in quick jagged movements as they looked around.

Then, from below the water there came a rushing sound. Bubbles erupted from the milky surface of the lake. The bubbles burst as they came into contact with the air, sending gouts of yellow flame up towards the ceiling of the cavern. The Seer's fingers flicked once again, and more eruptions of smoke and fire sprang from under the water's surface.

The dragons went wild with anger and fear. Their wings thrashed and thrummed the air as they tried to escape the explosions below. Some renewed their furious attack on the Seer, tangling themselves in her hair and biting down with a terrible wrath.

Others were hit directly by the firestorm from the lake and burst into flame themselves. Many of them panicked and flew into the walls. Some plunged down towards the waters to try to douse the fire licking at their leathery bodies, but by now the lake was one boiling mass of flickering reds and yellows. The power that T'yuq Tinyaz had unleashed was unlike anything that Serrion had ever seen before.

'Go, go now!' she cried.

Hideous shadows fought on the walls and ceiling in the guttering light. The Seer disappeared from view behind the remaining dragons and the flames from the lake.

Yelling out in fear and frustration, Serrion turned and fled.

As he ran headlong down the corridor he heard her final words echoing around the cavern. He tried to make out their meaning, but they were distorted by the distance and the shrieks of the remaining dragons. All he could hear was:

'Elasp ottewan tew ear!'

He arrived upstairs and burst into the tapestried corridor just outside the great hall. Cannish and a couple of the other guards saw him immediately and came running towards him. The shock on their faces was clear and he realised he must be presenting quite a sight. His clothes were ripped from the attack of the dragons, and he could still feel a warm trickle of liquid down his face that he knew must be his own blood.

Just as Cannish and the others reached him, there was a familiar droning sound in the hallway that made the ground vibrate. The pulver guards all had their swords drawn in an instant. They surrounded Serrion in a tight, defensive circle.

'Now what?' Cannish spoke under his breath. 'Is the attack on the field not enough? Are we to be threatened with yet more devilry on this day?'

A brilliant white column of light that heralded a pathway shot up from the ground. Everyone shielded their eyes. Only Cannish, who held onto his sword even more firmly, did not avert his gaze. He was ready to attack, whatever this 'new devilry' proved to be.

The column of white light dimmed and from out of it stepped Orianna. Everyone breathed a sigh of relief.

She staggered as she tried to get her balance and Cannish stepped forwards to steady her.

Orianna glanced around at everyone and her eyes fell upon Serrion. Her mouth hung open as she stared at her brother. The expression on her face was halfway between puzzled confusion and shock.

'Why are you looking at me like that, Orianna?' he asked.

'Serrion! What's happened to you?'

He realised that she was not looking into his eyes as she spoke. Her attention was focused just above, at the top of his head. Her eyes flickered around his face once more. She shook her head slightly, disbelieving.

'Tell me, please, Orianna, anyone,' he said as he looked around at the others. 'I've been through enough already today. You're starting to scare me. What is it?'

She gulped quickly before speaking.

'Your hair,' she said. 'Look at your hair.'

Serrion grasped the end of his long hair and raised the strands in front of his face. He stared at it for a moment. Realisation dawned on him and he reached out to take hold of the handle of Cannish's sword. It was polished and gleaming and reflected as well as any mirror. Drawing it towards him he held it the broad blade up to his face. Even though he had already guessed what he would see, he still gasped with surprise. Every hair on his head had now turned completely white.

Discussing the Danger

'We should have been expecting such an attack. It was foolish of me not to place extra guards around the cavern.'

'They must have created a pathway to send the dragons through. What could we have been done to prevent that? It is pointless to blame yourself.'

They had all gathered in Matt's study. Serrion and Orianna joined Helen and her parents around the large table. It was less than half an hour after the attack on the Seer's cavern. A pulver guard was positioned at each of the two doors that led to the room. Both were heavily armed, and silverscreens flickered in their hands so that they could keep in touch with further guards who were positioned outside. Beltheron was on high alert.

'Were those dragon creatures after me?' Serrion asked.

Matt shook his head. 'I don't think they were pursuing you Serrion. I think they were sent to stop T'yuq herself. Atros needed to silence her before she could tell us anything else.'

'They knew how important her visions were.' Jenn added. 'They couldn't risk her spoiling their final plans. I think it was just your bad luck that you got in the way.'

Serrion thought about this for a moment. It made sense. Then another thought came to him.

'So why didn't Piotre and Sophia try to get rid of T'yuq before? Surely it would have been easier for them if she had been safely out of the way?'

Helen had been quiet all this time, but now another thought occurred to her.

'What if they left T'yuq alone because they were getting information from her too?' she asked. 'Harrow was always going down there into the caverns to speak to her. Is it too much to think that he didn't pass on what he found out to the Andresens? He was willing to kill me to hide the secrets of what he had done. Those things must have been pretty bad, don't you think?'

Matt nodded slowly. 'I suppose you're right. Although, even after all that I have heard, I still find it hard to believe that the Cleve would betray us all in such a fashion.'

'You didn't see the look on his face as he was chasing me,' Helen said.

No one could argue with that. They all sat silently for several moments.

Serrion was still thinking of the last things that T'yuq Tinyaz had called out to him as he fled from the caverns.

'What about her final cries?' he said at last. 'I've been trying and trying and I still can't figure it out.'

Matt ruffled through some papers on his desk. 'Yes, that's strange. I wrote it down but I haven't been able to decipher its meaning as yet.'

'I thought it might be some kind of spell,' Serrion added. 'I asked Orianna, but she had never heard it before.'

Orianna shook her head, to confirm that she was just as confused by the words as everyone else.

'The most obvious thing is that you misheard in all the confusion and fear,' Matt concluded.

'*Elasp ottewan tew ear,*' Serrion repeated. 'I know I was scared and confused, but I know what I heard.'

'It's just nonsense,' Helen said. 'I can't think how we would ever find out what it means.'

'Not at the moment at any rate,' her father agreed. 'But we must put the Seer and her visions to one side for the time being. There is more news, a more pressing danger that is not so difficult to decipher and understand.'

Everyone knew what Lord Matthias meant. They all turned and looked towards Orianna.

'Yes,' she said. 'We need to consider the threatened Darkness.'

Once more she took out the scrap of paper which she had taken from the Andresens' house. Without a word Matt held out his hand to take it.

'The Darkness,' he mused. 'We do not know how they will strike with it, and have no time to prepare a defence.'

'What is the Darkness, Dad?' asked Helen.

'A cruel sorcery,' her father replied. 'The Darkness is a cloud of misery and sickness. It begins with the particular illness of just one individual in a city and then spreads rapidly.'

'It spreads an illness?' Serrion asked.

Matt nodded. 'It brings on a terrible lethargy and depression in those it touches. You only have to be surrounded by it, touch it, breathe it in, and it saps the life out of you as if you were nothing but a rag doll.'

They all shuddered. Just the *thought* of it was horrible.

Orianna had been considering how such a spell might be made to work. Already her quick mind was working on ways around this magic. 'And does it kill you?' she asked. 'Is this Darkness dangerous to your physical health as well as to your mind?'

Jenn spoke up for the first time. 'I have only come across it once before,' she spoke carefully, trying to remember it all properly. 'If it remains untreated, if the original person whom the Darkness used as a target is not healed within a handful of days, then everyone else begins

122

to sicken. The person who was poisoned weakens even further and dies, followed by all the others.'

'That's evil,' Helen whispered under her breath. 'No one would do that... would they?'

A heavy silence hung over the room. Finally Matt cleared his voice gruffly and spoke. His voice seemed suddenly loud and shocking to them all. Even Serrion jumped at it.

'Jenn has just told you all that we witnessed this once before. Gretton Tur perfected this evil, and his first use of it was upon the city of Maraglar.'

'The Silver City?' Serrion whispered.

Matt and Jenn nodded.

'Yes my boy,' the Lord of Beltheron continued. 'That is how the city of Maraglar was ruined and abandoned. It was left empty and desolate for years.'

Serrion himself had spent a short period of time in Maraglar, hiding on the run from the rish.

'It was a beautiful place,' he murmured as he remembered the tall towers of silver and glass, and the way they had reflected the brightness of the afternoon sun. 'Even when I saw it – when it was empty. It must have been incredible when it was full of people and noise.'

'It was,' Jenn agreed. 'Maraglar was one of Beltheron's most magnificent achievements. That is why Gretton Tur chose it as one of his first attacks on our people.'

'But surely there must be something that we can do?' asked Helen. She was getting impatient. It was right to be worried and anxious over the threat of this Darkness thing, but worrying was no way to solve a problem. 'We have some of the best brains of Beltheron sitting in this room,' she grinned. 'I don't believe that we can't come up with some kind of solution.'

Jenn smiled at her. She was so proud of her daughter's

attitude at times like this. She hoped that the threatened Darkness and the horrors that might accompany it would not change her daughter's positive view of the world. Jenn shared the same fear that every parent has; that the world will not be kind to their children, and that their innocence and joy of life will be twisted out of them by cruel experience. It was amazing to Jenn that Helen had still managed to hold onto that joy, even after the terrors she had faced. She never seemed to let anything get her down for long.

It was getting late. Matt gazed around the table. He saw eyelids drooping, and concentration begin to waver. He himself felt exhausted after the day's events.

'I suggest we all go home and get some rest.' He announced. 'I will call a council first thing tomorrow morning. Then we will discuss these matters further with the elders of the city.' He turned towards one of the pulver guards in the doorway. 'Spread word through the city,' he told him. 'There is to be a curfew tonight. Everyone is to stay indoors until daylight tomorrow. We do not know what other tricks that Atros might have in store for us.'

'At once my Lord,' the guard bowed low and left the room.

'That goes for all of us,' Matt continued. 'We must get behind our own locked doors as quickly as we can. Orianna, Serrion, I will send guards to escort you back here tomorrow morning for the Council.'

The other pulver stepped forwards. Matt quickly organised them to take Jenn, Helen and the rest back to their homes before it grew dark. He then bent over his desk and began to write messages to his advisors, calling them to the great hall the next day.

The Council of Matthias

Matthias held his council early on the following morning. Jenn sat by his side, and the highest ranking pulver soldiers and a handful of Beltheron's most trusted advisors were present. So too were Orianna and Serrion Melgardes. Both brother and sister had vital information to share; Serrion from his visions, and Orianna from what she had discovered from the witch in the Andresen's house on Earth. In fact, the council would have been impossible without their presence.

Although she had not been officially invited, Helen had eventually managed to persuade her dad that she should be there as well. She reminded them that after Jacques Andresen's death she was the only surviving member of the twenty-third generation of the Select Families of Beltheron. As such she insisted that it was only right and proper that she should attend the council. Matters of great importance to all the Belthronic people were being discussed. Helen felt that she had gone through so much in their defence recently that it was only fair she should be there alongside her parents and the all others.

Matthias had sent word that the council would begin at seven thirty sharp, but even before seven in the morning people began arriving in front of the great tapestry in the corridor of the great hall. They came singly at first, then in pairs and small groups. Everyone had been shocked by the extent of the attacks on the festival, and news of the death of the Seer of Beltheron had filtered out during the previous evening.

They all talked in reverent whispers about what had happened over the last twenty-four hours, and what more was to come. Cannish was on duty and ushered them through as they arrived, checking their names against a long list that Matthias had hastily put together.

Everyone gathered around the long carved table which had been placed in the centre of the hall. Orianna and Serrion were already standing behind their places at the table, and there were gasps of surprise at Serrion's hair as people entered and saw him for the first time.

When everyone was present, Matthias gave a nod to Cannish, who closed the old oaken doors behind them with a heavy thud. He turned a large brass key in the lock before moving to the side of the table next to another guard, a large, bald giant of a man called Husk.

'Friends,' Matthias began. 'We are facing the darkest time in Beltheron's whole history.' No one around the table missed the reference to the threat of the coming cloud. 'Atros could attack again at any time. We need to gather as much information as we can, together around this table, so that we can best decide how to counter these attacks and defend our people.'

Everyone nodded seriously. There was anxiety etched on every face. All knew the life or death situation that they were facing.

'My daughter must be the first to speak,' Matt said. 'I have told her she can be brief, as what she has to tell you is painful for her, and difficult to speak of.'

Helen got to her feet nervously and told them about Harrow and Ungolin's plotting and secrets. She spoke of how they had used the advice of the Seer and convinced the Andresens to kidnap Serrion to take their own son's place in Beltheron while he was raised by Gretton Tur. In a breaking voice she then related how Harrow had attacked her when she discovered his plans. Her father put his arm around her when she had finished and she sat down quickly.

'I have also brought Serrion Melgardes to the table, as the information he has received through his visions is vital.' Matt continued after Helen had finished. 'The way forward may lie in what he now has to tell us. I urge you all to give him your fullest attention. Serrion?' Matt turned towards him before sitting down. Serrion gulped. It was his turn to speak. His heart hammered in his chest and his tongue felt glued to the roof of his mouth. He coughed and rose to his feet.

Over the next half an hour he told them about the cloud he had seen in his vision. He was questioned about this and asked about details of the Seer's death. Finally he spoke about his premonition of Harrow kneeling before the throne of Atros. At this there were gasps of amazement and disbelief.

'And what else do you see, Serrion?' asked Matt. 'Can you summon up more information about Cleve Harrow that might tell us more?'

Serrion shook his head. There was no way he was going to tell them about the other part of that vision; the one where he himself bowed down to Piotre and offered him the golden staff. He suddenly realised that he was already doing what T'yuq Tinyaz had done. He was filtering out news, deciding what to tell people and what to keep to himself. 'Is this how it starts?' he wondered. 'Is this how you begin to lose your life in deceit and double meanings, just like T'yuq did?' He shivered at the thought.

'I've tried,' he said to the whole table. 'Please believe me, I've tried so much. I can control my visions more than I could before. T'yuq Tinyaz was right, it is possible to focus my mind on them, but I still can't control how *much* I see, or what they are going to show me. I'm...I'm sorry.'

'No need, my boy, no need,' said Matt hurriedly. You have already done so much for us.'

He turned back to the table and spoke to everyone again.

'Serrion's new vision suggests that Cleve Harrow has been working for Piotre and Sophia all along.'

'But that can't be right,' Tarawen interrupted. 'I'm sorry if I speak out of turn, my Lord, and I have every respect for what our young friend tells us. But we saw Harrow help Parenon to kill Gretton Tur on the plains outside Atros City two years ago.'

This comment was followed by a chorus of voices from all around the table.

'That's right.'

'Yes, it's true.'

'Everyone saw it.'

'He wouldn't, *couldn't* have killed Gretton Tur if he had been working for Atros all along.'

Jenia suddenly waved her hand for silence. The voices abruptly stopped.

'Have any of you thought of this possibility,' she asked them all. 'Did Piotre and Sophia want Gretton Tur dead themselves?'

'What?'

'My Lady what are you suggesting?'

'Impossible!'

'Explain what you mean.'

Jenia waved again for silence, and when she spoke again her voice was low. It had dropped to a whisper and was deadly serious. 'Think about it,' she continued. 'Was Harrow helping Piotre and Sophia to get rid of the Wild Lord so that they could place themselves on his throne?'

'They were already members of the Select Families of Beltheron,' one of the advisors butted in. 'That means that they already had power, right here in Beltheron itself.'

'That's right,' added another. 'Why should they sacrifice all of that just to gain similar power on Atros?'

'But it would *not* be a similar power,' answered Matt. He had been thinking about Jenn's idea. He realised that what his wife said could be true. 'It's not the same kind of power at all. That is the whole point. Our power here, on Beltheron, is limited. It is controlled by democratic decisions about what is best for everyone, as all power should be.'

'That's right,' Jenn added. Our place as members of the Select Families has always been to help and serve, not to dominate.'

'It is one of the principles of our life on Beltheron which we hold most dear,' another older member of the council agreed from the other side of the table.

Jenn continued. 'I know my sister,' she said as if she was speaking to herself. She looked embarrassed by what she was telling them. 'There was jealousy between us. I can understand how she and Piotre might wish for more power than being a member of the Select Family could give them. I am sure they have a desire for *complete* power.'

'And they could only achieve that by taking over the throne of Atros,' one of the advisors continued. 'As Matthias has just reminded us, the structure of government and our way of life here means that no one – not even a member of the Select – could ever achieve complete control over Beltheron itself.'

A second advisor who was sitting on Helen's left shook her head sadly. 'Absolute power,' she murmured.

It was almost as if she were speaking to herself. 'That would prove a dreadful temptation indeed.'

'So it *is* possible that Harrow could have been tricking us all along. That would mean he himself could play an important part in that absolute power on Atros,' Matt concluded. His expression grew angry and dark. 'What Helen tells us of how he attacked her would seem to be proof. He certainly wasn't acting like the Cleve that I know when he threatened to kill my daughter.'

'And that certainly backs up what the Melgardes boy says about his visions of Harrow kneeling before the Andresens,' one of the pulver captains added.

Helen had been deep in thought. So far, she had not said very much after giving her own evidence of Cleve Harrow's behaviour. Now however a slow suspicion that she had been considering during this part of the debate started to take a more solid shape in her head.

'What if...' she began, '...what if he wanted to become the Lord of Atros himself?'

'Who?'

'What does she mean?'

'Does she mean Cleve Harrow?'

'Cleve Harrow? Lord of Atros?'

There was immediate uproar around the table once again.

'Harrow as Lord of Atros? Unthinkable!'

'Ridiculous suggestion child!'

'The very idea!'

Matthias raised his hand to silence them.

'Remember that my daughter has already suffered at the hands of the Cleve,' he said. The thought of what Helen had gone through was still uppermost in his mind. 'Let her speak.'

Helen had been shocked by the outburst that her

words had caused. It took her a couple of moments to regain her confidence and speak again.

'Think about it,' she said. 'Harrow had information from T'yuq Tinyaz. She told him so much, over years and years. What's to say he didn't decide to use that information, that knowledge, for his own good?'

'Harrow trained with Gretton Tur when they were both no more than children,' added Matthias. He spoke slowly, working out this new idea in his head. 'They grew up together and both studied the same skills and ancient knowledge. They knew much of the same magic. If what my daughter suggests *is* true, then the thought of Cleve Harrow as a new Wild Lord would be a fearsome thing indeed.'

Everyone at the table was now perfectly silent. Each person was deep in their own thoughts. They knew that what Lord Matthias said was quite believable. Shocked by the possibility of such a betrayal from someone at the heart of Belthronic society, and lost in deciding what could be done to prevent further catastrophe, it was a long time before anyone added anything else to the discussion.

The morning wore on. Arguments and questions went back and forth. A direct attack on Atros was discussed. The evacuation of Beltheron City was suggested. Ideas for the best way to defend the city were put forward.

Finally one of Beltheron's oldest advisors pushed back his chair and got to his feet.

'My dear friends,' he began. 'It seems to me that we are entering a new phase in our struggle against Atros and the Andresens. Their attacks are more blatant, more violent and personal than we have seen before. It makes me think that we are close to the final battle.'

Matt turned to Cannish who was standing a few paces behind his chair. 'My friend, I fear that is true. It means that you and your colleagues must stand in the path of great danger once more.'

Cannish nodded. 'Whatever is required my lord,' he said.

'Go, gather a small group of your most trusted men,' Matt instructed. 'Tell them to ready themselves for attack.'

Cannish gave a short bow and he and Husk hurried from the hall.

Matt turned to the rest of the table. 'Let us pause to think and take some food,' he announced. 'We should clear our heads and consider our next course of action. Return here in one hour.'

There were murmurs of agreement from everyone as they rose from their places.

'I have books at home recording the attacks on Maraglar,' Jenn said to Orianna. 'I would like you to study them, to see if your sharp mind can muster a solution to our new problems.'

Orianna nodded. 'Anything that may be of use,' she said.

Jenn turned to Helen. 'Go home,' she told her daughter. 'I need to stay here with your father until the council begins again. Bring me the leather bound books marked with the words 'Maraglar' on the spines. They are on the middle shelf by my desk in the study.'

'Yes Mum,' Helen replied as she started to leave.

'Wait a moment,' Jenn continued. 'If you are going home you might as well bring these back with you too.' She started to scribble down the names of several herbs on a piece of paper. 'We will probably be talking late into the evening,' she explained. 'I will use these herbs to brew a drink that will sustain us and keep our minds focused on the discussions.'

Helen took the paper and started to run from the hall. 'I'll come straight back,' she called over her shoulder.

The room had now emptied apart from Matt, Jenn, Orianna and Serrion. All four sat silently. They stared into space ahead of them, each lost in their own thoughts.

Familiar Intruder

Crudpile crept quietly through the house. He made his way to the kitchen. It was dusk, but enough daylight remained outside for him to make out objects in the gloom without having to shine a light. Lord Andresen had told him to be careful, not to draw any attention to himself. Crudpile shivered at the Lord of Atros' warning.

'If you fail me in this Crudpile, your life will be a tortuous misery from this day forwards. Do not think you can hide from me, anywhere, in any of the Three Worlds, if you displease me in any way.'

Crudpile had whimpered his understanding, and repeated his loyalty to the Andresens before scuttling off on his mission.

That mission was to deliver the real plan of attack, Lord Andresen had said. 'When you have succeeded, Crudpile, all of Beltheron will quake before me, and the dreams of Gretton Tur, the Wild Lord, will finally be realised.

'My forces will provide a distraction in Beltheron.'

'A distraction my Lord?'

'Something that will keep the pitiful Lord Matthias and his attendants preoccupied while you creep in to the city.'

That is why Crudpile now found himself in the kitchen of Matt, Jenn and Helen's house in the middle of

Beltheron city. This was his great chance, he knew it. No matter how scared he was he knew that if he succeeded here then he would be given respect, a worthy place in Atrossian society and, most importantly of all, money. Crudpile craved money. He had never had much, and what little he had always seemed to disappear in bars like the Hunter and Holva on Atros, or into the pockets of people who were better at cards than he was.

He had been given careful instructions before Piotre Andresen had opened up the pathway which had taken him straight to the city gates. A crumpled street map in his pocket had shown him to the house. He had been told to stay hidden during the day of the festival when the attack would be made. He had heard the explosions and seen the black smoke rising over the field outside the city walls.

After this great diversion he knew that Matthias would be busy spending much of his time in the great hall and that Jenia would be with him. He had overheard a conversation from two passers-by that a council was to be held in the great hall. He grinned to himself. The lords of Beltheron would be so caught up in trying to deal with the aftermath of the attacks on the festival that they wouldn't return home until late in the evening.

That only left that brat of a girl, Yelenia. She had crossed his path too many times before, Crudpile thought, and every time she did it always ended up the worse for him. Well this time he would have the last laugh. This time he would use his opportunity well and get revenge on her and her whole dratted family.

It wasn't that Crudpile was particularly evil or cruel, but he was weak. Weak and greedy, and that is sometimes a deadly combination.

He had waited patiently in the shadows under the eaves of a low building at the end of the street. Pulver guards stood outside the house the whole night after the attacks on the festival. There was no way he could enter the house while they were there.

Crudpile must have fallen asleep in the early hours of the morning. He was still snoozing in his hiding place when the whole family had left early in the morning for the council. He only woke up when Helen returned to the house later in the day. Crudpile cursed himself for missing his chance. Finally Helen came out of the house again and walked towards the main piazza. She was carrying a small bag in one hand. Crudpile could see plants and herbs sticking out of the top. It looked as if Helen was heading back to the great hall. She hadn't even glanced in his direction. He grinned to himself. He wouldn't waste another chance.

It was an easy thing to use a piece of wire to pick the lock of the house and soon he was inside.

He gazed around the kitchen. There were the usual pots and pans ranged on shelves and hanging from hooks in the ceiling. Cupboards which would be stacked with food, and drawers filled with cutlery and other cooking utensils. But Crudpile was looking for something in particular. His eyes roamed around. There, on the large oak table in the middle of the room, was a glass pitcher filled with water. There was a gauze cloth covering the top to keep out dust and insects, and a couple of glasses laid out ready next to it.

Crudpile grinned. This was going to be easier than he had dared to think. He lifted the gauze from the pitcher and placed it carefully on the table top. Licking his thin lips with concentration he reached into another pocket of his ragged jacket, taking out a small vial of clear liquid. There was a wax seal on the stopper. He snapped it off and poured it slowly into the water. There was a small hissing sound as the two liquids began to mix, and a faint steam rose out of the pitcher. Crudpile waved his hand backwards and forwards over it a couple of times until the steam had disappeared. Bending down he then looked intently into the pitcher. It was perfectly clear. No one would ever have noticed that there was anything strange about the water inside it.

Satisfied that his job was done, and done well, Crudpile turned and headed for the door.

Helen had only got halfway to the great hall before she remembered the books about Maraglar that her mother had asked her to fetch for Orianna. Groaning and rolling her eyes in frustration at herself and her poor memory she turned and headed back towards home.

As she reached the top of her street, which wound away from the main market square and down a side road, she saw a thin figure who appeared to be lurking around her house. As soon as she laid eyes upon this skulking thing she knew he was up to no good. Not only that but there was something about the way he looked around furtively; something in the set of his shoulders and his jerky movements that seemed familiar to Helen.

Then, as he stepped out of the shadows of the eaves that ran down the rooftops of the houses on Helen's side of the street, she caught a good glimpse of his face. Now there was no mistaking it. She had been right! She knew him instantly. His thin meagre expression with the mouth drawn out into a thin suspicious line; the mean way his eyes darted from right to left; his long grasping fingers clinging to the stonework of the wall as he crept along told her everything.

'Crudpile,' she gasped. 'You old villain. What are you doing here?'

One thing was certain – this scoundrel from Atros would be up to no good.

He was making swift progress, in spite of his secretive stealth and already he had almost reached the end of the street. Helen ducked herself into the shadow of a doorway and watched as he slunk across the cobbles to the opposite side, before slipping down a side alley between the houses.

Helen reached into her pocket. She fumbled around for her silverscreen but, like the book for Orianna, she had left it behind at home. 'Stupid,' she told herself. 'Yet again girl, stupid, stupid, stupid!'

She had not seen any pulver in the streets that she could call on for help and it would take her too long to go back to the great hall to fetch help. By the time anyone could get back here to follow Crudpile, he would have slunk away into the shadows, possibly never to be found.

'It's down to me,' Helen thought. 'I have to keep an eye on him. I don't need to challenge him, or even get close,' she reasoned to herself. 'As long as I can keep him in sight, get an idea of what he's up to, or even find out where he's hiding himself, then I can report back to Dad.' In her head she began imagining that she was like a pulver spy – working bravely for the good of her city – even though she knew that girls didn't become pulver guards or spies.

She tore herself away from these thoughts as she realised that Crudpile had already disappeared into the shadows of the alley opposite. Helen hurried across the street, and threw herself against the wall of a small thatched cottage. Centimetre by centimetre she edged herself to the corner of the wall.

As she peeped around the corner, she could make out Crudpile in the dim shadows. He was moving even more swiftly now and she realised she would have to run if she was going to keep up with him.

Helen increased her pace, but immediately saw Crudpile begin to turn around towards her. She dove into a doorway, hitting the wood with a thump that shook her limbs, before flattening herself into the shadows.

'He must have heard that,' she thought as she clenched her teeth together to stifle the cry of pain.

Controlling her heavy breathing she tried to stay completely immobile and silent. Had he heard her? Was he even now making his way back up the alley to find her?

More than thirty seconds dragged by. Still nothing. No sound of footsteps approaching. 'Come on, girl,' she coaxed herself. 'You're giving him more than enough time to get away! No matter what, you've got to risk a look and then get back after him.'

Cautiously she peered around the doorframe. There was no sign of Crudpile anywhere. 'Idiot!' she berated herself. 'You let him escape!'

In frustration she set off down the alley at a run. In less than another fifty metres ahead of her she knew that it opened out into a wide, circular forecourt surrounded by a two large crescents of terraced houses. There was no other exit unless you ran to the street on the far side of the crescents. She guessed that it would have taken Crudpile longer to get there than the delay she had spent hiding in the doorway. If he wasn't in this alley, then she would be able to see him as soon as she ran into the crescent.

Bang! With a shocking thud, Helen felt herself being driven off her feet and down onto the hard cobbles. Her head hit the floor and a sudden stabbing pain in her skull drove out all other thoughts for several seconds. When she started to regain her senses, she found Crudpile on top of her, his hands around her throat. As she struggled and reason started to return to her shaken brain she realised he must have been hiding in ambush, in one of the doorways. She had been so busy running on ahead that she had not thought to look into any of them.

She tried to cry out, but he was blocking her windpipe and all she could manage was a low rasping sound that would not be heard more than a couple of metres away.

Helen managed to get a grip around her attacker's wrists. She tried to pull his grip away from her throat, but he was too strong. 'That's no good,' she thought, trying to stay focused, even though she felt herself begin to grow faint as he continued to cut off her supply of air. 'I have to do something else.'

As the last air in her lungs started to run out, and she felt the desperate struggle to breathe becoming more and more urgent, she grew frantic. Panic was driving her now. Fear as great as any she had ever known began to overwhelm her.

In this desperation, Helen started to flail about with her arms and legs. One hand grasped the back of Crudpile's hair. With what little strength she had left she jerked it back suddenly. Crudpile gave a sudden yelp of pain, but continued to hold on to her throat grimly. His expression was set in an evil, fearsome leer.

Her other hand found its way around to the front of his face. She stabbed upwards with her fingers, towards his eyes, sticking them hard into the sockets.

This did have an effect. With a scream, he pulled back, letting go of her to roll away over the cobbles, his hands now clutching at his face as he cried hysterically in pain.

Helen gulped huge, gasping breaths into her lungs. She coughed and coughed as she tried to get more air. Rolling onto her side she looked to see if Crudpile was going to be any further threat. He was already rising to his feet, but still clutched at his face. He took his hands away and Helen saw blood trickle from one of his eyes as he blinked and shook his head wildly from side to side. The other eye was red raw, but it was clear he could still see through it.

With a snarl of anger, pain and hatred, Crudpile made another move towards her. But now, at last, Helen had found her voice again.

'Help me,' she croaked at first, then louder with each breath. 'Help me. Please, please help.'

She heard a couple of doorways open further down the alley. Voices cried out in alarm and concern. Rapid footsteps approached.

Crudpile did not hesitate. He began to stagger off, one hand still to his face, rubbing his eyes.

'Stop! Stop right there!'

The angry shouts just spurred him on to run faster. By the time Helen turned to look, he was gone and a small group of people was gathering round her. She felt herself being lifted gently to a sitting position by a middle aged man with a kind face, worry carved into his eyes as he began speaking.

'Lady Yelenia? Gracious, are you alright?'

'What has happened to you?' others began to chime in.

'Who was that creature who attacked you?'

The questions continued as they helped her to her feet.

'I'm fine really, thank you. But I must get home.'

'Do you need us to contact your family?' the older gentleman asked.

'Yes, Lord Matthias must be told,' another blurted out behind her.

She managed to reassure them. 'It's alright, I promise. I am going straight back now. Believe me, the very first thing I am going to do is contact my Dad.'

She left them in a worried cluster on the street, calling back a final 'Thanks!' as she sped towards home.

Within a couple of minutes she was safely inside once more.

Helen reached for the silverscreen where she had left it on the table. Her fingers danced over the surface until the image of her father appeared.

'Dad, you'd better get home quickly.'

His face clouded with worry as she looked at the screen.

'What's wrong? Are you alright? What has happened?'

'I'm fine, Dad, really. But you and Mum should get back. I've seen someone, here, in Beltheron, and I need to talk to you about it.'

No matter how she was trying to disguise it, Matt knew instantly from her tone and the look in her eyes that his daughter was scared.

'Stay in the house. Lock the doors. We'll be there in five minutes.' Her father's voice was quick and fearful. She nodded in reply and switched off the screen. Placing it back on the table she moved to the door. As usual, the initial thrill of racing ahead into adventure had started to fade, and now she began thinking about the danger of following Crudpile. 'Stupid, stupid, stupid,' she said to herself. 'Helen Day, will you never learn?'

She turned the key in the lock and peered briefly through the window at the side of the door. By now though, with the lamps up bright to light the room, all she could see was her own reflection staring back at her from the darkness outside. Shivering suddenly with the thought of what might still be out there, looking in, Helen reached out and quickly pulled the curtains closed. She stepped back into the centre of the room, feeling the comfort of the light glowing from the lamps

'Mum and Dad will be here in just a couple of minutes,' she reassured herself.

The chase through the streets and the sudden, violent encounter with Crudpile had left her breathless. As she stood waiting for Matt and Jenn to return her hands moved to her throat which was still very painful and bruised. She realised she was extremely thirsty. She needed a drink. Walking through to the kitchen she reached for a glass and the jug of water sitting on the table...

An Awful Discovery

Matt wasted no time after speaking with his daughter. He was through the door, clicking his fingers for Cannish to follow him before the fading silverscreen was even back inside his pocket.

'Jenia!' he called out to one of the side rooms where his wife was poring over a large book of herb-lore. 'We need to get home.'

'What's wrong?' her face was immediately filled with worry.

'Helen's fine,' he replied, knowing that his first concern – their daughter – would be uppermost in her mind too. 'Something has unsettled her though. She wants us back at home. We need to go straight away.'

It was only a short three minute walk from the great hall to where they lived; across the main piazza, past one of the time tower mirrors, down a market street and along one of the avenues leading off it. Not even worth riding a flycar or mounting a horse. The three of them moved swiftly, Cannish looking around constantly into the shadows of the deepening evening, his hand on the hilt of his sword.

Despite her husband's reassurance, Jenn was almost running by the time they could see the house. Both of them felt a dread growing in the pit of their stomachs. Lights gleamed through the chink in the curtains. Then, as they approached, they heard a faint crash from inside.

In another moment they were at the door, unlocking it as quickly as they could. Cannish's sword was out, and Matt reached for his own dagger.

'Helen? Helen!'

The first room was empty. There was no reply.

'Jenn, stay here. Cannish, check upstairs,' Matt was already racing through to the kitchen as he barked out his commands.

He stopped in the doorway and gasped. Then he ran through.

'What is it?' Jenn's voice crumbled with fear as she rushed after him. Her hand flew to her face at the sight before her.

Helen was lying on the kitchen floor, her legs twisted at a strange angle, one hand clutching her stomach. The other arm was outstretched and the remains of a shattered glass were scattered across the tiles just beyond her fingertips. Her face was very pale.

Matt and Jenn knelt next to her.

'Helen? Helen!'

There was no response from their daughter. Matt carefully lifted her and carried her through to the main room. Cannish had come hurrying back down the stairs as soon as he heard their cries. He helped Matt lay Helen down on the cushions of the couch. Jenn took her face gently in her long fingers and raised it to look into her eyes. What she saw made her recoil in shock.

Helen's face was nothing but a blank featureless stare. Her eyes were open but there was no expression in them. They stared incomprehensibly without any sign of emotion.

Jenn tried raising Helen's right arm, but it dropped limply to her side the moment she released it.

She lifted Helen's arm once more, cradling her

daughter's hand lovingly against her cheek. 'Wake up, my love,' she whispered. 'Please, come back to me.'

Helen did not stir. Her eyes remained open and only the slightest breath came from her half-parted lips.

'She breathes, whispered Jenn. 'Thank the Three Worlds, she still breathes.'

Jenn continued to cradle her daughter's head in her arms, rocking her softly backwards and forwards.

Matt stood close by, gazing down at them. He felt helpless. His fists were clenched tightly together and his jaw trembled. Both mother and father were blinking back tears. Matt turned to walk back through to the kitchen and over to the broken glass. He bent down and dabbed his fingers into the dark stain of liquid that was seeping into the rug. He brought his fingers up to his nose and sniffed.

'Like lemons,' he said as he moved back to the others. 'But with a trace of almonds and...and...something else. I can't tell what.'

'Something sharp?' Jenn questioned him urgently. 'A bitter scent?'

Matt nodded silently.

'I have seen this once before,' Jenn said. 'Years ago. I know what this is. It acts like a sleeping death.'

'Sleep? You're saying that Helen is asleep?'

'Yes, but not an ordinary sleep. Our poor girl's dreams will be dark and frightening.'

As if to prove her mother's words, Helen gave a low tortured moan. At the sound Matt felt as if his world was crashing down around him. All his power, his position as the new Lord of Beltheron, meant nothing. In fear for his daughter he slammed his clenched fists on the table.

'There must be something we can do. Is there any hope?' he asked, terrified of the answer that his wife might give. He swallowed hard and asked again. 'You said you had seen this before. Is there anything, *anything at all* that will help?'

Jenn nodded. 'Yes, there is a cure. I know which plants and herbs are needed and I think I remember how to mix them. In any case Orianna has the books where the remedy is written down.'

Matt turned immediately to Cannish. 'Bring Orianna here, straight away. Raise an alarm, get people off the streets. Place pulver guards on every city gate – no one goes in or out of Beltheron without my word.'

'Tell Orianna to bring her copy of *'Floralia Belthronis,'* Jenn called out from her position by Helen's side.

Cannish nodded once and was out of the door.

Orianna almost felt grateful as she raced through the streets following Cannish. At least she now had a distraction from the spiral of sorrow and fear from which she had been unable to escape. The loss of her mother, followed so closely by the death of Parenon had left her stumbling through a maze of memories and reminiscences. These memories of happier times were the only thing that she clung onto, and yet the very thought of the two people she had loved so much were now painful. They stabbed at her mind rather than comforting it.

These feelings had only grown worse after the attack on the festival. They had all lost so much, and had made such sacrifices, and yet the forces of Atros still attacked them. Had her mother and Parenon given their lives for nothing?

On top of this, as the oldest surviving member of her family, she had now been thrust into a new area of care and responsibility for Serrion. She had never turned away from this responsibility, but it weighed heavily on her mind.

'He's been through so much, yet he's still so young,' she told herself twenty times a day. 'I have to look after him, I *want* to look after him, but how can I manage it when I feel like this?'

For the time being at least, these thoughts were pushed to the back of her mind. On their way through the streets Cannish had told her the outline of what had happened, and how important it was for her to follow him.

As they ran towards Matt and Jenn's home, he filled in some more of the details about the attack on Helen.

Orianna recognised the symptoms at once.

'If Jenia is right,' she panted to Cannish as they raced along. 'The cure is written down in here,' she gestured to the heavy volume of *Floriala Belthronis* in her hands.

It was quite dark by the time they reached the house. Cannish gave a brief single knock and the door was immediately opened by Matthias. One look at his grim features told her all she needed to know: the situation had not improved for Helen.

'Over here,' he said, crossing the room quickly. Orianna followed while Cannish looked back out into the street before closing and locking the door firmly behind them once more.

Orianna took in the scene at a glance; Helen, motionless on the couch; her mother sitting next to her, holding her hand and gently stroking her forehead.

'Where is the jug of water?' she asked Matthias. He showed her through to the kitchen where she knelt down next to the broken vessel and dipped her fingers into the spilt water, just as Matt himself had done less than half an hour ago.

She sniffed at it and nodded immediately. 'I know what this is. Jenia was right; the remedy *is* in the *Floriala*.

Orianna moved to the kitchen table and opened up the

book towards the back. She hastily thumbed through two or three pages of the index before reaching the particular place which she had been searching for. Her gaze swept over the page, searching the tiny print as her finger moved rapidly up and down the columns. She whispered the names to herself over and over as she searched: '*Belther Aberum, Belther Abus, Belther Acanthus, BELTHER ACFERONIS!* Here it is!' she cried. 'Belther Acferonis, page fifty six, illustration on page fifty seven.'

Matt moved closer to the table and peered over her shoulder as she thumbed through the book to find the relevant page where details of the Acferon plant could be found.

Orianna began to read out the passage. She recited the opening sentences rapidly.

'*Belther Acferonis*, known commonly as the Acferon plant, is a native flowering herb found mainly in the hills between Beltheron and Maraglar. It has bright yellow flowers in high summer. The leaves and stalks are most often used as tasty ingredients in cooking stews and soups, but the most useful part of this hardy plant lies in the seeds. Many plants were grown in Maraglar itself, and stored in the mage's tower next to the central pillars of silver.' Here Orianna slowed down her reading, to make sure that everyone else understood the vital pieces of information.

'More recently however, word has come of the Acferon plant also being cultivated in the land of Atros. It is believed to be used here for experimental purposes, and as an antidote for a variety of potions and spells developed by the followers of Gretton Tur the Wild Lord...'

Jenn stepped back from the book. 'Our enemies already know of the antidote,' she said. 'They have known all along.'

A chill ran through them all. Everyone in the room was thinking the same thing. It was Orianna who finally voiced their fears.

'Do you think they will have destroyed the plants near to Maraglar?' she asked.

'Sophia is sly,' Jenn nodded. 'She will not have overlooked this. If they knew of the plant's power, they would not want us to be able to use it. I fear now that we will find nothing when we try to find the Acferon plant near Maraglar.'

'You think they will have taken them all? And ruined our chance of curing Helen?'

'I'm sure of it,' she said.

Matt clutched his wife's shoulder. He spoke a few quiet comforting words in her ear that no one else could hear. Then he turned and spoke to the whole room.

'Nevertheless, we must go there to Maraglar to find out. That is still our best hope.'

'Let me go,' Orianna offered. 'I know what I am looking for, and I feel I must have something to do or I will go mad.'

Matt and Jenn both nodded.

'Thank you Orianna,' Matt said. 'Cannish, you must go with her.'

'Sir!'

'Guard her well. You must leave immediately. You have supplies to hand, Cannish?'

'Always at the ready sir,' the pulver replied as he patted the small kitbag that hung from one shoulder. His other hand gripped the hilt of his sword firmly.

'Then leave at once,' Matt commanded. He was already crossing the room to a chest of drawers in one corner. He took out a vial of liquid and something that looked like a sliver of shining glass and bright metal.

'Hold this,' he said, handing the glass and silver fragment to Cannish. 'It is made from the same substance as the buildings of Maraglar. We can use it to make a pathway that will take you there.'

Orianna and Cannish nodded to show they understood.

'Search for the high tower next to the central pillars of the city,' Matt continued. He looked back towards Helen. 'We may yet find luck on our side; some plants may remain there to cure our daughter.'

Maraglar Deserted

Orianna and Cannish arrived in a searing column of white light that reflected sharply against the glass and silver walls of Maraglar. As the light faded they both looked around. Even abandoned and deserted, Maraglar was still beautiful. The last rays of sinking sun shone low in the sky, colouring the buildings in a deep rosy glow.

'Come,' Cannish urged. 'I can see the towers in the distance.'

He pointed towards two shining spires rising into the dark red sky: the two central pillars of silver.

'That is the place,' he said. 'The mage's tower is next to those spires. If there are any Acferon plants left, your book tells us that this is where they will be stored.'

They began to move through the silent streets. Shadows deepened around them and Cannish fumbled in his kitbag for a small lantern. He soon had a bright glow coming from it. They raced on, with the flickering light throwing their shadowy reflections onto the smooth walls. Orianna shivered at the eerie quality of these silvery buildings that changed to a shining black as the dark of the evening descended.

Neither the student nor the soldier spoke. Their footsteps were the only sound as they hurried on. Down the empty streets they moved, Cannish alert to the slightest movement. But no movement came. It was clear they were completely alone.

The two pillars grew larger each time they glimpsed them through gaps in the buildings. Even in the dark of the evening they seemed to glow, as if they were lit up from inside. It made Orianna shudder. She felt cold all of a sudden. Eventually they rounded another corner and there were the pillars, directly in front of them at the far end of a wide avenue.

'I read that the Acferon only ever grew in one patch of garden between the pillars,' Orianna said as they began to run down the avenue. 'All varieties of the plant were then stored in the mage's tower next to them.'

Cannish squinted ahead. His keen pulver eyes scanned the flat space in the shadows around the pillars. From this distance he could see nothing that looked like a tower nearby.

As they drew nearer, they could see that the ground in between the pillars had indeed been laid out as a formal garden. There were still the outlines of flower beds, but nothing grew here now. All had been trampled and destroyed.

'There's nothing here,' Cannish said. 'No plant, no clue, nothing.'

'Worse still, I cannot see anything nearby that might be the mage's tower,' Orianna added, echoing Cannish's own thought.

'Was there no description of the tower in your books?' he asked.

Orianna shook her head. 'There was nothi...' her voice drained away as she stared down the wide avenue that continued in the other direction beyond the pillars. The colour drained from her face. 'We have failed,' she said.

'What do you mean?'

'Look.'

Cannish turned to follow the direction of her gaze.

Some way off they could see a low pile of rubble, shattered glass and mangled metal. It was darkened and charred, unlike anything else in that shining city. They realised they must be looking at the remains of the mage's tower. It was obvious that it had been blasted by a huge explosion.

Cannish began running towards the wreckage of the building.

'Wait,' Orianna stooped down to the churned earth at her feet. Almost completely buried under the soil was a piece of paper. She worked it free of the ground with her fingers and lifted it up to her face to take a closer look.

'There is something scribbled down here,' she murmured. Cannish bent in towards her, eager to see what his companion had found.

As Orianna looked at the untidy lettering on the scrap of paper, her face grew hard at the cruel joke written there; just two words that robbed them of any hope of success.

What does it say?' asked Cannish. 'I cannot make it out.

'*Too late!*' Orianna replied. 'It says 'too late'. Matthias was right. The Andresens got here before us.'

'Those devils!' Cannish murmured under his breath. 'As if it weren't enough for them to put us all into this deadly affair, they have to mock and taunt us too!' His voice rose to a shout and he shook his blade furiously. 'Would that they were at the end of my sword's length right now!'

Orianna hung her head. A deep despair welled up inside her. Things were as bad as they could have feared.

The two of them turned away from the shattered plot of ground. Even Cannish realised it was no good spouting empty words of vengeance and anger.

'Come on,' Orianna said. 'It's useless to stay around here any longer. It's clear that the Andresens have beaten us. We need to get back to Beltheron to tell the others the bad news.'

'Do you have the vial?' she asked him.

It is here my Lady,' he confirmed. 'Take my lantern for a moment.'

He handed the light to her as he reached for the glass vial that would take them home through a pathway. Orianna was watching him when something stirred at the edge of her vision. The movement was so small that even Cannish almost missed it. He was instantly alert however, moving in front of Orianna to protect her, his sword at the ready. Orianna held the lantern up over his shoulder so that it shone in front of them both.

'What is it?' she asked him in a whisper.

'I cannot tell; the movement was very quick.'

'There it is again!'

They had both seen it clearly this time. It was lit up briefly in the flickering shadows cast by the lantern; a ragged shape behind the ruin of the mage's tower.

'Stay behind me,' Cannish hissed. 'Hold the light steady.'

He moved forwards slowly.

Orianna could not see anything now. Had they imagined it? Perhaps it had just been the wind, lifting some discarded paper or fabric, or just shadows and her overheated imagination. All was silent.

No! There was something or some*one* there again. A dark and ragged figure rose to its feet in front of them. It was hard to tell at first if it was a woman or a man. A thick cloak was wrapped around it, and it moved heavily.

Then there was a cackle of laughter. 'Too late! Too late!'

Cannish moved his weapon to point aggressively at the figure.

'But not too late for me,' the voice continued. 'I saw it

all. Oh yes I saw them take it.'

'Who are you, and what did you see?' demanded Cannish.

'Do you know where the Acferon is?' Orianna said.

The strange figure lifted the hood from its face and they saw that it was an old woman. Her face was lined with experience and pain, but her eyes were still bright and mischievous in the guttering light.

'I know what you seek, my friends,' she said. 'And I can help.'

'How do we know we can trust you?' asked Cannish.

'Oh don't worry. I am no friend to Atros,' came the reply. 'My home was ever here in Maraglar. How I hate what has happened to it; how I fear what *will* happen to Beltheron if you do not succeed.'

Orianna stepped closer to the crone, lifting the lantern higher to see her face more clearly.

'Careful, my lady!' Cannish spoke a warning.

'What did you see?' Orianna repeated her question.

'I saw a woman in purple robes,' the old stranger said.

'Sophia!' guessed Orianna.

'Yes, yes, the Andresen woman.'

'When was she here?'

'Days and days ago.'

'And did she do all this?' Orianna swept her hand around to indicate the ruin of the garden and tower.

'Yes, yes. She destroyed everything.'

'And the flower. Where is the Acferon flower?'

'Find Fordan Hamel,' the old woman whispered. 'He will help. He knows where the flower is hidden.'

'Fordan Hamel?' Cannish asked. 'Who is he?'

'Matthias knows. Tell him to go to Fordan,' the old woman said. Her voice now had a hard edge of seriousness to it. 'Fordan will help. Fordan knows everything...'

She continued to call out to them even after they had disappeared; even after the last light of their pathway had stopped reflecting on the walls of the Silver City, and she was left alone once more in the solitude of Maraglar.

'Thank you both,' Matt said. 'You have done well.'

They were back in the great hall in Beltheron. It had only taken them a handful of minutes to return and tell every detail of their mission to Maraglar.

'Do not feel badly,' he continued. 'It is no fault of yours the plant could not be found, and you have discovered vital information.'

Orianna and Cannish both made a bow towards Matt, but he dismissed the gesture with a wave of his hand. It still made him feel uncomfortable to see anyone bow to him, especially people he considered friends as much as anything else.

'I know of this Fordan Hamel of whom the Maraglarian woman spoke. He has long been a friend of ours. Cannish, would you be so good as to fetch Captain Tarawen here with whoever else you think you may need for an urgent, undercover operation on Atros. Orianna, please fetch your brother.'

She nodded and hurried from the room. Cannish clicked his fingers towards a guard in the doorway. After a quick, whispered conversation, the guard disappeared through a doorway.

It took Orianna several minutes to find her brother. By the time they returned to the great hall Matt was already speaking to a group of three pulver. Serrion knew Cannish of course, and Tarawen had also become a familiar face to him through his friendship with Parenon and his brave service to Ungolin. Tarawen was well known for his hatred of the rish and his lifelong search for vengeance and justice for what they had done to his family. However the third and final pulver was unknown to both Serrion and Orianna.

'Ah Serrion,' Matt stopped giving his instructions to the pulver and turned his attention to him. 'I will speak with you in a moment. I was just giving Captain Tarawen, Cannish, and Husk here their orders.'

He gestured with his hand to each of them as he spoke, in an act of introduction. Husk was the third pulver. The one Serrion did not know.

Husk was tall. Like most pulver he stood at just under two metres. But unlike others that Serrion had met, like Vishan, and of course, poor Parenon, Husk was also broad and thickset with tight muscle. He was completely bald without even eyebrows or eyelashes. This just served to make his eyes – which were a startling grey – stand out even more. Husk stood silently with very few movements of his huge frame as they all continued to listen to Lord Matthias' orders.

'I will create a pathway that will drop you on the coastline some five miles from Atros City itself. You will see a high tower among the cliffs further down the coastline. Under the shadow of that tower is a collection of houses around a harbour. There dwells Fordan Hamel, an old fisherman. You will probably find him tending to his beloved boat on the shoreline. If the old woman in Maraglar spoke the truth, then he will be able to tell you where to find the Acferon plant.' Matthias paused for a moment before continuing; 'If anyone can.'

'Then this must be done without any further delay,' Tarawen continued.

'Exactly so,' Matt said. 'I have everything prepared to create a pathway immediately.' He turned to Tarawen for a moment. 'I trust Captain that your men have all their necessary equipment here?' he gestured to the rucksacks and assorted bags that were stacked up in a neat row near to the door of the great hall.

'Yes, Lord,' Tarawen stood up even straighter as he answered. 'All is prepared. My men and I are ready to set off for Atros right now.'

'Good, then gather your packs and come.' Matt stood and walked to the centre of the hall. He took a vial from his pocket and began to unwind a locket on a chain from around his neck.

'Serrion, I believe that your part in the future of Beltheron is about to become clear. I want you to go with these men to Atros.'

'Me?' Serrion gasped. 'But what can I do?'

'Tarawen and the others are quick, brave and skilled,' answered Matt. 'But they do not have the power to see what might be around the next corner. They do not have your powers of foresight and seeing, my boy.'

The pulver quickly slung their rucksacks on their backs and formed a tight group in front of Matthias. His arms were now spread wide, and he had already removed the stopper from the vial of liquid. With a brief look at each of them Lord Matthias began to scatter its drops around them. At the same time Serrion heard the familiar droning sounds that indicated a pathway was being created. He held his breath and closed his eyes as the white light of Matthias' magic enveloped them all and he was sucked upwards into the swirling vortex that would take him to Atros.

Arrival on Atros

The group of pulver stepped down from the cover of the trees and onto the sand. Serrion followed them. They all paused at the edge of the beach, casting their eyes backwards and forwards. Serrion squinted into the sunlight. The coastline to their right continued straight for some way before curving around in a vast, wide bay until it rose up into rocky hills almost directly in front of them, over three miles away. There was a gradual slope up one side of this black rock face. Sitting atop of it was a high white tower. The tower was sheltered from the sea and wind on the western side by a tall outcrop of sharp, jagged rock. This rock stabbed upwards into the sky like a bony finger pointing out of the sea. The other side of this natural barrier dropped away in a sheer cliff face down to the crashing waves over two hundred arm-spans below.

Cannish pointed towards the tower. 'That's where we're heading for,' he said. 'That tower marks the southern tip of Atros City.' It looked a long way off to Serrion's eyes. Before you even got to the long, slow incline that led up to the tower there were at least two miles of the beach to cross. Probably more, with the curve of the beach, he thought to himself. His heart sank.

'Why didn't Matt get the pathway to drop us closer?' he grumbled. 'Surely we're wasting time having to cross this beach?'

'Lord Matthias has to weigh speed with caution,' Tarawen replied. 'We do not know if the agents of Atros are watching. It is safest to drop us into the forest where there is the least chance of the light from the pathway being noticed.'

'But now we have to cross the beach in broad daylight,' Serrion commented. 'Surely that will be just as dangerous if anyone is watching us from that white tower?'

'Your caution is wise,' Tarawen answered. 'But we are not heading straight there.' He pointed to a place down the beach where the forest grew closer to the shoreline. There a range of low rocks and rubble led up to a number of houses painted a surprisingly bright colour. Each one looked as if it had been freshly whitewashed.

The windows of the white fronted houses winked at them in the sunlight. There was a row of fifteen to twenty of the low buildings stretching along the shore between the tree line and the sea. Down on the short stretch of beach in front of these dwellings a cluster of several small fishing boats had been drawn up out of the water.

'That is where we have to get to first,' Tarawen told them.

'See over there,' said Cannish. 'There are people moving around the houses and boats. We will not be noticed amongst them, even if eyes do watch us from Atros.'

'The forest is too thick, even at its edge, to make for a comfortable walk. Therefore we must walk along the sand,' Tarawen suggested. 'If we keep within the shadows of the trees here, right at the edge, we will not be seen. Come, it will not take us long.'

The sand on the beach was powder dry and Serrion sank ankle-deep into it as they walked, making each step he took a weary effort. Could this really be easier than walking through the woods he wondered?

The rest of the pulver didn't seem to mind it. They trod lightly upon the sand, Husk leading the way with his long strides. He was getting further and further away from Serrion with every minute. The boy wanted to stop, to ask if they could rest, but he knew that he had to keep going. The image of Helen, sick and feverish at home, made him forget about the aches in his legs and back as he trudged on.

High clouds sped across the pale sky, throwing light and dark shapes of blue shadow across the water. Pink-feathered gulls wheeled in the air above them, curling on the warm updrafts of air.

After a mile or so, Cannish called a halt. He turned to Serrion.

'We had better be prepared for what might be waiting for us ahead,' he said. 'Do you see anything Serrion?' he asked.

Serrion un-slung the pack from his back let it drop to the sand. Grateful for the chance to rest he sank down and sat next to it. He gazed in front of him, focusing his mind on a small, round pebble sticking up in the sand a few metres away. As Serrion stared at the pebble, trying to free his mind of everything else, it began to glow a bright red. He relaxed, letting his thoughts flow towards the stone as T'yuq Tinyaz had shown him. As the focus of his mind surrounded the stone he allowed the light within it to grow. Serrion picked it up and held it tightly. He felt a strange warmth coming from it as the light grew brighter still. The seering had begun.

Within a few seconds the red had misted his whole vision and the pebble began to melt and change shape. It grew upwards, rising from his hand, and formed the shape of the tower that they were making for. In his mind's eye, Serrion was hurtled towards the doors of the tower...

...He could see two large guards standing in front of the entrance. He had not come across creatures quite like this before yet the name for this terrible breed, 'the harch' came to him immediately. They looked like large rish hunters, but were covered in thick black hair. Like rish they each had four arms. They had no need of weapons though. The lower pairs of these arms were much shorter than the upper ones and had claws at the end which looked like a crab's pincers sprouting out of them. The longer arms above came to sharpened spikes, like lances. The oval shape of their heads ended in a long snout with wide nostrils that twitched repeatedly. Serrion realised straight away how important these noses and a strong sense of smell must be to the harch – for they had no eyes to see with...

He tore his Seering away from these beasts and pushed it forwards to the heavy metal doors at the base of the tower. They opened in front of him, showing a wide staircase leading up. Once more he pushed his vision further, focusing on the lower steps of the staircase. He felt himself directing his premonitions in a way he had never been able to manage before. For the first time he began to understand what T'yuq Tinyaz had meant. Grasping the pebble tightly and concentrating even harder, Serrion's viewpoint surged swiftly onwards, up the stairs to a round room at the top of the tower.

...There stood Piotre and Sophia Andresen. They were dressed in their finest gowns, the brightly coloured silk of their robes rippling gently in

the morning breeze. Sophia's dark hair had been untied and it billowed out behind her in waves. Serrion could smell her heavy perfume, like flowers on the wind.

Then came the roaring cheers from the plains below the tower. Grunts, roars and shouts of victory rose up until they were deafening. Piotre held his hands out in front of him, palms wide and fingers spread. His gesture immediately silenced the avid crowds...

Serrion felt his vision lurch and tilt, as he lost control of it for a moment. In a red swirl of colour he was lifted up above the heads of the Andresens until he was looking down vertically to the wide plain.

The image that now met his Seer's gaze made him reel.

...Massed across the plain, as far as his eyes could see, were armies of rish and harch. They had formed into row after row in blocks of troops...

Each row must have numbered almost five hundred, Serrion thought. The sheer scale of the forces that the Andresens were now marshalling numbed him with shock.

His real self staggered backwards, and he shook his head to clear his vision. But instead there came one final image. This was one that he had seen before.

..A flicker of red and yellow deep in evil eyes that looked directly into Serrion's own.

'You are with us then?' a cruel voice whispered into his ear. 'You will serve us on Atros after all?'

A wicked smile spread across thin lips as Serrion realised that this stranger with the odd eyes was reading his mind...

At last the red began to fade and he could see Cannish's face again, close to his, with a pinched expression of concern etched upon it.

'What is it, my boy? What have you seen?'

Serrion couldn't speak for a moment. He was still gasping for breath. He sat down heavily, one hand on Cannish's arm for support. In his other hand he was still clutching the pebble. He glanced down at it and saw that it had shrunk and faded back to its normal shape. It was now cool as he turned it around in his fingers.

'I don't know,' he said to Cannish. I don't know what it means. But we must hurry. Piotre is gathering a huge army against us.'

He hurriedly gave them whatever details he could remember about the massing of the Atrossian forces. He did not say anything about his final vision. For now he wanted to keep that to himself. He did not want anyone else to know that he might one day be questioned about serving Atros.

The pulver stood silently, their faces grim, as they listened to him.

Finally Cannish spoke.

'It seems from what Serrion has just told us that the poisoning of Lady Helen, and the release of the Darkness, is just the first part of the Atrossian attack.

'In that case, we do not have a moment to lose in our search,' added Tarawen. 'Our break here is over. Let us double our pace and head off on our way once more.'

They walked for another hour. To Serrion it seemed more like a relentless trot. The pulver had upped their pace, as Tarawen had suggested and they succeeded in covering a great distance.

Eventually they came out over a range of low rocks and rubble onto a wide beach. There were the cluster of buildings and houses they had seen earlier. They made their way to the group of fishing boats nearby.

Two or three lurched over on their sides in the sand, but most were propped upright, looking in good repair and ready to sail.

Out to one edge of the cluster of boats was a smaller vessel. It was raised high up on a wooden frame so that it was possible to walk underneath to clean the hull and clear the keel of its heavy crust of barnacles and seaweed.

Sitting on the deck was an old man. He was hunched over, working at a white piece of canvas sail spread out across his knees. Serrion could see his fingers moving quickly as he moved a large needle up and down, repairing the fabric with thick, strong thread.

Gravel crunched under the pulvers' feet as they approached him. Looking up from almost directly under the hull of the boat, Serrion had to squint into the sunlight to see properly.

Tarawen called up to the man.

'Greetings friend.'

A head with a grizzled beard and straggling grey hair appeared over the edge.

'That word should not be used so easily in these parts.'

'What word, *greetings*?'

'No. *Friend*.'

'That is true,' Cannish replied. 'Friendship is something that has to be proved, and not only on Atros.'

'I used to live here, close to Atros City,' Tarawen said. 'I was one of the rebels who worked against Gretton Tur.'

'Anyone could say that,' was the short reply from the

man in the boat. 'Don't waste my time, come back with proof of your friendship, or leave and don't come back at all. I'm a busy man.'

The head disappeared back over the side of the boat. There were sounds of scuffling and scraping on the deck.

Cannish had a thought. He raised his voice and called up to the boat.

'Matthias says hello.'

The sounds above them stopped immediately. There was a moment of silence while the group of companions on the beach held their breath expectantly. Then the old man's face reappeared. He looked up and down the beach, checking to make sure no one else was nearby before he spoke.

'You know Matthias?'

They all nodded. The man's eyes narrowed as he studied them closely.

Now it was Serrion's turn.

'We are all supporters of Lord Matthias of Beltheron. I am close enough to him to be allowed to call him *Uncle Matt*.'

For a moment the man didn't move. Then his lined face opened out into a broad grin. A high, thin laugh escaped from his mouth.

'Well come up, come up,' he chortled. 'What are you standing around down there for?'

He stepped back from the side of the boat to give them chance to climb up and join him.

'Fordan's the name,' he introduced himself. 'Fordan Hamel the fisher.' he told them as Husk, bringing up the rear as usual, made his way over the side and into the boat. In another moment they were all gathered together on the deck. In turn they introduced themselves then asked him how he had ended up there.

'I know it is partly my own fault,' Fordan explained. 'I've been stranded here a long time. I was tricked by that wretched Piotre Andresen into working for him. He told me I would be helping to find a cure to assist the rebels – to help men like you, Tarawen. It never occurred to me not to trust Andresen. I didn't ever think that I would be helping that evil dog Tur and his pack of rish scavengers.'

He gazed into the distance; lost in those memories of so many years ago. 'Before I knew it I was trapped here, under their control,' he continued. 'I'd given them the Acferon plant, shown them how to cultivate it themselves, aye, and other useful flowers too. Then, by the time I'd learned the truth of who Andresen and his painted butterfly of a wife were really working for it was too late. I was already under one of her enchantments. She stopped me from ever travelling through a pathway to get back home to Beltheron.'

He gave a deep sigh then looked around the group of friends once more. His face broke into a grim smile.

'But now I've got a chance to put that right haven't I?' he grinned. 'I can tell you how to get to the Acferon plant.'

They all huddled closer to hear his words.

'I'm afraid it means travelling to Atros City itself,' Fordan continued.

'Aye, I feared as much,' Tarawen grunted.

'You know of Ragosh, the barman?' Fordan asked them.

Tarawen nodded. 'He and I go back a long way.'

'His inn, *The Hunter and Holva,* is the still the safest place to head for once you are inside the city walls,' the old man told them.

'And once we are there, what then?' Cannish asked.

'The Acferon is grown in Sophia's own herb garden, high up amid the rooftops of Gendrell.'

Serrion's heart quailed at this. He had been to Gendrell before. It was the castle at the very heart of Atros City; once home to Gretton Tur himself.

'You know of the exact whereabouts of the plant that we need?' Tarawen asked Fordan excitedly.

'Aye,' he nodded in reply.

'Then why do we not just create a pathway there now,' asked Cannish. 'We could be back in Beltheron with the Acferon, and Lady Helen could be cured by nightfall.'

'No!' warned Fordan in a loud cry that shocked them all. 'You cannot try to create a pathway within the walls of Atros City.'

'Why not?'

'Andresen has protected his stronghold with strong defences,' the old fisher replied. 'Deadly defences.'

Tarawen's eyes narrowed. 'Explain,' he said.

'Piotre and Sophia talked carelessly about their plans,' Fordan continued. 'They were boastful, proud and confident. They didn't care that I heard.'

'And what did you hear?' Cannish's voice came in an impatient growl. He was getting tired of waiting for this old man to get to the point.

'A spell has been placed within the city walls,' Fordan Hamel answered. 'Any attempt to create a pathway within the confines of the city will distort.'

'Distort?'

'Aye. It will twist into another, unknown pathway; one that can be controlled by the Andresens. Try to travel a pathway in Atros City and you are at the mercy of its Lord and Lady. They can send you anywhere they choose, and there will be no way back.'

They all sat silently, considering this for some time. Finally Tarawen spoke. 'It cannot be helped,' he said. 'Even with this enchantment on the pathways, we are still in a better position than we were. We now know exactly where to find the Acferon plant, and Fordan's information about the threat of the distorted pathways means that we will not fall into that particular trap. Thank you sir, for your hospitality.'

'Stay a little while longer, rest yourselves here,' the old man invited them.

Tarawen shook his head in regret. 'Unfortunately there is no time, my friend.' He got to his feet. 'Come,' he said to the others. 'We must continue our quest without further delay.'

'That is nonsense, and you know it,' Fordan replied. 'The boy is already exhausted,' he said as he gestured towards Serrion. 'And even the brave pulver would benefit from a short sleep if they are to go into possible battle. There is no point travelling any further before you rest. I will wake you in two hours, when it is growing dark. You are only a short distance now from the city walls. In any case it will be safest to approach at night time.'

They all knew that this made sense. With relief, they allowed their new friend to fuss around them, fetching blankets opening up a small cupboard high up on the side of the boat, and handing around savoury biscuits.

Soon Serrion was curled up in a blanket. He sank into a grateful sleep on one of the narrow bunks along the side of Fordan's boat.

Dark Dreams

Serrion awoke with a lurch. He sat upright, gasping for breath. Cannish and Tarawen were sleeping in bunks above and behind him. Husk was still awake, on guard. He turned to Serrion, his expression unchanged as ever. Serrion threw back his blanket and got to his feet. He gestured with his hand to let Husk know that he was ok. The giant pulver nodded briefly.

Serrion stepped a few paces away from the others. A terrible dream had disturbed his sleep. A dream, or a vision, he was not sure which at first. It had started as words, and then images of people he knew had flooded his sleeping mind...

> ...*Piotre Andresen spoke first. 'I will strike vengeance on those that have done this to my son. I will raise a despoiling cloud over that vile city! A dark breath of miasma that will sicken and weaken all who live there.'*

'The Darkness,' Serrion thought to himself. 'The cloud that I saw in my vision.' He continued to concentrate on the memories. The fact he could recall them so easily, even after waking, suggested that they had not just been a dream. That would have faded as quickly as he had got to his feet. Another familiar figure now appeared.

...Sophia was silent at Piotre's side. Her husband was so intent upon his ranting fury that he did not notice her reluctance to join in. She was distracted, Serrion noticed, her mind elsewhere.

'Then my loyal soldiers,' Andresen continued. 'When the puling, whimpering citizens of Beltheron are sickened and weak, then we will mount our final attack. We will fall upon that city with all the might and fury of Atros at our beck!'

A mighty cheer rose up to them from the ranks of Atrossian forces below...

The voices grew in volume until they were deafening in Serrion's ears. He clutched at his temples to try to free himself from their terrible raving sound. As he did he realised he was holding the pebble that he had picked up earlier on the beach. He dropped it from his fingers and his vision faded just as quickly as it had come.

Once again he felt feverish and weak. His limbs trembled. He felt as if he hadn't slept for days. These premonitions were starting to take more out of him with every day that passed. He wondered if this was because he was drawing closer to the source of the evil, or if they were just taking over more of his life after his visit with T'yuq Tinyaz. Whatever the reason, they were getting harder to ignore. Almost without thinking, Serrion picked up the pebble again and thrust it deep into his pocket.

Husk was at his side. His hand was on his shoulder, comfortingly. The others were waking up. The patch of sky he could see through the round porthole window was darkening as the pale sun set. Night was coming. It was time for them to complete their journey to Atros City.

*   *   *

On Beltheron, Helen was also dreaming. She gave a cough and started to gasp for air. With every breath she took, a dark cloud of thick vapour began to rise from her mouth. These small clouds hung in the air around her head and then began to seek each other out, gathering together and joining to make a heavy fog that soon covered the whole ceiling.

Jenn felt the air turn cold around her. She looked up and saw the dark cloud above Helen's head growing thicker. 'Oh no,' she gasped. 'They wouldn't, they COULDN'T do that, not even Piotre and Sophia.' Even after all she had heard in the Council, there was still a small part of her that refused to believe the depths of wickedness that her sister was capable of sinking to.

She now realised that this illness that had attacked Helen was not the one she had seen before in Maraglar; it was much worse. 'They've changed the potion,' Jenn thought. 'They've made it worse. They're using Helen to create the Darkness.'

She clutched at her daughter tightly, murmuring soothing words to try to comfort her. Helen was still breathing deeply, the clouds of dark breath multiplying all the time and joining that higher up in the room. Jenn looked up and saw that the darkness was now seeping out of the room through the top of the doorframe.

Jenn knew the next stage of the Atrossian attack had started. After a few moments she became aware of voices from outside on the street. There were calls of terror and outrage, then, from further off on another street, a distant scream.

Jenn placed Helen's arm back on the cushions of the couch and moved swiftly to the window. A gnawing suspicion had entered her mind, like a half remembered glimpse of a bad dream on waking.

Even as she reached the curtain the room grew suddenly dark. Jenn looked out and gave a short hollow moan of despair. What she saw made her insides clench with fear.

Outside the sky had blackened with an immense cloud. It moved steadily over the rooftops of Beltheron, its twining fingers, like thick smoke, began spiralling down towards the houses and streets. At the same time, the dark breath from Helen's lips that had seeped out through the doorframe spiralled up into the air to join this new cloud. Jenn saw people staring upwards and pointing in fear, their mouths wide in shock and incredulity. Many were dropping limply to the ground, like puppets whose strings have been cut. This did not seem to affect everyone at first though, and others were running to help those who had already sunk down onto the floor. Jenn recognised with horror the same blank expressions on the features of the fallen as that she had seen on Helen's face.

'It's here at last,' she whispered in terror. 'The Darkness is upon us.'

Over the wall

It was late in the evening when Serrion, Tarawen and the pulver arrived outside Atros City. Slate grey clouds slumped over the rooftops, fading to darker, almost black streaks towards the eastern horizon.

The first few spits of a cold, thin rain had started to fall. They mottled the worn, rutted cobbles on the paths leading up to the outside of the city walls, making the uneven surface slippery and even more treacherous underfoot.

Serrion, Tarawen, Cannish and Husk kept to the shadows close by the city's high outer wall. As they made their way towards the heavy iron doors the pulver instinctively arranged their formation so that Serrion was in the middle. He knew this was to protect him, yet the threat of what was beyond those gates, and the dangers he knew they were about to face meant that Serrion did not feel much comfort. 'It will take more than a few pulver blades – no matter how skilfully they are used – to save me from what's in there,' he thought to himself.

The idea that men such as these – brave, honourable people like Tarawen and the rest, were willing to risk their own lives to protect him was still something that he couldn't get used to. As far as he was concerned he still hadn't done much to deserve such loyalty and courage. It made him feel guilty and uncomfortable.

As the rain began to fall harder they hunched their shoulders down further into their cloaks. Fordan had given them several pieces of dark old canvas from his boat to help hide them in the shadows.

'Glad we're in disguise,' Cannish mumbled under his breath. 'Hate to think of our noble pale blue cloaks being sullied by this stinking Atrossian piddle.'

Tarawen grinned. 'Yes, doesn't matter what happens to these rags,' he said. 'In fact I look forward to staining them with some rish blood before much longer.'

'We have to find our way in first,' Cannish replied. 'Can't exactly go knocking on the door here can we?'

'Not at all,' Tarawen agreed. 'We need to keep our arrival as secret and silent as we can, for as long as we can. I fear we may already have made too much noise'

Husk was silent, staring up at the walls next to the gates. His expression remained exactly the same, except for a slight narrowing of his grey eyes as he noticed something high up on the wall.

He touched Tarawen gently on the shoulder and pointed upwards. Tarawen followed his gaze. He squinted up into the rain for a few seconds, not sure what had caught Husk's attention. Then, as the misty rain swirled away for a moment, he saw it. Tied around the heavy stonework at the top of the high wall was a rope. The rest of its length was hooped and curled around a sword that had been forced between a narrow gap in the stones. The handle of the sword gleamed in the growing darkness of the night; a bright pale blue, the colour of the pulver!

'It seems that someone has left us a way in,' Tarawen whispered. 'Thanks to your sharp eyes, Husk, we will not have to fight our way through the sentry at the other side of this gate.'

'But who left it there, I wonder?' Cannish asked.

Tarawen shook his head. 'I do not know, and yet it seems we might find allies in the strangest of places.'

He turned to Serrion. 'Do you think you can use your skill to release the rope from the sword, my boy?'

Serrion nodded and stepped forwards. He raised his hand towards the sword and felt the beginning of that familiar tingling at the tips of his fingers. But after just a moment the sensation began to burn painfully. He drew back his hand, flexing it into a fist then spreading and shaking his fingers again, as if to get rid of pins and needles.

He tried again, but within a few seconds he had to stop. Serrion clutched his hand to his chest, huddling over it as if to cushion it.

'What is wrong,' Cannish asked him urgently. 'Are you alright my young lord?'

Serrion shook his head. 'I don't know,' he replied. 'I feel exhausted all of a sudden. As if trying to move the sword has drained all the energy from me. And my hand,' he flexed his fingers again, wincing as he did so. 'My hand feels as if it is burning.'

Tarawen's expression had grown grim. 'Lord Andresen's work no doubt,' he commented. 'He must have warded the walls and gates to his city with magical defences. Probably another part of the magic that Fordan told us about. We can't get in through a pathway, for fear of it being distorted and sending us to who knows where, and we can't use your Belthronic powers Serrion. His magic is blocking you.' He turned to his companions. 'It is no use trying again,' he said. 'We must find another, more ordinary way to follow the path left for us. Cannish, can you release the sword with one of your arrows?'

Cannish nodded. He was already notching an arrow to his bow.

The pain in Serrion's arm had faded and he looked upwards again. He saw that, if the sword could be knocked out of the wall the rope wound around it would fall down towards them, but the other end should remain securely tied around the stones at the top of the wall.

'Husk,' Tarawen continued in a whisper. 'Can you catch the sword as it falls, before it hits the ground and alerts the guards?'

Again Husk did not speak. He merely held out his broad arms and flexed his fingers. This gesture was all that Tarawen needed. He knew that Husk was ready.

Serrion craned his neck upwards once more as Cannish pulled back the drawstring of his longbow. His left hand made a small movement to alter the angle of his shot, then, with the slightest movement of the fingers of his left hand he released the arrow. It sped silently towards its target.

They all held their breath. With a small 'chink' sound the tip of Cannish's arrow struck the blue handle of the sword. There was enough force in the blow to lift the sword and move it sideways a few centimetres, but it remained lodged in the crack between the stones. The arrow twisted a couple of times in the air, then began to fall back towards them. Husk took a step to one side, held out his hand and effortlessly caught it. He handed it back to Cannish.

'Thank you my friend,' he breathed. 'We'll try again shall we?'

Once again he notched the arrow to the bow; once again he released it; once again they held their breath as the arrow sped upwards.

They groaned silently to themselves as the arrow found its mark, moved the sword fractionally to one side, but yet again failed to release either it or the rope.

'Let's change the angle a bit,' Cannish said to himself as Husk handed the fallen arrow back to him a second time.

He took another arrow from the leather quiver at his side and strung both of them side by side, the first held to the bowstring between his index and middle fingers, and the second arrow between his third and little fingers. Pulling the string taught, Cannish altered his grip on the handle of the bow with his left hand so that he was able to control the direction of the second arrow head with his thumb.

He took two paces to his left, adjusted his aim again, and released both arrows at once. They shot skywards, their courses separating slightly in flight so that both struck the sword simultaneously – one hitting the handle and the other striking the silver blade. This time the force was enough to tilt the sword to such an angle that it slipped from the stones. It tumbled down towards them, releasing the coiled rope as it fell.

Husk caught the sword in one hand as if it weighed nothing at all, before reaching up to catch the first of the returning arrows. Cannish looked at the way the second arrow was falling towards him, and held out his quiver to catch it. Making barely a sound it dropped cleanly inside to join the others.

'Show off,' grinned Tarawen.

'Practice,' Cannish replied.

Tarawen took hold of the rope. He pulled firmly a couple of times, tugging it to the right and left. The knots in the stone above him held firm.

'I will climb first,' he said to the others. 'Stay here until I send the signal that all is safe.'

Serrion watched as Tarawen placed his feet against the wall and then moved swiftly hand over hand up the rope and into the gathering gloom.

Serrion's heart began racing. He had trained in swordsmanship and even a little bit of hand of hand combat with the other pulver, and he knew that his strength had increased in these practice sessions. Even so, he was not sure he would be able to make such a climb.

'But you have to,' he told himself. 'You can't let them down, not now when everyone believes in you so much.'

He continued to watch as Tarawen disappeared into the misty darkness above them.

When he reached the crest of the wall, Tarawen could see that the stones along the top were thick enough for them to walk along without fear of falling to either side. Keeping his body low against the stones he craned his neck to look down the other side, down into Atros City itself.

Almost directly below him, just as he had expected, two rish guards patrolled the inside of the gate. He could see the top of their pale, domed heads and heard the grating rattle of their chain mail armour as they moved. Casting his eyes around further he saw the main street running straight ahead in front of the guards towards the main section of the city. Other side streets ran off in both directions leading to a variety of dwellings, inns and barracks for the rish army.

As far as Tarawen could make out, all the streets were quiet. Apart from a couple of figures moving between houses here and there the rish guards were the only creatures that he could make out. If he and the others could get past them and down into the city streets without too much disturbance to raise the alarm then their search for the flower might not prove too difficult.

But *how* to get past them? Tarawen looked down the route that the top of the stone wall took as it wound around the city perimeter. The position above the gate where he was crouching dropped down on the inside – the city side – to a broad walkway about a man's height below him. This followed the entire length of the wall as far as he could see. For the first time Tarawen now noticed slits in the brickwork of the wall and realised that this walkway was for patrols to pace up and down, able to look out through the slits to watch for anyone coming to attack the city. 'And a perfect path for us to get away from the guards below,' he considered with a new glow of hope.

His eyes ranged further along the top of the wall. About one hundred paces away he noticed a series of steps cut from thick slabs of rock leading down to the street below. Tarawen now had to squint into the darkness which was growing thicker by the minute. The base of the steps that he had just seen led onto a small open courtyard that was blocked from the rish guards' view by the curve of the city wall. In turn, this courtyard led to a quiet side street.

'Our luck still holds,' he thought to himself. 'That is the route that we must take.'

Leaning over the outside of the wall, Tarawen waved a gesture to the others below, beckoning them to follow him.

Cannish climbed as agilely as Tarawen, and within moments he was crouching down beside his captain.

Serrion was the next one to climb the rope. Husk stood at his side as he started to ascend, steadying the rope with one strong hand, the other still on the hilt of his sword as he gazed around at the bare plain of Atros.

The first few metres of the climb did not present any problem for Serrion. He tried to do just what he had watched the others achieve, going hand over hand up the rope, with his feet walking up the side of the stones and helping to keeping him balanced at the same time. It was hard work though, and even before he was halfway up the muscles in his arms began to ache. They screamed at him to stop. Even though the rain had now eased off the rope was still slick and wet, making it even more difficult for him to keep a firm hold. Half way up his foot slipped on the stones and his right leg slammed against the wall.

The jolt made him cry out with sudden, piercing pain. Serrion gritted his teeth and adjusted his grip. He set off once more until at long last he felt himself being pulled up the final metre by strong hands under his shoulders.

He sat on the top of the wall for a few moments to rest his limbs and get his breath back, while Husk clambered up after him with a surprising agility for someone of his size and weight. He hauled the rope up after him, untying it from the stones and looping it over his shoulder.

In whispers, Tarawen explained their situation and pointed down the line of the wall towards the alley that he had seen earlier. Treading carefully on the slick stones of the high walkway, they began to make their way down towards the steps that would lead them into Atros City itself.

Thankfully they were not challenged from below. The darkness of the evening, and the clouds from the storm helped to cloak them in shadow as they made their perilous way. Serrion concentrated hard on his footing. The stones were uneven and the combination of that with the darkness and the slippery surface made every step treacherous.

Eventually they reached the curve of the city wall and crept down the steps to street level.

All four of the pulver looked around continuously, but Tarawen was confident that they had been quiet enough to go unnoticed by the guards. They hurried into the shadows of a deep recess under a heavy granite archway.

'It has been some time since I was last here,' Tarawen whispered to his companions. 'But I think I have a decent memory of the layout of the streets.'

He poked his head out from their hiding place and looked briefly to left and right.

'As I thought,' he continued. 'If we go right here to the end of this passageway, we open out onto one of the major thoroughfares. That leads us to the heart of Atros, and to the place where we are most likely to find shelter for the evening.'

'A major road will likely be busy,' Cannish added.

'Aye, we must take extra care,' Tarawen agreed. 'Eyes and heads down lads and keep all in a group. If we're challenged leave it to me to speak.'

'Serrion, get in the middle of us lad,' Cannish moved him between himself and Husk.

'Where are we heading for?' asked Serrion.

Tarawen grinned. 'To some it is the most disreputable and dangerous place in all of Atros. An inn called *The Hunter and Holva* where you will find the most aggressive and unpleasant guests this side of the Caves of Despair. They are thieves, murderers, cutpurses and brigands all. Keep one hand on your dagger and the other on your money at all times.'

Cannish grunted, and nodded in agreement.

'That's right. It's the last place I'd choose to go for a quiet drink.'

'Then why are we all going there?' asked Serrion.

'Because lad, it is also probably the only place in this whole stinking city where we will find anyone sympathetic to the cause of Beltheron. I know it well from the time I spent in this land working with the rebels.'

Cannish nodded, 'I remember tales that Vishan told about it too. He said that *The Hunter and Holva* was the only place he could be sure that his presence would be kept secret.'

'I just hope the owners haven't moved on somewhere else' Cannish joked under his breath, 'I hate it when you find somewhere you really like and then you go back and find new management and everything's changed.'

'Enough talk,' Tarawen cut them short. 'Time to go.'

With a final glance to right and left, Tarawen made his move from the shadows and onto the street. 'Stick close by me, Serrion. Everyone keep your eyes and ears alert from now on. No more words until we reach *The Hunter and Holva.'*

Bar Brawl

The ramshackle building loomed up ahead of them out of the shadows. Serrion peered into the evening light at the broken sign that swung above the inn door.

Ragosh the barman wiped his hands on the greasy cloth that he carried tucked into the belt of his stained apron. He jerked his head briefly towards a table in the shadows towards the back of the inn. Even Serrion had to duck his head to get under one of the thick low beams that supported the roof. Husk almost had to bend double before he could squeeze himself into the chair in the corner, his back to the wall. Tarawen and Cannish also took their places, turning their chairs around slightly so that each one of the three pulver could survey what was going on in the rest of the bar.

As soon as they were seated, Ragosh came shuffling over.

'Yes gents?' he asked.

'Four ales,' Tarawen replied simply.

'Four ales coming straight up.' He disappeared in the shadow.

'Tarawen,' Serrion spoke shyly. 'I'm not really old enough to drink ale.'

Tarawen and Cannish grinned. Even Husk's eyes narrowed in amusement.

'Don't worry my lad,' Cannish said. 'Ragosh won't really mind, and the regulars here won't report you.'

'Besides, you have to fit in as best you can,' Tarawen clasped his shoulder reassuringly as he spoke.

Ragosh brought their drinks and slapped them down in front of them. Serrion stared at the liquid in his glass. Lifting it to his nose he sniffed suspiciously. It didn't smell too bad, like a slightly 'off' cough mixture. He was about to take a sip, but before he could, Tarawen touched his arm. 'Think of the drinks as a disguise,' he whispered. 'It doesn't mean you actually have to drink the vile stuff.'

With a touch of relief, Serrion placed his glass back down on the table and looked around the room.

The place was less than half full. Two or three shady looking characters leant heavily on the bar itself, the remains of their drinks in grubby glasses and tankards in front of them. At a couple of the other tables, furtive figures noisily chewed their food or gulped greedily at their own drinks. Some just stared blankly into the distance, lost in their thoughts, their drinks untouched.

All in all this was a horrible, depressing place, Serrion considered. Dull and dark with only one thin finger of muddy evening light spilling through a small window high up in one wall. The only other light came from a few stubby guttering candles on the bar and a few of the other tables. These just gave off a dim yellowy glow that seemed to succeed more in throwing shadow onto the scene than illuminating it.

As his eyes adjusted to the darkness around him, Serrion glimpsed another figure. He was sitting alone at a table deep in the farthest shadows at the opposite corner of the inn. This table was half-hidden in a small alcove behind a supporting beam of oak wood. There were no candles at this table. 'That is where you would choose to sit if you wanted to be left alone,' thought Serrion. 'Left alone – or not noticed at all.'

The man was slumped over the table with his head in his hands. His whole body trembled, whether through fatigue, pain, or drink it was impossible to say. His hair fell down over his forehead so it was difficult to make out his features. Even so there was something strangely familiar about him that struck Serrion instantly. Before he had time to consider this though, Serrion noticed his companions stiffen. He looked at Tarawen and the others next to him. They were keeping all of their attention focused on a group of rish guards who had just entered the bar. Now Serrion pulled himself back from studying the strangely familiar figure at the distant table so that he could concentrate on the newcomers as well.

There were five of the creatures. Smelly, dull grey cloaks hung down from their wide, bony shoulders and Serrion could make out the hard notched chain-mail armour that they wore underneath. Each one held a small iron shield on one of its upper arms. Axes or swords with a roughly serrated cutting edge were hefted in the hand of the other. The hands at the end of their lower pairs of arms were empty, but the thick, gnarled fingers and hard, calloused skin on their knuckles looked just as dangerous. Serrion felt himself gulping in fear, and his stomach lurched at seeing these beasts at such close range.

The rish paused in the doorway of 'The Hunter and Holva'. Their large hulking figures looked even bigger and more threatening hunched under the low ceiling of the bar.

Tarawen and the other pulver lifted their glasses to their mouths or hung their heads – making a good job of looking like everyone else in the bar.

Serrion felt Cannish's hand on his shoulder as he reached across and pulled his hood up to cover his giveaway white hair. He cast the pulver a quick glance, but Cannish merely winked and gave him a brief nod.

With a frightening flash of thought, Serrion realised that he was the one would look most out of place in such a setting as this, and therefore the one most likely to catch the attention of the rish.

It seemed however, that their enemies were searching for someone else. As soon as they had looked around the room one of them gave a grunt of recognition and the group moved directly towards the table in the corner, where Serrion had noticed the oddly familiar figure. All eyes followed the rish as they overturned a couple of tables and chairs. Serrion's gaze flicked over to Ragosh. He saw that his face was set into a stern expression of resignation. He did not say or do anything at this invasion of his premises. 'He probably knows that it's no use trying to intervene,' thought Serrion. Getting in the way of the servants of the Lord of Atros would just cause him more trouble – or his life.

The rish were now surrounding the table.

'Yow, G'rupp,' the largest of them grunted in a deep, growling voice that sounded like thunder overhead.

The figure didn't move.

Serrion sensed Tarawen, Cannish and Husk all move their positions slightly around him. He glanced down to see that Cannish's hand was already on the handle of his sword, and Husk had edged forward in his seat, ready to leap up.

'Get ready to move boy,' Tarawen whispered in his ear. 'To the door and out if you can. We'll deal with this.'

The rish repeated his command, his rasping voice growing louder. 'I said G'RUPP!'

The figure remained seated, but he began to slowly raise his head. Serrion craned his neck to see around the rish who was standing immediately in front of him, blocking his view. As the man's face came up, Serrion made out the features for an instant. He gasped in sudden recognition. Vishan! Immediately, Serrion felt Tarawen's hand close tightly over his mouth, preventing him from calling out. Serrion's eyes darted to Tarawen's face, to see him give the briefest shake of his head, his finger on his lips.

Serrion nodded and remained silent. His head was swirling with memories of the last time he had seen Vishan, tumbling from the bridge in Maraglar, and disappearing under the water, as he fought with Sophia Andresen.

Across the room, the rish growled for a third time. 'Gi'rupp, powlver Shcum!' it bellowed.

Then, several things all seemed to happen at once.

Serrion was hurled to his feet by Tarawen's hand gripping his tunic in the small of his back.

His other two companions leapt forwards, blades flashing in the flickering yellow light.

The rish all turned around in surprise – their attention broken away from Vishan – to look at this interruption.

Vishan leapt swiftly from his chair, all pretence at illness and weakness gone. He jumped onto the table, sword in his right hand, dagger in his left.

Beside the bar, Ragosh reached up and pulled down sharply on a thick coil of rope that had been hidden away on a shelf beside the bottles and jars. As he did, Serrion saw a trapdoor open in front of him.

Tarawen, Husk and Cannish were halfway across the room, ready to draw battle with the rish.

The Atrossian beasts recovered from their surprise immediately. Thick clubs were swung in Vishan's direction, but he swiftly sidestepped the attack by leaping onto the next table. A large candle flickered there. He kicked it towards the rish, sparks and hot wax hitting the face of the one closest to him. It snarled in fury, doubling the strength of its next club stroke.

Vishan put his dagger between his teeth and leapt upwards, grabbing onto one of the wooden beams supporting the ceiling with his free hand. With his other hand he slashed away at his attacker with his sword. Swinging himself up and out of the immediate reach of the rish, he balanced along the beam until he had reached the far side of the room, where Serrion still waited, mouth agape with excitement.

'Good evening Serrion!' he grinned. 'How are you my boy?'

Across the room, Tarawen, Husk and Cannish were proving more than a match for the rish. The small space of the rooms in *The Hunter and Holva* made it difficult for the larger creatures to use their weapons effectively. Their multiple arms were more of a hindrance than a help, and as they struggled to overcome this surprise attack, they all got in each other's way. One even struck his companion a sharp blow behind the head with his cudgel as he swung it towards Cannish's face.

Husk was so strong that he only had to punch one of the rish in the midriff with the flat of his hand to have the beast stagger backwards and fall, winded and unable to stand.

Tarawen was like a whirlwind. His blade flashed and flickered. The memory of what the rish had done to his family years ago filled him with vengeful fury. He showed no mercy to the creatures in front of him.

'Vishan!' he called across to his old friend. 'We'll hold them here for now. Make for the tunnels with the boy!'

'Quick,' Vishan said to Serrion. 'Follow me.'

Even though Serrion felt a little put out at being herded around by the others, and being dismissed by Tarawen as just 'the boy,' he realised that he had no choice in this situation but to do as he was told and follow Vishan.

They made their way to the bar where Ragosh was waiting for them. He raised a wooden section to let them through and pointed to the open trapdoor.

'I think you remember your way,' he grinned at Vishan.

'What about the others?' Serrion asked.

'Right behind you,' Cannish called.

Serrion glanced back and saw that his companions were indeed now racing towards the bar. All of their attackers were lying around on the floor, or slumped over tables, dead or wounded.

'Many thanks once again, my dear Ragosh,' Vishan said as they disappeared down the steps and into a dim corridor underneath. 'Yet again I owe you a debt of gratitude I feel I can never fully repay.'

'There is no such thing as a debt between me and you my friend,' Ragosh called after them. 'Just keep doing what you do. You keep up the fight against these creatures and I'll keep on helping.'

'Our grateful thanks, nonetheless,' Tarawen said as he ran past. 'Glad to see that *The Hunter and Holva* is as interesting as ever.'

'You should see it on quiz night,' the landlord laughed.

They were soon out of earshot. Tarawen and the other pulver ran down the steps behind Vishan and Serrion. Husk, the last one through the trapdoor, had to bend almost double under the low ceiling as they descended.

Cannish and Tarawen both grabbed torches from the walls as they passed. There were also a number of iron hooks running down the length of the walls from which hung an assortment of weapons and replacement arrows in quivers. Vishan ran straight towards them, as if he were expecting to find them there.

'Did you know about these?' Serrion asked.

'Ragosh likes to keep his rebel friends happy with supplies of more than just warm beer,' Vishan grinned as he unslung a fresh quiver from its hook and swung it over his shoulder.

The companions made their hurried way down the corridor into the shadows beyond.

Chucking Out Time

The group of friends sped down the tunnel away from *The Hunter and Holva.* They did not pause for breath or to look behind them until they knew they must be well clear of the streets around the inn above them. At last they rested and listened for any sign of pursuit behind them. There was nothing to hear. All breathed a sigh of relief.

For the first time, Vishan was able to greet them all properly. He shook hands warmly with the other pulver, using the traditional double-handed grip reserved for companions who had fought together.

Finally he came to Serrion. The two looked at each other in silence for a moment. Then Vishan grinned and clasped the boy's hand firmly in both his own, echoing the greeting he had used with the others.

'Good to see you safe, lad. I worried about leaving you standing on the bridge like that back in Maraglar.'

'You too,' Serrion replied. 'How did you escape from the water, and... and what happened to... to...'

He found it hard to speak Sophia's name.

'I don't know the details myself lad,' the pulver spy answered.' All I know is I woke up chained to a chair in one of her dungeons, with her and that husband of hers gloating over me.'

'She's alive then,' Serrion muttered, almost to himself.

'Aye lad, she lives still. More's the pity.'

Serrion was filled with questions. 'So how did you escape from the dungeons? How did you manage to get to *The Hunter and Holva*?'

Vishan grinned.

'My escape? That reminds me of something.'

Reaching under the folds of his cloak, Vishan began searching through his pockets.

'A mutual friend told me to give this to you,' he said.

'A mutual friend?'

Vishan nodded.

'You mean Cleve Harrow don't you?' Serrion's expression had hardened. 'I'm not sure if he's a friend anymore.'

'Don't be too quick to judge him Serrion,' Vishan urged. 'There is much to explain and now is not the time. Here.' He brought a small vial out of his pocket and handed it to Serrion, who took it warily.'

'What is this,' he asked.

'Something to help you, the way it did me.'

Serrion's suspicious expression did not change.

'Did Harrow give this to you?' he asked. He looked at the small glass bottle uncertainly, as if it might contain liquidised slugs.

'Yes, but don't worry. It is safe to drink.'

Serrion was still unconvinced. His visions and what he had recently heard about Harrow's actions made him fearful.

'Have your powers been affected since your arrival here in Atros?' Vishan asked him.

Reluctantly, Serrion nodded.

'As were mine,' the pulver continued. 'You know we share certain gifts, our ability to move objects, open doors and so on?'

'Yes, but what has this to do with...'

'Harrow somehow came to my cell. He freed me and gave me some of this liquor. Immediately I felt stronger, and my powers returned. I would not be here now, helping you, without the aid of the Cleve.'

'Sorry Vishan, but I have seen so many visions of things that Harrow will do in the future I cannot trust...'

'There is no time!' Vishan's friendly patience was now wearing thin. 'My word as a pulver is honest and truthful. I promise you Serrion that you *can* trust the Cleve. You *must*! Drink this. It will help.'

The others looked on. Serrion caught Tarawen's eye. He nodded encouragement at him. Cannish spoke a brief; 'Go on lad.' Even Husk's eyes narrowed slightly as if to say 'go on'.

'These people have risked their lives several times to protect me,' Serrion thought to himself. 'There is no way they would encourage me to drink this if they thought there was any danger.'

The time for thinking was over. He unstoppered the vial and lifted it to his lips. He drank it all back in a quick gulp. The liquid was thick and syrupy and had a tarry, burnt taste. He shuddered as he felt it slip thickly down his throat. Then he felt a sweetness flooding his mouth.

'It will only take a few moments,' Vishan said. 'You should feel your power returning almost immediately.'

As if in response, Serrion lifted his hand and pointed towards the sword in Vishan's belt. It twitched for a couple of seconds, then the clasp holding it unfastened itself with a loud click and the sword shot into Serrion's outstretched palm.

He grinned.

Vishan and the others all breathed a sigh of relief. It was good to see Serrion with a smile on his face again.

'Can you use your visions as well?' asked Tarawen.

'I'll try,' Serrion replied.

He relaxed and allowed his thoughts to clear. He took the pebble from his pocket and clutched it tightly in his hand. Serrion stared with all of his attention at it until he felt the familiar swirling red of his visions.

'I can see Piotre and Sophia addressing huge numbers of soldiers,' he said. I have had this vision before, so it seems that my seering is working as usual.'

'Good,' Tarawen announced. 'Now we must press onwards. Every minute that we delay here could give more power to our enemies.'

'If only we could just make a pathway up to Sophia's gardens,' Cannish muttered.

'But you know we cannot,' Tarawen answered. 'The information that Fordan Hamel gave us was thorough. We must heed his warning. Any attempt to create a pathway within Atros City could be deadly. We have to make it on foot from here.'

'Follow me,' Vishan said. 'I have travelled these tunnels many times. I know the swiftest way into the castle.'

He turned and led them down the dark passages.

Jenn sat by Helen's bed. The dark breath had continued to curl out of her daughter's mouth for several hours, seeping from the room and joining the immense cloud over the city. Late in the night Helen gave another spluttering cough which seemed to release her and she settled into sleep, breathing normally again.

That had been two days ago. Since then Jenn had only left her daughter's side to refresh the towels she had used to mop her face, and now her head was drooping with exhaustion. Her eyelids were almost closed, and sleep had just about taken over when she was startled back into wakefulness by a low moan.

Helen had begun to thrash her arms weakly above her head. Her face had become even paler. Jenn reached out to calm her and recoiled with shock as her fingers touched her daughter's skin. She had been cool before, but now her temperature had dropped so much that it was like touching ice.

'She's getting worse,' Jenn thought. 'The next stage of the illness is upon her. Serrion and the others must find the Acferon plant and return with it soon. We're running out of time.'

Out in the streets of Beltheron City, the Darkness was having its effect. There were hardly any people outside. Nearly everyone had heeded the warning and stayed behind firmly closed doors. Window frames and gaps under doors had been tightly sealed with blankets and towels, so that no hint of the debilitating fogs outside could seep in. Only a handful of foolhardy individuals had ignored Matt's orders and continued to go outside as usual. Even they made their way quickly and furtively about their business, holding thick cloths up to their mouths and noses to keep out the smoke of the Darkness. They cast worried glances up to the skies, and doubled their pace if they caught a glimpse of a darker shadow curling around a rooftop, or appearing at the end of the street.

The hospital was full. Extra beds had been brought in to serve the large numbers who had fallen ill on their first breath of the dark smog. Even so, several men and women were lying on the floor, wrapped in whatever spare blankets could be found. Many coughed and spluttered, others just shivered, quaked and groaned as dark dreams and haunting images flayed their minds.

Matt was making a visit to the hospital, to lend his support to those who were working so tirelessly to help the sick.

He walked down a corridor with one of the doctors. The faces of the sick were what shocked him most of all. Most had blank expressions, their eyes staring sightlessly into the distance. Some moved their heads constantly from side to side like animals confined in a small space and unable to escape, while others mouthed silent words in an unending litany of fear.

'This is a terrible thing,' the doctor shook his head as he spoke to his lord. 'I have tended to the wounded from fields of battle, and cured sufferers from any number of dreadful diseases. But this...This is...' his words faded into nothing as he failed to find a way to express his horror at what the Darkness was doing.

'I know,' Matt said as he placed his arm on the doctor's shoulder. 'You are doing whatever you can my friend. I appreciate that.'

He turned away with a guilty thought gnawing at his conscience; everyone else was doing whatever they could, but what was he, the Lord of Beltheron himself, doing to help?

Harrow's Message

Orianna was turning an idea around in her head. At the moment it was no more than the fragment of a memory; it sat at the back of her thoughts like a dream that still lingers after you have woken up and got out of bed.

The thought that troubled her was about the woman they had met in Maraglar. Was it something about the way that she had been dressed that stirred Orianna's memory? Every time she tried to focus on the thought, it moved away from her again. Was it her clothes, or the way that she had moved perhaps? Or was it just something that she had said? Time and again Orianna tried to work out what it was that bothered her. She was sure it was important, and knew that she had read about it somewhere in one of her books that she had studied with Cleve Harrow. But what was it? There was only one way to find out. She had to return to Harrow's room to search.

She moved with care through the shadows of the streets to avoid the fingers of the dark clouds above her. The smoke of the Darkness moved threateningly around the rooftops, as if it were some silent creature hunting its prey. There was no one else around. All was shuttered and locked. Several times she had to turn back down a side street as a whisper of smoky cloud curled around a building up ahead or gathered in a thick haze that blocked her path. Eventually she reached the crumbling tower where Harrow had his study looking out over the rooftops of Beltheron. Orianna craned her neck upwards to the top of the ancient building. There was no smoke surrounding it that she could see. Cautiously, she began to climb the steps. At long last, and out of breath, she made it to the top. She was the only one apart from the Cleve himself who was allowed a key. Turning it in the rusty lock she creaked the door open.

The moment Orianna was inside she took her cloak from her shoulders. She folded it and placed it along the floor at the bottom of the door. 'That should keep the Darkness out, if those clouds come searching for me,' she thought.

It always comforted her to spend time in this study. She loved her work for the Cleve. For her to come here, and be surrounded by so many volumes filled with ancient knowledge and stories was a thing she always looked forward to. Today however, there was a more serious purpose to her visit.

Standing in the middle of the circular room she spoke aloud to herself. 'What were you? Where can I find you?'

As Orianna thought about it, she began to wonder if the clue she was searching for hadn't been in a book at all. She made a decision and moved to a stepladder leaning against one of the high bookshelves. She lifted it over to a stack of cupboards. Climbing up she opened the doors and began to sift through a thick pile of old documents and letters. It took her four trips up and down the ladder to lift down every document from the cupboard. She transferred them all to the oak table in the middle of the room. There was quite a pile by the time she had finished. It would take too long to go through every piece of paper, but she knew she could be selective. She immediately discarded all the bills and scraps of receipts that Harrow seemed to hoard as if they were golden coins. Then she quickly skimmed the letters and papers between Harrow and various traders in Beltheron before dropping them on the ground beside her chair. There was nothing of interest in those either. Soon, there was a stack of unwanted documents scattered on the floor around her feet, and the pile on the desk in front of her was much more manageable.

Even so, she had to go through the remaining papers twice before she noticed the small envelope tucked inside a bundle of yellowing files. There was just one word written on it: Hamel.

This was it! Orianna knew at once she had found the thing that had been troubling her. Fordan Hamel. The name the woman on Maraglar had given them. The man that Tarawen, Serrion and the others had gone to find on Atros. It hadn't struck her until now, but she was suddenly certain that she must have seen this envelope before, or maybe she had once overheard Cleve Harrow discussing its contents.

Breathlessly, she tore at the seam of the envelope. With trembling fingers she picked out the pages within.

There were three sheets filled with Harrow's unmistakable handwriting. She began to read feverishly.

'So now the truth is known, and the ultimate plan of the Andresens starts to become clearer. They intend to mount a variety of attacks on our beloved Beltheron. Not just with their mighty armies of rish, brannoch and harch, but with treachery and betrayal also. Sophia's skills with herbs rivals that of her sister Jenia, and she has discovered the truth of the Acferon plant's powers. She will not rest until that power is in her own hands.

The flowers grow now in Sophia's own gardens. They lie atop the towers of Gendrell, riven by the winds of Atros.'

Here was extra information, Orianna realised. If they had only known this, they could have saved so much time! She carried on reading.

'The plant is vital to turning back the Darkness. The threatening clouds will clear and the danger will recede when the first victim is cured by the seeds of the Acferon.'

Underneath this, Harrow had scribbled a few words that leapt out at her. Her eyes grew wide as she read them. She gasped and almost dropped the pages in her shock. What Harrow had written next changed everything.

'Hamel told me this. But that was before the Andresens got their claws into him. Who knows what they promised him, or with what terrors and tortures they flayed his mind. However it was, we now know that Hamel can no longer be trusted. He is an agent of Atros, and given the chance he will betray us all to our doom.'

Why had Harrow kept this a secret, she wondered? The answer came in the following passage.

'T'yuq Tinyaz has made me swear this to secrecy. She has told me to write this down, for discovery by you, Orianna.'

Orianna almost dropped the paper in her shock. T'yuq knew this would happen all along! She had planned the whole thing! She had made Cleve Harrow write this for her to discover! Hurriedly Orianna read on.

'T'yuq knew that you would find this letter, and that you would know what to do when the time came. Trust your instincts, in this my dear. Do what you feel to be right. You have an important part to play too.'

Here the letter ended. Orianna knew that she must act immediately. Forcing the letter into a pocket of her robe she ran to the door. As soon as she was outside she cast her eyes around for a flycar. She hated riding in them, but climbing back down the many uneven steps which wound dangerously around the outside of the tower would take too long. There in the distance was a pulver pilot skimming by over the dark clouds. She began waving her arms to him. He spotted her and spun the vehicle around to fly towards her. It only took her a few moments to give him a quick outline of the urgency of her mission. He nodded to her to hop on.   The flycar leapt into the air and they raced down towards the rooftops of the city. He expertly avoided the swathes of grasping smoke that tried to reach out at them. After circling around a particularly dangerous looking whirlpool of smoky blackness he dropped into a narrow passageway, burst out into the main square and through the sidestreets. Soon the pulver's vehicle pulled up outside Matt, Jenn and Helen's house.

Within moments the door was flung open and Orianna was led inside by an anxious Jenn.

'Harrow's books and papers back up everything that we have thought so far,' she began. 'They say that the Darkness will disappear, and all those under its influence will recover, once the first victim is cured.'

'The first victim being Helen you mean?'

'That's right,' Orianna nodded. 'It seems that it all stems from her. If Serrion and the pulver can return with the Acferon in time, we will be able to cure not just Helen, but everyone else as well.'

'*If* they return in time,' Jenn repeated. '*If* can be a very big word Orianna.'

'There's something else,' Orianna continued. She took a deep breath and told them of Fordan Hamel and his treachery.

Matt stood deep in thought for a moment. 'It appears that we have no choice but to trust Cleve Harrow after all,' he said. 'It is possible that our friends might have fallen into Hamel's trap already. I'm sorry, Orianna, but it seems your brother might be in the gravest danger even as we speak.'

'I know,' Orianna replied. 'And that is why I ask that you will send me to Atros. I know where the plant is to be found, and I might still have a chance to warn Serrion and the others before it is too late.'

'And if it is too late for them, perhaps you can succeed where they have failed,' Jenn thought to herself.

'Go immediately,' Matt ordered. 'Take the golden staff with you. Find the flower as quickly as you can.' He was already reaching for a vial to create a pathway.

'Here I go again,' thought Orianna to herself as Matt thrust the golden staff into her hands and she felt the swirling white column surround her once more.

Orianna landed with a jolt that drove the wind from her lungs. She had landed awkwardly on an uneven stone floor. Her legs had twisted painfully under her and brought her to her knees.

'One day I'm going to arrive through a pathway in a more dignified manner,' she thought to herself.

Thankfully she still had a firm grasp around the golden staff and she used it to support herself and raise herself back to her feet.

It was not an uneven floor, she realised. It was a stone staircase. One foot had landed one step higher than the other. As she stood up she became aware of movement and noise below her. It sounded as if a large group of people were running up the staircase towards her. Filled with fear that she had been discovered by her enemies and that her mission had failed before it had even started, she spun around to face the danger.

Danger Above, Danger Below

'Directly above us is the castle of Gendrell itself. At the top of one of the towers is the rooftop garden where Sophia grows the Acferon.'

Vishan was speaking to them all in a low voice. He had led them down corridors and tunnels for what Serrion thought must have been hours. They were now standing in a low-ceilinged cavern. There was a small wooden trapdoor in the centre of the roof just above their heads.

'From here we must be even more watchful,' Vishan continued. 'Our enemies could be within inches of us even as I speak.'

They all nodded silently. They understood the predicament they were in.

'Give me a hand up onto your shoulder Husk,' said Tarawen.

The huge pulver lifted Tarawen easily onto his shoulders so that he could inspect the fastenings on the roof trapdoor.

'It seems an easy thing to open,' he whispered down to the rest. 'I can see a small clasp through this gap which I can easily break with my sword.'

Already he was working his blade backwards and forwards through the trapdoor until they all heard a loud snap. They held their breath, expecting hordes of rish to fall in upon their heads at any moment. Nothing happened.

Tarawen breathed a sigh of relief, replaced his sword in its scabbard and slowly began to lift the trapdoor.

They all watched as, centimetre by centimetre, the trapdoor was lifted.

'What do you see?' hissed Cannish.

'Nothing, it's all darkness in there,' came the reply. 'That's good. I think it's safe to go up,' he whispered. 'Husk, give me another leg up.'

Tarawen was hoisted through the trapdoor and disappeared into the gloom.

Long seconds went by. Everyone in the tunnel remained motionless. Then a light flickered and Tarawen's face appeared in the open hatch of the trapdoor. He grinned.

'Come on, it's quite safe. What are you waiting for?'

Within a minute, all of the companions had been lifted up into the room by the great strength of Husk. He then raised his arms, took a grip on the side of the opening and lifted himself up and through without any expression of effort or exertion on his face.

Serrion looked around the room. It was all murky shadows. He couldn't make out anything.

'Is it alright to shine a light in here? He asked.

Cannish nodded and handed him a glass globe about the size of an orange. Serrion had seen objects like this before. He knew that Helen was an expert at making them work and do all sorts of magic. All he needed though, was a bit of light.

'Ilumen,' he whispered into it.

A greenish glow began to spread from the globe. He held it up so that the others could see as well.

The light threw weird, threatening shapes onto the walls. Serrion jumped as a looming figure hunched over his shoulder, then almost laughed out loud as he realised it was only his own shadow.

The pulver all had their own green light globes and were now holding them aloft, like Serrion. Their eyes adjusted to the new light levels and they made their way cautiously through the corridors. Vishan and Tarawen led the way, with Serrion in the middle and Cannish and Husk bringing up the rear. Husk spent as much time glancing behind him, to make sure they were not being followed, as he did looking ahead. All was silent. Serrion remembered the last time he had been here, when this castle had been made of old, crumbling stone; it was cold and ancient. Now it had been remade by the Andresens and their minions. Smooth grey marble covered the floors, and walls and pillars of metal and gold surrounded them.

No one spoke. It was clear that Vishan and Tarawen knew their way and there was no need for words.

Slowly, carefully, they proceeded. Through three doors and up two short flights of steps they went; along sloping corridors, always moving upwards. Up, up into the very heart of the castle.

At long last they came to a larger door. It was made of thick wood with heavy iron fittings that locked it securely. Tarawen and Vishan whispered to each other briefly, then nodded to each other. Vishan held out his hand and the familiar green glow spread from his fingers. The light spread around the door handle and it lifted slightly. Vishan twisted his fingers in the air, but the handle did not budge any further. He tried again and Tarawen leant into the door, listening intently for the sound of a click as the lock was released. Nothing. Vishan tried a third time, and Serrion noticed a film of sweat forming on his forehead with the effort. Again the only thing that happened was the metal handle lifting slightly, vibrating, then dropping down again. The door remained firmly locked.

'Is there nothing we can do?' asked Cannish. 'Is there another way?'

Vishan shook his head. 'This door leads to the wing of the castle that Fordan Hamel showed us. This is the way we have to go if we are to reach the gardens and the Acferon plant.'

Tarawen turned from the door and gestured to Serrion. 'The locks holding this door are strong,' he whispered. 'Who knows, they may also be warded by Atrossian magic. Maybe your skills can help Vishan here, my boy.'

Serrion nodded and stepped forward. He was glad to be given the chance to do something.

'At the same time as me, Serrion,' Vishan said. 'Are you ready?'

With another quick nod of his head, Serrion made it clear that he was. Both of them lifted their hands towards the door handle.

The familiar tingling feeling in Serrion's fingers made him twitch with nerves. What if this didn't work? What if they couldn't unlock the door? They might *never* find the Acferon.

He needn't have worried. As soon as they both held out their hands towards the door his power was added to Vishan's, and they heard a grinding creak from inside the lock. The pulver nodded a signal to Serrion and they twisted their fingers at the same moment. The handle lifted again, but this time the door did swing open.

Tarawen put his hands on their shoulders. 'Well done,' he whispered.

'Well done indeed,' came a familiar voice from the darkness beyond the door. 'You made it at last. We've been expecting you.'

From out of the gloom stepped Fordan Hamel. He was flanked by two rish guards. They each held spiked swords and studded cudgels in all four of their hands.

Serrion and the others stared in disbelief. Tarawen groaned as he realised the truth. Fordan had tricked them. He had been working for Atros all along!

Vishan silently cursed himself. If only he had been able to discover more about Piotre and Sophia's network of agents. Then he might have discovered Hamel's treachery. But even as he thought about this he knew how fiendishly the Andresens had plotted to keep all of their allies and spies separate. It was essential for them to work in that way, so that if any one spider in their web was caught, there would still be others to continue in the service of Atros.

'So everything you told us was a lie?' Serrion asked Fordan furiously. 'The spell on the pathways, the Acferon plant, everything?'

'No, not everything,' came the reply. 'The Acferon plant is here, just as I said. And many walls and locks of the castle *have* been warded by Lord Andresen's magic. But the pathways themselves are safe.' He laughed cruelly. 'There is no spell on *them* at all. You could have been here, in and out of the castle, and home again with your prize within five minutes of leaving my boat! But I had to delay you, to give me time to get here myself and lay this little trap.'

'So the Andresens know we are here?' Vishan asked.

Fordan shook his head. 'Not yet, I wanted to catch you myself, with the aid of my assistants here,' he gestured towards the rish. 'Then I knew Lord Andresen would be so delighted that I could name my price for a reward.'

Tarawen was the first to speak. 'I hope they do pay you well, fisherman, because you'll need all the Atrossian gold you can get your hands on to escape me. I'll make sure that you're tracked down to the ends of the Three Worlds for this.'

'Words, words, words,' Fordan Hamel replied with a leer. 'Worthless from the lips of a dead man.'

Husk drew his sword, but before he could do anything else they heard the heavy padding of many feet behind them. The group of friends turned to see a horde of rish approaching.

Vishan turned to Serrion desperately.

'You know where the Acferon is,' he said in a rushed whisper. 'Use your seering to help you. Make your way to the rooftop. I will send assistance if I can.'

'What?' Serrion couldn't understand what Vishan meant.

'Trust me,' Vishan replied. 'And trust Cleve Harrow.'

Before Serrion had time to respond, Vishan had grabbed a vial from his pocket. In a swift blur of movement he thrust it into Serrion's hands. He leant in so that his lips were close to Serrion's ear and whispered 'A gift from Cleve Harrow. Good luck lad.'

Serrion felt Vishan press down sharply on the vial. It cracked and a hot liquid seeped onto Serrion's fingers as Vishan was pulled away by one of the rish. A blinding white light surrounded Serrion and he heard the battle cries of Tarawen and the others begin to fight. Another of the monstrous rish guards reached towards him. Then he was plucked away into a twisting maelstrom of light and sound. His stomach lurched as he clutched tightly onto the cracked vial and it spiralled him upwards into a pathway.

The light of the pathway confused the rish for a moment. They stared blankly at the scorch mark on the ground where Serrion had been standing only a moment before. It was enough time for Tarawen and the others to gain the upper hand. Led by the mighty form of Husk, swinging his sword around madly, they ran through a gap in the gang of rish in the doorway. Tarawen lunged at Fordan Hamel with his own sword, eager to act out his revenge for the betrayal. Surprisingly the old fisherman was too quick. His age did not stop him from leaping agilely out of the way, and down a dark side corridor. Tarawen yelled in frustration, and was about to head after him, when Vishan's voice stopped him.

'No time! That way takes us down; we need to climb up! Finding the Acferon comes first.'

Tarawen nodded his agreement and they hurtled up the stairs. Husk and Cannish were below them, climbing backwards as they swung their swords to delay their pursuers.

They had not gone very far before there was a swirling sound like rushing wind above them. Around the bend in the stairwell they saw a bright flash of light.

Another pathway had opened up just ahead. But who was it? Who would be landing on a staircase in the middle of the castle in Atros City?

Tarawen edged up another couple of steps, peering around the bend. There, in the fading white light stood Orianna Melgardes, with the golden staff of Beltheron in her hands.

'Thank goodness it's you!' she cried.

'What in the Three Worlds are you...?'

'No time to explain!' she yelled back at him. 'Follow me.'

Together they all raced up the stairs, with the rish in hot pursuit. At the top of the staircase was another door, Orianna pointed the golden staff at it as she ran.

'*Egress*!' she shouted. A bolt of fire sprang from the tip of the staff and the door swung open. They poured through and with another flick of the staff the door slammed behind them, striking the faces of the two rish who had been the closest to catching them. Vishan pointed his fingers at the door and the heavy metal bolts slid into place, melting and melding the door closed as his fingers twitched with sparks.

Orianna gasped to get her breath back and looked around the group of pulver. Standing in front of her were Tarawen, Cannish, Husk and – to her amazement – Vishan! He was still alive! But her relief at seeing Vishan was short lived. Where was Serrion? What had happened to her brother?

'About time you got here,' Vishan grinned at her. He jerked his head towards the other pulver. 'Working with these grunts is fun,' he laughed. 'And I must admit Husk's muscles have been useful. But I reckon that we'll be needing your brains from here on in.'

Piotre's Room

Serrion landed heavily. His foot twisted under him and he struggled to stay upright. The light of the pathway went out. After a few moments he steadied himself and looked around.

Strange shapes surrounded him in the gloom that was only partially lit by the green glow coming from the globe that Cannish had given him. A looming figure appeared from the shadows, suspended by a rope from the ceiling. With a jolt of horror, Serrion thought at first that it must be the corpse of one of the Andresens' victims, but with a sigh of relief he realised that it was only a mannequin of some kind, a little bit like a shop window dummy. Still, he thought, it's a strange thing for them to keep here, in the middle of the castle of Atros.

He continued to make his way across the wide hallway, holding the green globe in front of him. There were a number of swords and other weapons in racks. 'Perhaps I'm in some sort of store room,' he thought.

Why had the vial brought him here he wondered? Perhaps it was just some kind of sidestepping, to get him out of the danger of the rish, and landing here was purely chance. He bit down on his fear and realised that he had no choice but to trust what Vishan had done to save him.

Then, Serrion stiffened. Very faintly, in the hallway beyond the door he heard approaching footsteps. Looking around the shadows, Serrion noticed a heavy curtain covering an alcove. He hurried towards it, extinguishing the light of Cannish's green globe as he ran.

As soon as he pulled back the curtain and stepped into the alcove, he heard a click and the main door began to swing open behind him. In panic he pulled the curtains closed, hoping he wasn't making any sound.

A heavy voice spoke a single word, 'Ilumen,' and the room was instantly flooded with light. Serrion peered out through the thin crack of the curtains.

Piotre Andresen strode into the middle of the room. He was dressed in loose-fitting breeches and a flowing shirt that allowed him to move easily. Over the top of it though, was a protective leather jerkin, with chain mail sewn into it. On his feet he wore long, sturdy boots of dark leather. In one hand Andresen carried a long, curving sword and in the other a hefty dagger with a serrated edge that glittered in the light. He passed so close to Serrion's hiding place that the boy could see the sharp teeth of the dagger. The thought of what they could do to human skin and the fragile flesh below made his head spin. Andresen took up his place in the centre of the hall.

In the light, Serrion could now see every detail of the place he had just been searching with his dim lantern globe. The things he had seen suddenly made sense. The room was obviously some kind of gym, or training area. Rows of sabres, long knives, epees and other fencing equipment were ranged across the entire wall on the far side. Placed around the hall were stands which supported collections of other weaponry, maces and clubs with sharp spikes sticking out of them, throwing daggers, bows and evilly carved arrows.

To the left of where Andresen now stood, the mannequin that he had seen swung gently to and fro, suspended from the ceiling on a length of thick, gnarled rope. Of course, the dummy was for fencing practice. Little painted circles and crosses were marked in various places on the mannequin's head chest, and stomach. They were targets, Serrion realised. As he continued to watch from the alcove, Piotre Andresen began to move in smooth, slow actions, flexing thigh muscles as he leant from one side to the other, and stretching his torso in a sequence of controlled, measured movements. As he moved, his arms turned and twisted, and the blades swooped through the air with a hissing, singing sound.

Serrion could hardly take his eyes off the man. His movements were so quick and fluid it was more like watching an expert dancer than someone taking an exercise in swordsmanship. Andresen's movements became faster and faster, until, in a lunge so rapid that Serrion did not even see it, he had plunged the sword into the mannequin. Andresen let go of the handle so that it vibrated in the very centre of the red target on its chest as he spun around. Pivoting on his right foot, he brought his left arm around in a wide, smooth arc, cutting with the dagger. The jagged blade of this second weapon sliced through the fabric and stuffing on the neck of the mannequin as if it were butter, decapitating it in one cut, so that it fell from the rope and landed at his feet with a dull thud.

Serrion quailed at the speed and strength of his enemy, this man who had once been his father. He moved back a step from the gap in the curtains, terrified of being spotted. He realised that he had stopped breathing. He knew of course that this was the vision he had seen under the Great hall in Beltheron, when Matthias had taken him to meet the Seer. He also remembered with a shudder how that vision had ended, with a dagger shooting towards him too quickly for him to avoid.

He almost whimpered with fear but bit down on his terror. He forced his mind back to what T'yuq Tinyaz had said to him on that day.

'These images that we see are not always visions of what will definitely be, but only hints of one of many possible futures. With knowledge of them we can act to change the outcomes, alter the path to create a different future...'

He forced himself to think clearly. Piotre Andresen still did not know he was there, behind the curtain. All he had to do was to remain still and silent, and soon the Lord of Atros would leave. The dagger did not *have* to come towards him, he reassured himself over and over. That was just one *possible* future.

But even as he was thinking this, he realised that it had now gone very quiet in the hall. Since he had stepped further back into the shadows of the alcove, he had not been able to see through the gap in the curtain. He could not see what the Lord of Atros was doing. He could be standing right there, on the other side, that deadly dagger still in his hand, ready to make the final, swift lunge forwards. Every nerve in Serrion's body was intent on picking up the slightest sound of motion on the other side of the curtain. Maybe Piotre had already gone? Perhaps Serrion had been so wound up in his thoughts that he hadn't even heard his enemy leave? Surely that was too much to hope for, he thought. And if the lights were still on, that must surely mean that Piotre was still there.

He waited for what seemed like another full minute. There was not the tiniest noise, not a breath, from the room.

'This is ridiculous,' he thought. 'I can't stay in here forever.'

Cautiously, moving his weight ever so slightly forwards, he lifted one heel to begin to step back to the curtain. There was still a tiny, thin chink of light coming through the narrow gap. If he could just move forwards another couple of centimetres, it would give him a view back into the hall. Raising his foot he took a step. He was sure he hadn't made a sound. Leaning his weight onto this forward foot, he then edged towards the chink.

Through the gap he could see about a metre wide across the room. There was the beheaded mannequin, now just a pile of fabric and sawdust slumped in the middle of the floor. The sword was still sticking out of it, straight up into the air. No sign of Piotre.

Serrion tilted his body to the left. The view through the curtain altered until, bit by bit, by moving further and further over, he had seen most of one side of the hall. It was empty. His left knee bent lower as he struggled to keep his balance. Still he had not made a sound. He began to tilt himself the other way. Back past the mannequin, centimetre by centimetre he scanned the rest of the hall through the gap. Still nothing. He began to relax. Piotre had gone after all.

Serrion was about to allow himself a deep breath of relief when his view brought him to the door. There stood Piotre Andresen, stock still, his hand raised to the handle. He had been about to leave the room. Serrion gave a gasp of shock as he saw him.

Andresen must have heard him, for now he turned his head to one side, so that Serrion could see his face in profile. The Lord of Atros was listening intently. As Serrion watched, he saw Piotre slowly lower his hand from where he had been about to push the door open. His fingers reached down to his belt. Serrion flicked his gaze down. Piotre was reaching for his dagger!

Serrion thought about the vision he had seen of the dagger flying towards him. Was that a premonition of what was about to happen right now? Was Piotre about to kill him?

Terror shuddered through Serrion. He felt his heart begin to race. But panic was no good. He knew that. He forced himself to concentrate. He tried to remain calm by focusing on what T'yuq Tinyaz had said to him.

'These images that we see are only hints of one of many possible futures. With knowledge of them we can act to change the outcomes, alter the path to create a different future...'

Piotre was still at the door, his head still cocked to one side, but now the dagger was out of his belt. He flexed his fingers around the handle, adjusting his grip ever so slightly, ready to throw, or lunge with it.

Serrion frantically tried to remember the details of his vision. He was sure that the blade had been coming directly at him – from shoulder height. It looked as if it had been thrown from a standing position... *one of many possible futures...* he too had been standing up when he had seen the image of the dagger coming at him... *act to change the outcomes...*

Piotre was coming towards the curtain. He was halfway across the room already, his hand lifted to shoulder height, the dagger held in a throwing grip.

...alter the path.

Serrion dropped to his knees as the dagger was released. It shot through the narrow gap of the curtain, passed over his head by several centimetres and struck the wall behind him before falling to the ground with a clatter.

Back in the room beyond the curtain, Piotre gave a sniff at the sound of the falling dagger. 'Huh, I could have sworn there was something,' he muttered. He stepped closer to the curtain, extending his hand to pull the drapes back and retrieve his weapon. Serrion froze in absolute terror on the other side. There was no space, no shadow for him to shrink into and hide. If Piotre took another step, he was bound to see him.

The door at the opposite end of the room opened. From his position crouched down on the floor, Serrion could see past where Piotre was standing. He could just make out the legs of an Atrossian guard in the doorway.

'Excuse me sir.'

Piotre spun around.

'What is it?' he asked impatiently.

'Alarm given, sir.'

'Alarm?'

'Yes sir. From the western end of the castle, sir.'

'Intruders?'

'Pulver scum by the look of it, sir.'

Serrion tensed. They could only be talking about Vishan and the others. His friends had been discovered!

'Numbers?' Piotre Andresen snapped the question.

'Five of them sir.'

'Five pulver?' Andresen asked.

'*Five?*' thought Serrion. 'Who is the fifth?' He strained to hear the guard's reply.

'Five intruders sir, but one of 'em... Well, one of 'em sir...'

'Yes? Come on man. Spit it out. One of them what?'

'One of 'em looks like a woman sir.'

'But you said they were pulver. How could one of them be a woman?'

'Yes sir, I know, but it's true, my lord. Young she is, with long white hair.'

Piotre cursed briefly under his breath and raced towards the door. He yelled out instructions to the guard as he went.

'Right! Lock down the city! No one goes in or out of Atros until I give the word. And send your men down to where they were spotted. Tell them to take a brannoch.'

'Yes sir.'

'We'll soon hunt them dow...'

Their voices were cut off sharply as the door slammed behind them and they sped down the corridor.

Serrion had gone cold at the guard's words. Long white hair! There could be only one person that he had been describing. But how had Orianna found her way into the city and found Vishan and the rest? And why had his sister come to Atros?

Serrion leapt out from his hiding place behind the curtain and raced towards the door to follow Piotre.

Tricking a Noetic

As soon as Serrion ran through the doors to chase after Piotre Andresen he realised he had made a terrible mistake. Hands clutched at his arms from behind. Cruel squeezing fingers pinched deep into his flesh.

He started to struggle, kicking out violently. The hands around his arms just held onto him more firmly.

'Nice try, but you will have to do better than that to escape me.'

Serrion recognised the voice immediately. It was Piotre Andresen.

Serrion had not waited long enough. Piotre must have heard him running across the floor even as he had closed the door behind him.

Serrion now felt himself being spun around by the grasping hands until he was looking up into the familiar, evil grin.

'How I've waited for this moment,' Andresen spat at him. 'How I've longed to repay you for what you did to my son.'

Serrion was propelled forwards by the strength of Piotre's hands. He struggled to begin with, but soon gave up and allowed himself to be taken through the corridors of the castle.

After many twists and turns – far too many for him to remember in case of possible escape – they came to a large oak door. Two rish stood guarding it. At a word from Andresen they threw the door open. Serrion craned his neck to peer inside, but it was too dark to see anything.

The arms holding him flung him forwards into the room. He lost his footing and fell clumsily onto the ground.

'Careful with the boy,' said another voice he recognised. 'He can still be useful to us.'

'Stay with him,' Andresen said. 'Guard him.'

'My pleasure, Lord,' answered the familiar voice.

The door was slammed closed. At the same instant, a bright light flooded the room, as if a switch had been turned on. Serrion lifted himself up and turned to look at the owner of the voice. He already knew who it was, a big part of him had suspected that he would be here all along, but Serrion still needed the proof of his own eyes.

Sure enough, there stood Cleve Harrow. There was a long silence between them. Serrion closed his eyes briefly. He reached into his pocket for the pebble that he had brought from the beach. Gripping the pebble in his hand he let a red image dance inside his head as he focused on a vision of the future. Opening his eyes once more he nodded up at the Cleve.

'It's alright,' he said. 'I know now that I can trust you.

Harrow's shoulders dropped with relief.

'Good. Thank you my boy.' He moved towards his young friend and helped him to stand.

'We don't have much time,' Harrow said urgently. 'Andresen will be back in a matter of minutes.'

'You didn't mean to hurt Helen, did you?' Serrion asked him. 'It was all just part of the plan, wasn't it?'

Harrow nodded.

'And you never were working for the Andresens at all, were you?' Even though he knew the answer to this, he felt that he had to hear Cleve Harrow tell him in his own words.

'No, I never betrayed you or any of the people of Beltheron,' Harrow replied. 'Not for a moment.'

'But the Andresens had to believe that you *were* helping them, and that Vishan was an agent of Atros too. That's right isn't it?'

'You know now don't you?' Harrow said. 'I had to get close to them. T'yuq Tinyaz showed me that this was the only way. All of the other futures that she saw ended in failure. There was even one future where the Andresens were assassinated before they could gain power. But in that future Gretton Tur and the forces of Atros lived on and destroyed Beltheron utterly.'

'So this is the only way,' Serrion said. It was not a question. He knew the answer already.

'Yes,' Harrow nodded. 'That is why we are both here together. It has all been leading to this.'

Serrion nodded. 'T'yuq Tinyaz told me things too. Well, she *showed* me, when she shared some of her visions.'

'But she didn't show you *everything*, did she my boy?'

'No,' Serrion swallowed hard. At last he was beginning to understand his place in the fate of Beltheron. 'She only showed me certain things.'

'Go on,' Cleve Harrow prompted him gently. 'Think it through, Serrion. It will help you to understand.'

'She showed me the things that would make me come to certain decisions.' He gulped hard. 'She was steering me here all the time, wasn't she?'

'If it makes you feel any better Serrion, she did it to me too. She steered all of us.'

'She used you too? Just like she used me?'

'Yes, my boy.'

Serrion knew he should feel comforted by this. The fact that even Harrow had been manipulated should have made a difference; it should have made him feel better. But it didn't. It was too late for that. He felt dead inside as he began to think about the mind of T'yuq Tinyaz once again.

'But why didn't you warn us about Fordan Hamel?' he asked. 'That would have saved us from some of the danger at least.'

'We had to lure Hamel here,' Harrow replied. 'It was vital that all of Atros' agents were in the castle together at the same time. The Seer worked out that this was the only way to achieve that.'

'She saw *everything* in her visions, didn't she?' Serrion asked.

'Yes,' Harrow replied softly. 'Every possible future.'
Every possible future.

Serrion's head reeled as he tried to imagine the burden of it. A shudder of guilt went through him as he remembered the terrible things he had said to the Seer, just before the attack of the dragons in the cave. He had accused her of doing nothing to help the fate of Beltheron. Now he knew how awful the tasks she faced must have been; how crippling the decisions she had to make, every single day. There was also a stab of fear as he remembered her words that soon, the responsibility of making those decisions would be his.

'So, if she saw everything, then she knew that I had to be here on Atros as well, with you, right now,' he said to Harrow. He was still working it out in his head as he spoke. 'There has to be a good reason for me to be here at this moment, otherwise she would have told you something different, or showed me a different path.'

'Yes, you have to be here Serrion, at this point in our history. The Andresens have built such defences around themselves; this was the only way to get you close enough to them. To all of them at once.'

'Yes, I know all that now, Cleve. I've just pieced all that side of it together. But why me in particular? *That's* the part I still haven't been able to see. *That's* what I still don't understand.'

Harrow looked behind him. There had been a sudden loud disturbance on the other side of the door. Their enemies were returning. He spun back towards Serrion. 'You will.'

'What?'

The noise outside increased. They could hear raised voices now.

Harrow gripped Serrion's arm. 'You will. When the moment comes you *will* understand.'

'But...'

'No time,' Harrow said. 'They are here.'

The door handle began to turn.

'Tell Helen,' Harrow continued quickly. 'Tell her I'm sorry I had to treat her that way. I'm so sorry I frightened her, but *everyone* had to believe that I was working for the Andresens. I hope she can forgive me.'

Serrion was about to open his mouth to reply when there was a crash behind them. The door burst open. Piotre Andresen rushed back into the room and stood triumphantly before them. He was still wearing the fighting gear that he had been practising in earlier. Serrion's heart faltered at the memory of how swiftly Piotre Andresen had moved with a blade. His premonition of the dagger flying towards his face came at him again.

Another figure now appeared behind Piotre. Hethaloner Rasp had hurried up the staircase in his master's wake. He wanted to get close to the Melgardes boy. He had to be able to look into his eyes.

Even Harrow quailed in fear at the sight of Rasp. He had known him many years ago, in his own childhood.

When he and Gretton Tur studied and played together, Rasp would join in their games and talks. That was before Gretton Tur had become fascinated with power, and turned to evil; before he had been banished from Beltheron and become the Wild Lord of Atros.

'Cleve,' Rasp whispered to his old companion. 'How good it is to see you again.' He gestured towards Serrion. 'And how I have waited for the chance to talk to our young friend here.' The mind reader's voice sounded like ice cracking over a frozen lake. The meaning behind it was just as lethal.

Harrow met Rasp's gaze as it flickered behind his thin spectacles. The yellow and red sliver of colour in the left eye fascinated Serrion and he struggled to remember where he had seen it before. Then it occurred to him. He *had* seen this man, but not in his real life, in a vision...

> *...A flicker of red and yellow deep in evil eyes that looked directly into Serrion's own.*
>
> *'You are with us then?' a cruel voice whispered into his ear. 'You will serve us on Atros after all?'*
>
> *A wicked smile spread across thin lips as Serrion realised that this stranger with the odd eyes was reading his mind...*

The truth hit Serrion with a jolt. This man from his vision, the same man now standing before him, was a noetic! He would read his mind, see his visions and discover everything!

'Lead him to my rooms,' Rasp ordered the rish. 'Chain the boy ready for my questioning.'

Don't harm him Rasp!' Harrow commanded as the rish stepped forwards.

'Rasp,' Serrion thought. 'His name is Rasp. Why is that familiar?' He struggled to remember where he had heard the name before.

He had no time to consider that now. Serrion's thoughts turned and turned on a more immediate problem. If this man Rasp could read his thoughts, and see his premonitions, then there was no escape, no way out. It all seemed hopeless.

Unless...

Unless Serrion could point Rasp towards a *particular* vision. If he concentrated hard enough on one thing, maybe he could steer Rasp towards a course of action. In the same way that T'yuq Tinyaz had steered him.

The thought of T'yuq Tinyaz brought another memory flooding back.

He thought of her last words echoing around the underground chamber. 'El asp ottewan tew ear!'

He started to break it down in his head, syllable by syllable.

El...asp...ot...e...wan...to...ear...

He knew that there were gaps in what he had heard as he ran away from the dragons. He had been so scared he hadn't even trusted his memory. But now he began to fill in the gaps with a possible meaning.

Asp... could she have said Rasp?

The meaning hit him like a bolt of lightning and he almost staggered and lost his footing as he was led down the corridor.

El asp... *Tell Rasp*

Ot e wan... *what he wants*

Tew ear... *to hear.*

Was that it? Was he right? The more he turned it over in his head, the more certain he was that he had worked out the Seer of Beltheron's last message to him.

'Tell Rasp what he wants to hear.'

Finally Serrion understood. He now knew why he was the one who could save Beltheron. No one else could trick the noetic and get close enough to the Andresens to defeat them. Rasp would read their thoughts, he would always know what they intended to do. But Serrion could divert his attention. He could trick Rasp with the temptation of knowing the future. Then maybe he could get past the Andresens' last line of defence.

As the chains bit into his hands and he and Harrow were led away, Serrion began to work out how he could use what was in his mind to trick the noetic.

'Tell me truthfully,' Rasp was saying. 'Why have you come here?'

'Why do you think?'Serrion replied scornfully. I wish to follow the Lord of Atros too.'

'You?''

'I am a Seer. I know what they have in store for me on Beltheron. They wish to imprison me like they did to T'yuq Tinyaz. They want to leave me in a dank cave underneath their great fortress. Cold and alone, while they enjoy themselves up above.'

'This is just what I expected you would say,' Rasp replied. 'A simple tale to trick us. Why should we believe you?'

It was clear to Serrion that he still had not convinced the noetic. But he realised how he could persuade him.

'I suppose there is only one way I can only prove it,' he said.

He noticed Hethaloner Rasp's eyebrows shoot up for a second. He had his interest. Here was Serrion's chance. He had to take it.

'I'll show you,' he whispered. 'I'll show you the future.'

Rasp went completely still. He might have been made of stone for all the movement he made. Then Serrion saw the expression on his face. Eager, greedy, and suddenly impatient. 'Show me,' Rasp hissed. His eye glittered. 'Show me now!'

His fingers grasped Serrion's chin. Serrion winced as the noetic's sharp nails cut into his face, drawing a thin line of blood across his jawline.

He focused on Hethaloner Rasp's left eye. He could tell from Rasp's avid expression that the chance of reading the mind of a Seer was too much to ignore. Serrion had guessed correctly. This was an opportunity that Hethaloner Rasp had dreamed of. If there was one thing more powerful than being able to read someone's thoughts, it was to be able to see the future!

'Show me,' Rasp repeated even more urgently. 'Prove what you have just said. Let me see what is to happen in the time to come!'

Serrion concentrated harder than he ever had before.

'Very well,' he said. 'I will.'

Yes, he thought to himself. He would show the noetic the future, but only one part of it. Only one possible future out of many. Like T'yuq Tinyaz had told him in her final words, Serrion would only tell Rasp that future that he *wanted* to hear.

As their minds connected, Serrion felt the same sickening lurch that he had sensed when T'yuq had shared her own visions with him. Nausea overwhelmed him as Rasp began filtering through his thoughts.

'Concentrate!' Serrion told himself desperately. 'Think about the vision, think about kneeling in front of Andresen! Nothing else, only that. Rasp has *got* to see that or he will never believe me.'

Then, all of a sudden, there it was. Clear in the very

front of his mind. He was kneeling with Cleve Harrow in front of Piotre Andresen's throne. Serrion focused every part of his mind on the idea of surrendering power to the land of Atros.

From deep within his vision, he heard Rasp give a cry of wonder, and of victory. He released Serrion, and the vision faded. The real room swirled around him in a blur and finally came back into focus. The noetic was still standing close to him. The flicker of red and yellow deep in Rasp's evil eyes looked directly into Serrion's own.

'You are with us then?' there was wonder in the cruel voice that whispered into his ear. 'You *will* serve us on Atros after all?'

A wicked smile spread across Rasp's thin lips as Serrion realised that he had succeeded. He had managed to transfer his vision to the noetic. Rasp had read his mind.

But only the part of his mind that Serrion *wanted* him to see. Only *one* future.

So far, Serrion's plan was working.

One Possible Future

'Hethaloner Rasp has informed me of everything,' Piotre Andresen said. 'Harrow was telling the truth, you are on our side after all. How bizarre! Who would have thought it?'

He was sitting on the throne that had once belonged to Gretton Tur, the original Wild Lord. The throne was made of dark, burnt bones. Sophia was beside him on a similar throne constructed from the same ghastly materials.

Serrion was on his knees at their feet. Harrow knelt at his side, his head bowed low in front of the Andresens. Serrion almost smiled to himself as he recognised this as the image he had foreseen in his vision. His face still burned where the noetic's fingers had scored deep scratches down his cheek and he felt sick from the filthy water that he had been given to drink.

Andresen made a gesture to one of the rish who was standing against the wall. The creature stepped forwards and untied Serrion's cords. He flexed his fingers as the blood rushed back into his fingers and palms.

'My apologies for such rough treatment,' Andresen said.

'However, there are things I still do not understand,' Piotre continued. 'Still so many reasons why I should just kill you here and now.'

Serrion found his voice, although it sounded weak and cracked in his own ears.

'But you know my mind now,' he said. 'You have seen the future. Rasp told you what was in my thoughts.'

'Then tell me this,' Sophia's voice cut in urgently. 'Why would you obey us, why would you want to serve us, after all that we did to you?'

Serrion swallowed hard. The trickery was not over yet. He still had to convince Sophia and Piotre themselves.

'Most importantly of all,' Andresen continued. 'What really happened with Jacques?'

'Yes,' hissed Sophia. 'Tell us the truth about what you did to our son.'

Harrow had been silent all this time. Now he spoke out. 'Perhaps I can explain something of that, my lord,' he said.

As he began to rise to his feet, Harrow leant against Serrion as if for support. His fingers held onto Serrion's shoulder. Was it just his imagination, Serrion wondered, or had the Cleve just squeezed his shoulder a little more tightly than necessary? Was he giving him a signal? There could be no doubt about it, as he felt Harrow's fingers grip his shoulder even more tightly for a fraction of a second longer than he needed to.

'Go ahead then Cleve,' Andresen was saying. 'We are eager to hear what you can tell us of our poor son's last moments.'

'Well,' Harrow answered. 'First you must know the truth about this boy here.' He looked directly at Serrion as he said this, and gave a wink that Serrion knew could not have been seen by anyone else.

In the next instant, Harrow threw a yellow ball of fire into the centre of the room. There was utter confusion; yells and shouts were everywhere. It was deafening in Serrion's ears. As the brightness of the explosion faded, he just made out Harrow's retreating form as he escaped through a door at the far end of the hall. Sophia pursued him with a scream of fury and disappeared through the same doorway. Serrion realised that everyone had forgotten about him for the moment. Piotre's attention was drawn towards his wife as she ran from the room. Serrion took his chance. He quickly felt for the pebble in his pocket. As his fingers closed around it the now familiar feeling swelled up in his mind's eye. He focused his vision on Harrow's retreating figure...

...and saw Harrow racing up the stairs to meet Orianna and the pulver. He heard them discussing the flower and saw Harrow begin to lead them towards the rooftop. Then a crowd of rish, led by Piotre Andresen, stood in the path of his friends, blocking their way...

Serrion wrenched his attention away from his vision. He dropped the pebble back into the folds of his pocket and looked around the room urgently. What he had just seen was only one future – it could be changed. But to change it he knew that he had to keep Piotre and the rish away from that staircase. If he was going to save his friends he had to hold the Lord of Atros' full attention for as long as he could.

'Forget Harrow!' he yelled at the top of his voice. 'And I'll tell you what you want to know about Jacques. I'll tell you the truth about what happened.'

Andresen spun around to face him. He reached up to grasp at Serrion's throat.

'Tell me,' he whispered cruelly. 'Tell me about my son.'

Orianna and the pulver raced along the corridors. They had beaten off the rish who pursued them, but now found that they were hopelessly lost in the confusing tunnels and staircases. Tarawen called a halt.

'This is no good,' he muttered. 'We could be going around in circles for all we know.'

'We have been wandering for over an hour,' Orianna agreed. 'Anything could have happened to my brother in that time. You said you needed my brains, so let's use them shall we?'

She took a deep breath and began to murmur a low incantation. A strange dark line began to form on the ground at their feet. The pulver gasped with astonishment. As Orianna concentrated and completed her spell, the lines joined together to become what looked like a thick arrow on the ground. The lines sped away from them and disappeared around a corner.

'I've never tried this spell before,' Orianna told them. 'But if it works it's our quickest chance of finding our way to the Acferon. Come on, we have to follow the arrow lines.'

They began to move off at a rapid pace. The ears of Tarawen and the rest were alert to any sound of pursuit behind them, or sign of a trap up ahead. On and on they went down the corridors and around corners, following the strange, moving arrow on the ground ahead of them.

Before long however, they heard the noise behind them that they had all feared; the heavy sound of many feet getting nearer and nearer. Husk turned around first, to face the attack.

Piotre's Last Trick

Andresen had one hand on Serrion's throat. The other reached down towards his sword.

'Tell me then!' he hissed. 'Tell me about my son.'

They were alone in the room. Andresen had sent the rish to follow Sophia in her pursuit of Cleve Harrow.

Serrion was terrified, but that fed an angry rage in him. He yelled back at his captor with all the fury he could summon up.

'Your son only got what he deserved!'

The grip tightened even more and Andresen's eyes narrowed.

'What did you say?'

'Your son was a bully and a coward,' Serrion continued. He did not care what he said now. He knew he was probably going to die very soon, and that nothing he did would make any difference. Now all he wanted to do was to yell, insult, and hurt his enemy however he could. At least that might keep Piotre Andresen here, so that he couldn't stop Harrow and Orianna.

'Jacques Andresen couldn't even fight me properly!' Serrion spat out. 'He was running away when he fell on the broken staff of Atros.'

This was only partly true, and Serrion knew it. Jacques *had* fallen onto the sharp edges of the shattered black staff, but it was Serrion himself who had pushed him onto it.

'Liar!' Andresen pulled back his hand to strike Serrion. There was a flare of madness in his eyes that gave Serrion an idea. It wouldn't save him, but it might just give his friends a little extra time.

'Your son was running away from me because he had discovered the truth!'

Serrion was busily making up ideas as he spoke. Even Vishan, the great spy and double agent, would have been proud of how this young man was improvising his story, playing his part to distract his enemy.

'He was scared because I told him that I wanted to serve you.'

'What? My son, scared?'

Serrion knew he had to keep talking. He had to invent a story that would hold Piotre's attention for as long as he could. He had heard the faint sounds of the battle on the staircase several floors below them. Piotre must not be allowed to focus on that. Serrion raised his voice to a shout so that Piotre would not hear.

'I told your son that I would make you prouder of me than you ever were of him. Your son was jealous of me.'

But now Serrion was running out of ideas. He couldn't think of what to tell Piotre Andresen next. The sound on the stairs grew louder. It was no good. Andresen had heard it! He spun to the door, realisation dawning on him that he had been tricked.

The distraction was enough for Serrion. As soon as Piotre's attention was turned to the battle below, he jumped up to his feet. He knew how quick Piotre was, and knew he couldn't waste a second. There was a row of swords, maces and throwing spears displayed along the far wall of the hall. Serrion ran towards them. He flung out his hand and one of the fencing swords lifted from the bracket that held it and flew across the room.

Andresen was already on the move. In three rapid paces he was back within striking distance. He used his forward momentum to spin in the air, straightening his arm and whipping his sword around incredibly fast. The sword that Serrion had just released from the wall deflected the blow as it flew into the boy's hand. If not for that, Andresen's very first strike would have ended the fight.

Piotre landed easily and lunged again. Serrion only just managed to get a firm grip on the sword in time to lift it to parry. The strength of Piotre's blow still drove Serrion off his feet. He stumbled backwards and landed heavily on the cobbles.

The sword in his hand clattered on the floor. It sent up a flash of red sparks from the stone. Red! Serrion gazed at it intently. An image of the future suddenly sprang into his mind. This was not the distant future however. This was not some unknown period of time. It was in this room, only seconds away.

In his vision, he saw Andresen leering down towards him, his sword raised.

Andresen began to speak. 'I have you now. There is no escape this time.'

Then, like an echo, he heard it in real time. 'I have you now. There is no escape this time.'

He was seeing only seconds into the future! He knew what Andresen was about to do. That meant he could anticipate his moves. Maybe there was a way to defeat him after all!

In his vision, Andresen's sword came down quickly, swinging towards Serrion's left hand side.

Serrion rolled over, picking up his own sword as he did so.

In real time, Andresen's sword came down quickly, swinging towards Serrion's left hand side. It hit the ground where he had been lying only an instant before.

Serrion was already on his feet again.

In his vision, Andresen lunged.

Serrion took a rapid step back.

In real time, Andresen lunged. Serrion was already out of reach.

Again and again, Serrion saw what Andresen's movements were going to be in the moment before he made them. Again and again he was able to parry the blows or step out of the way.

'I see what you're doing,' Piotre gasped. 'You can tell where I am going to strike next can't you?' There was a leer of madness in the Lord of Atros' eyes. 'That's all well and good,' he continued. 'But have you heard of the feint in fencing?'

'The *what*?' thought Serrion.

But there was no time to work it out. Andresen lunged with the sword. Serrion was still looking a couple of seconds into the future. He saw the blow coming to his left, and his mind's eye told him to dodge the other way. But at the last moment, Andresen altered his weight onto the other foot and with an unbelievably quick flick of his wrist rotated the blade so that it came at Serrion from the other side. Piotre had been so quick, that Serrion had no time to adjust his balance. There was no way he could avoid this blow and it struck him heavily on his own sword arm.

Serrion gave a cry of pain and the sword fell from his fingers.

Piotre laughed aloud. 'That's what I mean by a feint, boy! I have more than one trick up my sleeve!'

But so had Serrion. He had more than one gift. There was another special talent that he could now use.

All of the lies and deceit that he had been shown by this man burned in his head like fire. As Piotre Andresen closed in on him, his sword high in the air, Serrion raised his hand. With a flick of his fingers the sword turned in his adversary's grasp. Andresen lost his hold on the handle as Serrion flung his own hand sideways, forcing the sword high up into the air. Serrion pointed at it and it hovered over them. Then he made a small circular motion with his finger. The sword mirrored his movement, slowly turning until the tip pointed directly down towards the Lord of Atros. There was one moment of terror on Andresen's face as he looked up and realised that he had been beaten by this maggot of a child, then Serrion clenched his hand into a fist and the sword swept down, slashing through Piotre Andresen's body.

Serrion looked away at the last moment. He shut his eyes so that he would not see, but still heard a sickening wet sound, followed by a grunt of pain and shock.

When he looked again, Serrion saw Piotre leaning against the wall, his own sword piercing his breast. He sank slowly to a sitting position on the floor. One of Piotre's hands was raised towards Serrion. The Lord of Atros was attempting to cast one final spell.

It was no use. As Piotre tried to speak, his hand wavered in the air, and sank back down onto his lap. He uttered a sigh, then his eyelids flickered closed. His head dropped to his chest and his shoulders slumped.

Breathless, Serrion stood over him. He looked down for what seemed like a long time. There was a numb emptiness in his mind, and a dull sensation of fatigue through his whole body.

It seemed strange that he should not feel something more. 'Is this it?' he thought to himself. 'Is this what it was all about? Have I won?' There was no feeling of victory, or even relief. Just an awful sadness at all the things he had seen and done. A tremendous weariness overwhelmed him. All of a sudden he wanted to lie down where he was and sleep.

Serrion finally snapped his attention away from the dead man. Once again he became aware of the noises coming up the corridor. There were cries and angry shouts just beyond the door.

He spun around in time to see the door fly open. Sophia charged in, her dark hair flying out behind her and madness in her expression. It was clear she had not been able to catch up with Harrow when he had fled from the room.

Her eyes fixed upon the slumped body of her husband. She saw the growing pool of blood across the floor. She staggered for a moment and uttered a low moan of disbelief. Then, with a violent scream she launched herself at Serrion.

He was too exhausted to resist. He felt her fingers close around his throat as if it were happening to someone else. Her crazed eyes, so close to his own, appeared to be far away.

There were more sounds behind them. Sophia turned to look, and spat out a curse.

'Come with me,' she hissed at Serrion, and dragged him across the floor towards a black curtain at the far side. She thrust out her hand and the curtain parted to reveal a stone staircase leading to a higher part of the castle. Pushing Serrion through the opening they began to climb...

Up the Staircase

Moments later, Orianna, Cleve Harrow and the three pulver raced into the room. The moving map line that Orianna had created was still curling across the floor in front of them. Husk was the last, as usual. He came in backwards, still swinging his sword to bring down a harch in the doorway.

The companions looked around the hall and saw Andresen. Cannish ran across to him and bent down. He raised his fingers to the Lord of Atros' throat for a moment to check for a pulse. Then he turned back to the others and nodded.

'Dead.'

'Where are Serrion and Sophia?' asked Orianna. Her voice was filled with fear. 'Where is my brother?'

Tarawen's gaze fell upon the curtain and the staircase beyond.

'They must have gone that way,' he said. 'There is no other way in or out of this place.'

'Unless she used her magic,' Cannish added.

'Please no,' Orianna breathed. 'We can't lose them, not after all this.'

Tarawen was already by the staircase. He was listening intently.

'I think I hear footsteps above,' he said.

'Then come,' Cannish yelled, let's follow them.'

'Wait!' Harrow's voice filled the room. 'It will take my magic to defeat Sophia.' He turned to his young student.

'Orianna, give me the golden staff!'

She hesitated for a moment, before agreeing. 'Alright,' she said. She handed the staff to the Cleve. 'But he's *my* brother. I'm coming with you.'

He nodded. 'I would not expect anything else, my dear.'

There was another eruption of noise from the corridor.

'We will keep the guards busy down here for as long as we can,' Tarawen said. 'Vishan, Cannish, Husk, follow me.'

The four pulver strode back towards the door in time to see a new batch of rish guards appear.

'Go,' Tarawen hissed behind him. 'I have these devils in my sights.' He ran forwards, raising his sword to attack.

Harrow and Orianna didn't wait any longer. They ran to the staircase to follow Serrion and Sophia. Harrow was in the lead in spite of the limp which still affected his leg. He surged up the steps three at a time. Orianna had to bunch up her long robe to avoid tripping on the stair as she raced after him.

The stairs wound in a spiral around a central column. They were wide and uneven, but the rise of each step was shallow so they were not too hard to climb. Harrow was increasing his lead on Orianna and he had already disappeared around the curve of the stairs above her when there was a droning sound and a flash of bright light over her shoulder. She spun around.

Standing a few steps lower down, lit by the light of a fading pathway, stood Hethaloner Rasp. His eyes glittered behind the steel frames of his spectacles. Orianna gasped. Harrow had taken the golden staff with him. She had no defence, no way of fighting this man.

He grinned at her. 'I know what you are thinking,' he hissed. 'You are correct. You cannot defeat me.'

He moved towards her, lifting a dagger from his belt. His face stretched into a wicked leer.

Then his expression changed. The evil grin faded and the noetic looked surprised for a moment. Orianna noticed a wet red stain appear on his tunic front. He slumped down onto the steps, revealing the figure of Tarawen behind him. His sword was in his hand, and Orianna felt sick as she saw the blood soaking its blade.

'Not much of a noetic, was he,' Tarawen grinned mirthlessly. 'He didn't see that coming.'

'No but I can see more Atros reinforcements below us!' yelled Cannish who was just behind him. 'Let's get a move on shall we?'

With Orianna leading the way, they chased up the staircase after Harrow, Sophia and Serrion, fighting off rish and harch with every step that they climbed.

On the Rooftop

Sophia burst out onto the open rooftop garden with Serrion in her grasp. She flung him onto the cobbled floor and he rolled over, trying to get away from her. In the corner of his eye he saw a row of earthenware pots along the far side of the wall. Bright flowers grew in them. 'The Acferon!' he thought. 'I've made it, but I didn't expect to do it like this. If only I can get a chance to reach one of those flowers...'

His thoughts were stopped by a violent stinging sensation through his whole body. Sophia was lifting him from the ground in a magical pulse of blue and purple light.

'At last I have you where I want you,' she hissed. She turned her hand slowly and the light grew brighter.

The stinging feeling increased, as if he was being squeezed by a giant hand. He felt himself begin to rotate in the air, as Sophia teased him, twirling her fingers and building the pain even more.

'The light you are held in will grow tighter and tighter,' she said. 'In a moment I will snap my fingers, and you will feel a vice closing around you. You will be crushed into nothingness. There is nothing you can do. Even now you cannot move, can you?'

He realised that she was right. He was being squeezed tighter and tighter all the time. He couldn't move a finger, an eyebrow, anything!

He felt himself twisted around again, until Sophia was staring straight into his face.

'Now I take revenge,' she said. 'For my son, and for my husband.' She raised her hand in front of his face and moved her thumb and middle finger together, ready to click them and close the vice around Serrion.

However, even Sophia Andresen could not complete the killing of the child that she had raised without a single pang of sorrow. As she looked into his eyes, she showed a moment of sentiment. She hesitated.

That moment was enough.

Harrow burst out onto the rooftop. With a howl of vengeance for all that he had suffered, the Cleve flung himself towards her. Serrion saw him flying through the air for a moment as Sophia turned towards him. She raised both arms and a bolt of light shot towards Harrow. He was already falling towards her and it was too late for her magic to stop him plunging into her at the very edge of the parapet. Sophia grunted with the impact and both of them tottered against the wall. The golden staff fell from Harrow's grasp and clattered away from them on the ground. Sophia's fingers were around the Cleve's throat instantly, her dark hair flowing around them in the wind, whipping both of their faces. Blue fire flickered around their heads as they swayed backwards and forwards. Harrow's weight and strength should have been enough to overcome Sophia in a moment, but her rage and the fury of her powers held him in check. In fact, it seemed to Serrion as if she were already gaining the upper hand in the struggle.

As soon as her attention had been drawn away, Serrion felt the vice loosen around him. He dropped to the floor, choking for breath and clutching his aching ribs.

Behind them he could hear Vishan and Tarawen's voices, and swords clashing against the weapons of the rish in the crowded stairwell. They were getting closer, being beaten back by the numbers of their foes as they streamed up the tower. No matter how many the pulver drove back, more took their place, stepping over the fallen bodies of their fellows.

Serrion tore his attention away from the stairwell at a scream from Sophia.

'Help me!' She was forcing Harrow backwards again, so they were both now moving away from the wall.

'You?' Serrion yelled back. 'Why should I help *you*?'

Everything that Sophia and Piotre had done over the years now pushed him into action. Ignoring the pain he still felt from Sophia's magic and the wound on his arm, he ran towards the golden staff. He picked it up and gripped it tightly in both hands. He felt it pulse with energy. Serrion raised it and began to point it towards Sophia.

'Don't,' she pleaded, still struggling with Harrow to keep a safe distance from the edge of the parapet. 'Think of all we used to mean to each other.' Her voice had an old tone in it that he remembered from when he was little. 'Think of all I did for you. Please... Please help me...*Jack*!'

That was it. She had made a decision in that moment to try one last trick, to use that other name to remind him of his childhood with her. But it was a mistake.

'How dare she,' he thought. 'How dare she call me that.'

Serrion Melgardes raised the golden staff of Beltheron. He looked down briefly at the image of his own face carved into the precious metal, that ancient symbol of his importance in the struggle against Atros. Then he lifted his gaze and pointed the staff directly towards Sophia. He concentrated his attention on the tip of the staff until he saw it glow a bright red. The staff grew warm in his hands and he felt it vibrate with power.

'Jack... *Jack!* What are you doing?' Sophia shrieked. 'My boy, you must help me.'

'I told you once before,' Serrion said coldly. 'I told you on the bridge in Maraglar. I am *NOT* your boy.'

With these words he lunged forwards with the staff. Crackling fire burst from it, hitting Sophia in the shoulder and spinning her around towards the lowest part of the brickwork in the tower wall. The blow knocked Harrow away from her but still she managed to keep her balance. Her head twisted back to look at Serrion. Now there was no pretence in it as there had been a moment before. Any feeling of connection or love that might have been there was replaced by pure hatred and rage.

'How dare you, gutter boy!' she screamed. Her hand made a brief movement under her cloak. She was so quick that Serrion didn't even see the dagger as it left her hand. He didn't have time to deflect it with the staff, or move out of the way as it shot towards him. He only recognised it as the dagger from his vision in the last instant, as it struck him deep in the chest.

At first the feeling was more a sensation of surprise than of pain. For a couple of seconds it was as if someone had punched him, or pushed him sharply with the flat of their hand. But then he gasped as the piercing sting reached his senses.

Serrion dropped the staff and clutched at his chest. His hand came away and he looked down at it to see bright red begin covering it. At first he thought that this red colour must be the beginning, the opening, of another premonition. But then he felt the wet stickiness between his fingers, and knew it to be his own blood.

He looked up, as his sight began to fade, and saw Cleve Harrow, with tears streaming down his face, launch himself towards Sophia once more. She was still standing close to the lowest part of the parapet. Harrow careered into her at full speed. The force of the impact carried both Harrow and Sophia over the edge. As he sank to his knees, Serrion heard a final scream from the woman who had once been his mother. It grew fainter as they fell, but by the time the scream ended in a sickening crumpled thud far below, Serrion had already blacked out.

Vishan hurtled through the door at the top of the stairwell. He took in what had happened in one glance. Turning, he yelled out to his companions. 'Cannish, hold them on the stair. Orianna, get up here, now!'

'Glad to oblige!' Cannish yelled. With Tarawen and Husk he redoubled his efforts against the attacking rish. Orianna threw a last incantation backwards as she struggled up the remaining couple of steps and out onto the circular platform at the top of the tower.

Her face drained of all colour as she saw the scene. She gave a cry of horror at the dagger in her brother's chest.

Vishan had already wrapped his blue cloak around Serrion's body, which lay crumpled on the ground. He took the handle of the dagger carefully in his fingers. As he tried to remove the blade he started with surprise as it melted away in his fingers.

'What in the Three Worlds...?'

'She didn't use a real blade,' Orianna whispered as her eyes quickly scanned her brother's face and wound. 'She used an incantation instead! There is a spell working its way through him like poison.' Her eyes narrowed in concern and concentration. Then a grim smile passed briefly over her lips. She started to mouth strange words under her breath.

Vishan looked confused.

'What's going on, Orianna?'

'I know what she has done. I think I can reverse it. Give me room here!'

Orianna ripped off her cloak and pulled up the sleeves of her tunic. She began moving her hands swiftly. With her fingers only centimetres above her brother's body, she began to speak the strange words again. As she did, her eyes scanned the row of pots along the wall.

'The plant behind me,' she said. The one with the dark leaves and the tendrils climbing down the side of the pot.'

'I see it.'

'Bring it here.'

Vishan rushed to bring her the plant. Orianna ripped at the leaves, and pushed them into the wound in Serrion's chest.

Cannish, Tarawen and Husk appeared through the doorway. All looked completely exhausted. Cannish leant heavily on his sword, which was notched and cracked from battle.

'Vishan, I think that's most of them,' he gasped through panting breaths. 'But we're a wee bit tired, do you think you could manage to close this door here?

Vishan turned from Orianna's side and raised his hand. A burst of green light slammed the door closed as three more rish tried to scramble over the bodies of their fallen accomplices.

With another quick flick of his wrist, Vishan fused the metal of the lock together.

'That should hold the rest of them until you get your breath back.'

They all turned their attention back to Orianna and Serrion. Worry was etched on all their faces as Orianna worked feverishly to save her brother. She was murmuring strange words under her breath. None of the pulver could understand, or even guess at their meaning. Her fingers were moving over the wound as she dropped in more of the dark leaves.

'Please let me be right about this,' she whispered after finishing her spell. 'I've studied so hard, learnt so many spells. Please let it be of some use. *Please* let this work.' Her white hair fell down upon her brother's chest and tears soaked her face. 'Please,' she said once more. 'I can't bear to lose anyone else.'

Serrion did not move. Orianna's body began to shake as sobs overwhelmed her. The pulver stood around. All bowed their heads in sorrow.

Dark storm clouds were gathering over the rooftops of the castle. The rish still hammered at the door.

Vishan was the first to turn away. He strode over to Sophia's row of pots, and plucked the flowers, seed pods and leaves from the Acferon plant. 'At least we can save Lady Helen,' he thought to himself.

Tarawen placed his arm around Orianna.

'Come,' he whispered. 'We have the Acferon. We cannot stay longer.'

'No!' she said and pulled away from his hand. 'I'm staying with him.' she cradled Serrion tighter in her arms.

'My Lady,' Vishan pleaded. 'You cannot stay! Lady Jenia will need your help to cure Helen.'

Orianna was silent. She knew what they said was true. Saving Helen's life would at least give some kind of justice for Serrion's death. She nodded once and began to lower her brother's head to the floor.

As she did, Serrion's eyes flickered. He opened them and looked up into his sister's face. He was still wracked with pain and his vision was blurred, but he could tell it was her. He saw her face, covered in tears, and wondered what she was upset about. Then he saw her expression break into delighted joy and fresh tears spring into her eyes as she looked down at him.

He felt himself being squeezed again, but this time, it was his sister's arms as she hugged him, not Sophia's magic. This time it felt good. The best feeling he could remember.

Serrion felt himself being lifted up by many arms and then the familiar sensation of blinding white light and twisting up and away through a pathway. He did not know where he was going, he was still too confused from his injuries, but it did not matter. His sister's arms were around him, and that was all that mattered.

The rish and harch burst through the door and out onto the rooftop garden. They stared around, but there was no one to be seen. Loud thunder could be heard overhead. Some raised their eyes to see the thick dark clouds approaching Atros City. The last time such clouds had appeared was when Gretton Tur, the Wild Lord himself, had been defeated. That time, the whole castle had collapsed, and the power of Atros had been destroyed.

There was a low rumbling sound beneath their feet. The ground of Atros itself seemed to be shaking.

Fordan Hamel appeared in the doorway. The old traitor was breathless after his climb. He took in the shuddering, crumbling walls in an instant and his heart quailed with fear. The rish guards on the rooftop were uncertain what to do. Stones began to tumble from the parapets of the castle as the servants of Atros retreated down the staircase in fear and confusion, taking Hamel with them. He screamed out in fear and anguish as he was tumbled about in the press of rushing bodies.

Such was their haste to escape the destruction of Gendrell, none of them noticed the six dark, round scorch marks burnt deep into the stones under their feet...

The Darkness Recedes

Helen was dreaming. A black cloud of dense smoke was choking her. It felt as though her lungs were being squeezed by a giant hand. She coughed, and felt smoke surge up out of her throat and into her mouth. She spat it out frantically, and then gasped, trying to get her breath. She coughed again, spitting to get rid of the vile taste. She tried to swallow and a harsh rasping pain at the back of her throat made her wince with shock.

Then she heard voices.

'She's waking up!'

'Hold her head, she's choking.'

'She's trying to get her breath, lift her up!'

Helen felt herself being moved into a sitting position. She couldn't remember where she was but there was a delicious fragrance in the air, like the scent of strawberries wafted on a warm spring breeze. She had stopped coughing now, although her throat still felt sore.

'Helen? My love, are you alright?'

She recognised her mother's voice, and felt her arms around her. Helen opened her eyes.

She was in her own room. Her mother was holding onto her tightly and a huge grin spread across her face as she looked into her daughter's eyes. Just behind her, standing close to the bed, was her father. He took a deep breath, and his shoulders sagged with relief.

'Mum, Dad, what's been going on? Have I missed something?'

Laughter filled the room. Helen realised for the first time that there was quite a crowd there. Orianna and Serrion were in chairs along one side of the wall. They were both leaning forwards eagerly and Helen noticed a blue bowl in Orianna's hands with steam rising from it. She guessed that was where the glorious smell was coming from. Tarawen and Vishan were peering in at the doorway. They too looked relieved to see her awake.

'Yes you could say you have missed something,' Vishan laughed. 'But only the destruction of Atros, and the saving of Beltheron from the greatest terror it has known. Not much really.'

'That's right,' Tarawen added with a cheeky glint in his eyes. 'You were better off having a little nap!'

'Stop teasing her,' Matt spoke gruffly, but there was a happy gleam in his eyes. He moved forwards towards the bed and knelt down close to her face.

'There is a lot to tell you about,' he whispered. 'Both good and bad. But not now. There will be time for that later when you have recovered fully. For now it is enough to know that you are safe and well, and your friends here are all delighted to see you so.'

She was about to ask the first of many questions that were bubbling up in her mind, but her thoughts were distracted by the view over her father's shoulder through her window. It was so dark that at first she thought that she had woken up in the middle of the night-time. Now however it was getting much lighter in the room. Sunlight streaked in faster than any dawn, and she saw thick clouds that looked like smoke disappearing more rapidly than wind could take them. From the streets outside they heard shouts of relief and loud cheering.

'Look,' Serrion said excitedly. 'It's working! The Darkness is going!'

Everyone looked towards the window as the afternoon sunlight streamed onto their faces. It was so bright that Helen had to close her eyes again. She still felt very sleepy, and let her mother lay her head gently back down on her pillow.

Epilogue

'Step forward Orianna, or should I say, *Cleve* Melgardes,'
Matthias said. He held out a new staff towards her. This
one was made of a pure white metal. It shone in the early
afternoon sunlight that sparkled through the windows,
lighting up Orianna's hair with glints of dazzling silver and
platinum. She bowed her head as she stepped forwards to
take it from him.

Jenia was at her husband's side at the dais. She
beamed happily at him, and then turned with eyes full of
pride to look at her daughter, who stood close by on the
steps.

Helen was standing between Vishan and Tarawen.
She still looked a little tired and drained after her ordeal.
She was a little thinner around the face but that was more
than made up for by the excited gleam in her expression.
She kept herself upright, very still and straight. She did
not want to let the others down for she was now wearing
a pale blue cloak, a cloak of the pulver guard. Helen Day,
Lady Yelenia of the 23rd Generation of the Select Families of
Beltheron, had become the first woman ever to be accepted
for pulver training. She caught her mother's glance as Jenia
whispered: 'You just be careful!' at her. Helen nodded and
grinned back.

A young man stood on the steps at the back of the
hall. His position was set apart some distance from the

main crowd. Cannish and Husk, the two pulver with new badges of high rank on their bright blue cloaks, watched him closely from their positions by the doors to the great hall. The young man's long hair was pure white and flowed down over his shoulders. He wore a cloak of the same snowy white over a pair of jeans, scuffed trainers and a faded sweatshirt. From his place on the steps he was able to observe all that went on in that great historic hall on that great historic day. Serrion Melgardes, the new Seer of Beltheron, smiled at the scene.

He reached into his pocket and brought out the pebble which he had found on the beach in Atros. He focused all of his attention on it for a moment until it began to glow a bright vivid red. He gazed into the light, becoming absorbed by his vision as he looked forwards into the future. Into many possible futures.

After a long while, the red glow began to fade away. Serrion placed the pebble back into his pocket and raised his eyes to look at them all once more.

He caught sight of Helen across the other side of the room. She was staring at him curiously.

She mouthed a question silently at him. 'Is everything ok?'

He nodded back at her and smiled. He felt the heaviness of the pebble in his pocket and his smile grew wider.

'Yes,' Serrion thought to himself. 'Yes. Everything is fine.'

The End